If Gideon should ever find out the truth...

Rennie thought, staring at the gold ring, the symbol of their commitment.

His hand closed over hers as if to reassure her, but his touch only added to her fears. Her eyes flickered up to his face, then away. But that brief look told her enough. Beneath his calm exterior, Gideon was just as nervous as she was, though for far different reasons. After all, he was risking a lot, taking such a momentous step with a woman he scarcely knew.

Everything's going to work out, she promised herself. *I'll make it work. There's no reason for Gideon to ever learn the truth. So all I have to do is concentrate on being the best wife and mother I can possibly be from this moment on, and let the future take care of itself.*

But the tiny voice of doubt refused to be silenced.

MARRY ME,
Cowboy

GIDEON'S BRIDE

Amelia Autin

CONVENIENTLY
Wed

Silhouette Books

Published by Silhouette Books
America's Publisher of Contemporary Romance

SILHOUETTE BOOKS

ISBN 0-373-65327-1

GIDEON'S BRIDE

Copyright © 1995 by Amelia A. Autin

Visit Silhouette Books at www.eHarlequin.com

Printed in U.S.A.

AMELIA AUTIN

is a voracious reader who can't bear to part with a good book—or a good movie. She has over four thousand titles—including romance, science fiction, adventure and mystery—as well as hundreds of movies from the thirties, forties and fifties.

Gideon's Bride, Amelia's first novel, won the Romance Writers of America's Golden Heart Award in the long contemporary category. The setting for *Gideon's Bride* resulted from nine months spent in Wyoming—Amelia attended twelve schools all over the United States while growing up—where she fell in love with the people, the lifestyle and the picturesque landscape.

Please address questions and book requests to:
Silhouette Reader Service
U.S.: 3010 Walden Ave., P.O. Box 1325, Buffalo, NY 14269
Canadian: P.O. Box 609, Fort Erie, Ont. L2A 5X3

For my mother and father, with love—
You read and sang to me as a child, and proved
that lifelong dreams can come true.
And with gratitude to my RWA sisters—
The dreams were mine, but the skills were yours.
Thank you for sharing.

Prologue

"Jo, I've got a problem. And I only see one solution."

Gideon Lowell stood bareheaded in the deserted cemetery on the outskirts of the sleepy Wyoming town of Carter's Junction. His worn, gray cowboy hat rested atop a tombstone that read, "Johanna Lowell. Beloved wife and mother."

But she'd been so much more. Scarcely a day went by that he didn't miss her since he'd brought her home from Los Angeles to rest forever on this lonely, windswept hillside. At night he still reached for her in his sleep. He even turned around sometimes, expecting to see her, but she was never there. Wife, lover, friend. Mother of his children. He had loved her all his life.

"You know how hard it's been on the kids since you've been gone. Three housekeepers in less than two years. Shuttled back and forth between the Rocking L and your sister Emily's place whenever the latest housekeeper left. For myself, I wouldn't care, Jo. I could make do." He cleared his throat, his breath visible in the frigid February air. "But the kids, honey. For their sake I've got to break my promise to you."

If anyone had been around to see him talking to himself, Gideon would have been mortally embarrassed. But since he was alone on this snow-covered hillside, he could do as he pleased without worrying about his neighbors thinking he'd gone over the edge.

Gideon didn't come to the cemetery much anymore. With three children to raise and a thriving sheep ranch to run there wasn't a lot of time left over. Furthermore, it was a painful reminder of the worst day in his thirty-three years. But there were still times when he felt compelled to talk things over with Johanna. He'd always done so ever since they were kids, and even though he knew she was dead, Gideon didn't see why that meant he had to stop.

He crouched to brush away the snowdrifts from the bottom of the gravestone with his bare hand. "They need a mother, Jo," he continued, "not a housekeeper. Nicki still isn't talking, and the doctors say she's probably locked herself away from being hurt again. She needs a stable home life and a lot of love if she's ever going to come out of this."

His heart ached as he thought of their eldest child, Nicki. Their firstborn. He'd delivered her himself because Johanna had waited too long to announce she was in labor and they hadn't made it all the way into Sheridan in time. If only he could bring Nicki through this as easily as he'd brought her into the world.

"And then there's Trina. Losing you has made her afraid she's going to lose me, too. She cries whenever I leave her at Emily's. And Andrew…he's not even two yet, but still he knows there's something missing from his life. He hardly ever laughs."

He sighed deeply. "I've tried, Jo. God knows, I've tried. But I can't do it alone anymore. The insurance money paid off the mortgage on the ranch and the rest is in the bank for the kids' education, so their future is secure. But money can't give them what they need right now. They need a mother. Someone who won't pack up and leave when things get tough. Someone to be there for them, to love them and help me care for them."

Gideon stood up and squinted into the setting sun, ignoring the cold seeping into his bones. "So, as I said, honey, I've got to partly break a promise to you. I know I swore there'd never be another woman for me—that I'd remain faithful to you for always."

He leaned his weight on one hip in a casual stance belied by the harsh intensity of his tone. "I've never broken my word on that. But the kids need a mother, and the only way I can see to give them one without giving them up is to get married again."

The wind off the mountains to the west picked up, ruffling Gideon's golden brown hair and dusting snow over the grave he'd just brushed clean.

"Now, don't fret about it. It isn't anyone you know. As a matter of fact, it isn't anyone I know, either. I've thought it over, and I realized that the only way to do this, the only way I can bear to do this, is to advertise for a wife. That way, she won't be expecting things from me I don't have left to give."

Gideon pulled two long white envelopes from the pocket of his sheepskin jacket. "I've already written an ad for the Casper newspaper and a letter to one of those mail-order bride publications. You know, the ones we used to make jokes about. Somehow, it's not so funny anymore."

He cleared his throat again. "I won't lie to you, Jo. The loneliness gets pretty fierce at times. Our bed has been cold and empty for a long time. I *need* sometimes, Johanna. I dream of you and wake so hard and aching, that I think I'll die of it. I reach for you and you're not there. You'll never be there again.'' His voice deepened. ''And I'm only human, honey. I know there'll be times when I turn to her for relief. But she'll never be you. She'll never fill your place in my heart, I promise you. I'll love you till I die, Johanna. Nothing can ever change that.''

He stood for a long time in silence, his powerful body casting a long blue shadow over the snow. At last Gideon reached for his Stetson, settling it firmly on his head.

''I have to go now, honey. Emily has the kids again and I want to stop off to spend some time with them.'' He tapped the envelopes. ''And I have to get these to the post office before the mail goes out.'' Gideon glanced around, reassuring himself that he was alone, then placed his large, callused hand on the headstone.

''I love you.''

Chapter 1

Not quite three months later Gideon was regretting his decision to advertise for a wife.

After a hard day's work that had begun before sunrise, he sat on his front porch, his chair tilted back and his muddy boots propped on the porch railing. His hat shielded his face from the late afternoon sun. He looked relaxed, as if nothing more than enjoying the unusually warm spring day occupied his mind, but looks were deceiving.

What could have possessed him to place those ads? He'd endured the gentle and not-so-gentle teasing of his ranch hands, the whole town of Carter's Junction, and practically the entire county, for that matter. The reproachful looks of his sister-in-law, Emily, seared him with guilt. And his daughters had listened to his explanation in horrified silence, until Trina spoke for them both. "Don't you love Mama anymore?" Her childish voice had quavered, then dissolved into tears.

All this, and for what? To date he'd had twelve responses

to his ads. Three had shocked him with their suggestive language and explicit photos, five had been from city dwellers who'd never set foot on a ranch, two had been from women old enough to be *his* mother, for God's sake. The last two possibilities hadn't panned out, either. One had answered his ad only as a joke. The other seemed almost perfect on paper, but when she came to visit, Gideon could almost see her adding up his net worth as she toured the sheep ranch. He couldn't hustle her off his land fast enough.

"So what the hell do I do now?"

Almost as the words left his mouth, he spotted a plume of dust heading his way up the winding, two-mile drive from the main road. Gideon's mood lightened with anticipation. Was Emily bringing his kids for a surprise visit? God, he hoped so. He hadn't seen them in three days. He tried to get over to the Holden ranch at least every other day, although the seventy-mile round trip meant he was able to spend only an hour or so in the evening with his children.

But he'd known on Sunday that this week's hectic schedule probably wouldn't allow him to see his kids until Thursday night. It had been gut-wrenching, as always, leaving them with Emily, even though he knew he had no choice. But the situation was fast becoming desperate. If he didn't find someone soon…

To Gideon's disappointment, he realized it wasn't Emily's station wagon heading his way. In fact, he didn't recognize the car at all, which was unusual. The Rocking L was off the beaten track and they rarely had unannounced visitors.

Someone lost, or a salesman, maybe. Has to be. Well, I'm not buying anything, but I welcome the company. Anything to take my mind off my troubles.

Stretching, Gideon rose to his full six feet three inches and pushed his Stetson farther back on his head. He stepped down from the porch just as the driver of the expensive foreign sports car adroitly avoided the mud puddle nearest the house and pulled up in front of him.

A young woman with a cloud of dark hair got out. The quiet elegance of her clothes looked as out of place on a working ranch as her car, Gideon noted absently, even as he enjoyed the picture she made. His eyes started at her dainty feet and lazily worked their way up.

Nice legs. Tiny waist. Not much on top, but enough to give a man ideas. Pretty, too, in a quiet sort of way, and those dark curls make you want to tangle your fingers in them and—

Gideon caught himself up short. Where the hell had that thought come from?

She shaded her eyes against the bright sun and peered up at him. "Hi."

He nodded, touching his hat brim. "Ma'am."

"Is this the Rocking L?"

Gideon nodded again.

"Can you tell me where I can find Gideon Lowell?"

"You've found him."

"Oh." The woman's hand dropped to her side and she looked a little taken aback.

"Can I help you?" A sudden suspicion hit him but he waited.

"I came…" A puff of wind blew a silky curl across her face and she brushed it away, tucking it behind her ear. "Look, can we sit down somewhere?" She took two steps toward him. "I've come a long way to see you."

"Lady, if you came for the reason I think, you can just turn around and head back."

A flicker of—could it be fear?—touched her face. "What do you mean?"

"If you're here because of my ad, you're wasting your time."

"They said in Carter's Junction that you haven't found a wife yet. Were they wrong?"

"No."

"Then I don't understand. You haven't even given me a chance."

"I don't need to. I can see all I need to know." At her questioning look, Gideon continued. "You're too young, you're too puny, and your car and your clothes say 'city woman.' Do I have to go on?"

Her eyes narrowed, her chin tilted up, and she planted her hands on her hips. "I'm twenty-five, I spent the first fifteen years of my life on a ranch in Montana, and as for 'puny,' any woman would be puny next to a *mountain* of a man."

Her challenging stance reminded Gideon of a stubborn mare he'd once owned. He'd badly misjudged that horse and had the scar to prove it. Obviously he'd made a similar mistake here. He suppressed the urge to grin.

She must have seen something in his expression, though, because she relaxed a little and moved closer. "Please. Can't we sit down and talk about this?"

It was a perfectly reasonable request, but it was the soft, pleading note in her voice that persuaded him. Backing up, Gideon nodded toward the chairs on the porch, then followed the woman up the stairs. She headed for the seldom-used rocking chair. Johanna's chair. He shoved that thought from his mind and removed his hat, using it as an excuse not to watch her.

"How did you find me? The ads gave only a post office box in Carter's Junction."

She seated herself before responding. "When I arrived in

town I asked around. The waitress in the café gave me directions.''

''But why didn't you write first?''

She considered the question carefully, then said, ''I wanted to meet you in person, so I just…took a chance.''

Gideon nodded, accepting her answer. As he settled into his own chair he almost missed the odd look of relief that crossed her face. He wondered what it meant, but didn't pursue it. ''So, now you're here. Tell me about yourself.''

She fumbled a little at first, as if unsure where to start. ''I…as I said, I was born and raised on a cattle ranch in Montana, about two hundred miles from Billings. When I was fifteen, my father died. My mother sold the Circle F, which had been in my dad's family for three generations, and moved us to Los Angeles where she was from originally.''

Gideon couldn't hide his reaction to the name of the city, and she stopped. ''My wife died in Los Angeles,'' he said curtly. She said nothing and Gideon shook off the memories. ''Go on. Please.''

''I hated living in the city, but I had no choice. After two years my mother remarried, but she's dead now. Other than my stepbrother, there's really nothing to keep me in Los Angeles. I've always planned to come back to this way of life, but between college, and…and other things, it never happened.''

''I see.''

She leaned forward, her hands clasped tightly together in her lap as she listed her qualifications. ''I'm a good plain cook. My grandmother taught me, and she was a rancher's wife for almost forty years. I'd match my biscuits up against anybody's—the recipe is an old family secret. I'm a fairly good housekeeper, too, as long as cleanliness, not spotlessness, is your goal. I can muck out a stable, although it's not my favorite pastime. I can ride a horse like nobody's business.'' She flashed a smile. ''My father used to say I was born in the saddle.'' She paused, her expression turning soft and vulnerable. ''And I love children.''

Gideon studied her for a long time, liking the way her eyes met his. Up close she appeared older than he'd originally thought, but still younger than she claimed. Perhaps that was due to the slenderness of her body and her delicate features. But there was character in her face, and determination. This lady knew what she wanted, and surprisingly she wanted to be his wife. That made him suspicious.

''But you're young and pretty,'' he said finally, ''and obviously well-off. Most women want to fall in love before they marry. Why would you need to find a husband this way? What would you get out of this kind of marriage?'' Gideon's skepticism was obvious.

She chose her words with care. ''I was in an accident a while back.'' She raised a self-conscious hand, pushing the bangs off her forehead. For the first time Gideon saw the razor-thin scar that angled across it. Her hand then moved to her abdomen. ''I had internal injuries, too,'' she said quietly, with just a trace of some painful emotion evident. ''Because of them I can never have children.''

''I'm sorry. I didn't mean to—''

''It's okay. I've learned to live with it. But you see, there aren't a lot of men out there who want a wife who can't give them children. At least, not ones I'd care to marry.'' She smiled slightly. ''You already have children of your own. My problem wouldn't be a hardship for you.

''As for what I'd get out of this marriage, I'd get the chance I've been denied—to be a mother. I'd get the life I know and love and have longed for these past ten years. And I'd get a husband to whom my money isn't important.''

For an instant it looked as if she intended to say something more, but she didn't.

Gideon watched her for several moments, then stood. Her eyes followed him. "Okay, I'll buy that. There's just one more thing I have to know, one thing you need to do." He stopped, not sure exactly how to say what he had to say next.

"What is it?"

"I want you to come into the house," he said slowly, deeply, "and go upstairs with me to my bedroom." His eyes held hers, leaving no doubt as to his meaning. "After that I'll know for sure."

Bright color surged into her face, then drained slowly away. Visibly shaken, she swallowed several times before she managed to say, "I can't do that." Her words were so soft he had to strain to hear them. She swallowed again, regret and something else coloring her next words. "I just can't."

"Are you sure?"

She nodded, not seeming to trust her voice, then rose abruptly and started for the steps.

"Wait."

She swung around sharply, eyes wide with anger and a fear she tried to hide. He cursed himself silently. He hadn't meant to frighten her, but he had to know.

"Please wait."

She shook her head and backed away, forgetting the stairs behind her. She teetered on the edge for a panicked instant before Gideon's quick reflexes saved her from tumbling into the dirt. Through the silk blouse she wore he felt the firmness of muscle as she tensed under his touch. She might look as if a strong wind would blow her away, but there was substance beneath her soft exterior.

Gideon held her only long enough for her to regain her

balance on the porch step, then released her arm and backed off. "Please stay. I'd like to apologize."

Chocolate brown eyes searched his hazel ones. She must have found what she was looking for there, must have believed his sincerity, because she only hesitated briefly before reseating herself in the rocking chair. She perched on the edge, though, as if poised for flight.

"I'm sorry." Gideon's voice was rough with embarrassment. He hitched his chair closer to hers and sat down so he wouldn't loom over her. "I know how...crude my request must have sounded, but I didn't know any other way to find out what I needed to know. You *seemed* sincere, but I've been fooled before. And if you'd been willing to jump into bed with a stranger, then you wouldn't be the woman I want as mother for my children."

She sat frozen for a moment, then said, "It was a test?"

Gideon nodded.

"A test," she repeated. He nodded again, though it hadn't been a question. "Oh, God, I didn't know what to think. I thought you might—"

"I'm sorry. I wouldn't have said it if I'd known how you'd react, but I wouldn't have known otherwise, now, would I?" His convoluted explanation seemed to help. She took a deep breath and let it out slowly, her eyes closing briefly.

"Are you okay now?" Gideon felt like a first-class heel. Hell, he'd insulted her *and* scared her half to death, as well. *Good going, Lowell. She probably thought you were going to drag her upstairs and rape her. The one decent prospect you've had and now she'll probably tell you to get lost. And could you blame her?*

Her dark eyes were fixed on his face. "I'm fine," she assured him quietly.

"Are you sure? I feel terrible."

She laughed, a little shakily. "I can't say I'm sorry to hear it. I'd hate to think you could say something like that and *not* feel terrible afterward."

"Yeah, well..." Gideon wished he could do something to make it up to her. "Can I get you anything? A glass of water? A can of soda?"

She shook her head. "No, thanks, I'm fine now, really. But would you answer a question for me?"

Those eyes again. Gideon felt something tug inside him. "Of course."

"Why did you place that ad?"

Although expecting the question at some time, Gideon felt a rush of emotion at her words. He choked it off ruthlessly, then rose and moved to the porch rail, leaning against the sturdy post and staring with unseeing eyes into the hazy distance.

"I already told you my wife died. Johanna was almost eight months' pregnant, visiting her parents outside Los Angeles with our two daughters. I was supposed to be with them but something came up. No one really knows what happened. There was a car accident. Our girls were okay, but my wife was badly hurt. Andrew was delivered by C-section. Johanna went into cardiac arrest. She didn't make it." The choppy little sentences were the best he could manage.

She didn't say anything, for which Gideon was grateful. He struggled to regain his composure, unwilling to face her again until he had himself sternly under control. "Andrew spent the first month of his life in the hospital," he continued finally, his hand clenching the railing in remembered anguish. "I had to leave him there alone in order to bring my wife home to be buried. He doesn't remember it, but I do. And Nicki, my oldest daughter, hasn't spoken a word since her mother died. It's been more than two years now.

In that time we've been through three housekeepers. Each left for different reasons, but—"

"Why? Why did they leave?"

He frowned at the interruption. "The first left to get married, the second just couldn't take the isolation, and the last one quit about two seconds before I could fire her." Gideon moved impatiently. "The reasons aren't important as far as I'm concerned. The bottom line is that they all left. My children…" He stopped and hunted for the right words.

"Your children," she prompted.

"Yeah, my kids. I love them so much, it tears me up inside to be separated from them, but I have no choice. This ranch is our livelihood, and I can't take care of them and run the ranch, too. And I don't have a lot of options. My parents are both dead. My wife's parents live in a southern California retirement community, and aren't in the best of health, anyway, especially my mother-in-law. That's why my wife was visiting them two years ago. And I've imposed on my sister-in-law too much as it is—she has her own family to take care of. I could get another housekeeper, but who's to say she won't leave? My kids have already been through enough, lost far too much for me to put them through that again. So I decided to find a mother for them."

"A mother, but not a wife?"

Gideon sighed, shaking his head. "You can't have one without the other."

"I see."

"Do you?"

"I think so." She stood and came to his side, close enough for him to catch just the faintest hint of her delicate perfume. "But I'll ask you the same question you asked me. Why not look for someone you can fall in love with? Why go this route?"

"You want the truth?" At her nod he said, "I'm not

looking for a woman to love. My wife is dead, but in my heart she'll always be my real wife. There aren't a lot of women out there who can accept that. At least, not ones I'd care to marry,'' he finished, using her own words.

She nodded thoughtfully. "So what do you get out of this marriage?"

"I get a mother for my children. Someone to care for them and love them, to be there when they need it. Someone to do all those things a mother does for children she loves." Gideon rubbed his face, the late afternoon stubble of his beard grating a little, and wondered how to delicately say what needed to be said. "And if things work out the way I hope, I get a woman to share my bed at night."

Warm color suffused her face. It touched something in Gideon. Before he'd met her, when was the last time he'd seen a woman blush?

"So, it would be a real marriage, then. Not a marriage in name only, as they say."

"Yeah." Funny, but in all this time he'd never once thought about this arranged marriage from the woman's point of view. Never until now had he wondered how she'd feel about sleeping with a man who didn't love her.

Gideon knew he was no prize as far as appearances went. His face was too angular to be considered handsome, and his body, while honed to fitness from years of hard work, would dwarf hers, especially in bed. Add to that a well-deserved reputation for bluntness, and the whole picture did not add up to a man likely to sweep a woman off her feet.

She was speaking and Gideon forced himself to concentrate.

"So, you'd expect to…to…sleep with me."

"Yeah, but not right away," he quickly reassured her. "I wouldn't expect that. Despite what I said earlier, I haven't made a habit of jumping into bed with strange women. But

I'm a normal man, with normal desires. Living together in such close proximity, the subject is bound to come up at some time, so I figure it's best to have it out in the open now.''

Gideon watched with near fascination as her delicately pink cheeks deepened to rose. Unable to bear his steady gaze she looked away. "You're right, of course. It would be unnatural to expect either of us to remain celibate for the rest of our lives.'' She cleared her throat, darted a quick glance at his face, then looked at her hands. "And I don't think I'd want my husband looking elsewhere for...''

He touched her tightly clenched hands briefly, drawing her gaze back to him. Their eyes caught and held. "It's been more than two years for me,'' he said honestly. "There hasn't been anyone since my wife...and there was never anyone else while we were married.''

"You don't have to tell me this.''

"I think I do. I think it's important for you to know. I don't want you to have any romantic illusions about our life together. This is a business arrangement as far as I'm concerned. But I'll be good to you, as good as I know how. I'll treat you with respect, I won't ever lie to you, and I won't ever deliberately hurt you. And I'll be faithful to my marriage vows because that's my nature. But that's all I have to offer.''

A pregnant pause followed his words. Finally she said, "I can accept that.''

"After hearing all this, you're still interested, then?'' Gideon couldn't quite believe it.

"Yes, I...I think I am.''

He quickly made a decision. "Then I'd like you to meet my kids right away.'' He glanced at his watch and frowned. "It's too late to set it up today,'' he said. "But I was already planning to go over there tomorrow night. I can take you then.''

At her puzzled look he explained, "My kids are staying with my sister-in-law right now. That's my wife's sister, Emily Holden. The Holden place is about an hour's drive from here."

"I see."

"There's a motel in Carter's Junction where you can stay tonight. It's not fancy, but it's clean."

"I passed it when I came through town. I'm sure it will be fine. Do I...should I come here tomorrow or—"

"I'll pick you up. It's on the way."

"All right. What time?"

"I'll have to let you know."

"Fine." She gazed solemnly up at Gideon, her dark eyes having the strangest effect on him. He dragged his attention back to the matter at hand with an effort.

"If the visit with my kids works out and you're still willing afterward, we can get our blood tests and a license immediately. We can probably be married by the end of next week."

"So soon?"

"I want my children home with me where they belong. Do you have any reason to wait that's more important than that?"

"No, of course not. But don't you want...I don't know...references, or something? For all you know, I could be anyone."

He gave her a long, considering look, then shook his head. "No. I don't need references. For some reason, I believe you're exactly what you say you are. But if you're lying," he warned, his voice hardening, "walk away now. Hurt my kids in any way, *any* way, then God help you, because nothing else will."

If he hadn't been watching her so closely, he would have missed the faint tremor that shook her body in reaction to his threat, and his tone gentled. "But if you give my children the love and care they need, I'll give you everything that's in my power to give.'' Gideon paused for a moment, then, almost diffidently added, ''I didn't think to ask. Do you need references from me?''

''No, I...'' She seemed flustered, and a little embarrassed. ''I already asked about you in town.''

Gideon cocked his head. ''No kidding? What did they say?''

''You're honest, hard-working, a bad man to cross but a good man to have on your side, a loving father and a true friend.''

''All that, huh?'' He grinned, feeling inexplicably young again, almost lighthearted. ''Well, well. The things we never hear about ourselves.'' He held out his hand, still grinning. ''So, do we have a deal?''

She didn't respond immediately, and Gideon found himself holding his breath for her answer. Then she let his hand swallow hers. ''Deal.''

As if his smile were contagious, one escaped and flitted across her face. Something long dormant stirred to life within him. *Why, she's* more *than pretty when she does that,* he thought, gazing down at her, until a sudden realization chased the errant notion away.

''Hey!''

''Hey, what?''

His grin deepened. ''You've all but agreed to marry me, and I don't even know your name.''

She hesitated a moment. Standing this close to her, Gideon saw her pupils dilate with an odd emotion he couldn't put a name to, and it intrigued him. He filed that bit of data away in the back of his mind.

''Rennie,'' she said finally, almost defiantly, throwing her head back and looking him straight in the eye. ''Rennie Fortier.''

Chapter 2

At five minutes to five the next evening, Rennie walked
into the motel lobby to wait for Gideon. There was no one
at the front desk, but she didn't ring the bell on the counter.
She had no wish to encounter the curious clerk who'd
checked her in the night before, and who by now had probably heard all about Rennie.

She'd forgotten how quickly news could spread around a
small town. She had a casual conversation at breakfast with
the waitress in the motel coffee shop regarding the reason
for Rennie's presence in town, and by dinnertime it seemed
as if everyone knew she was Gideon Lowell's mail-order
bride.

The gossip itself didn't really bother her because she
knew there was no harm intended. Anything out of the ordinary was news in a small town, and when it was something as interesting as a mail-order bride, well!

She'd almost enjoyed herself today, strolling up and down
Main Street in Carter's Junction, making a couple of pur-

chases, and meeting a few of the town's 304 residents, as the town sign proclaimed. But every time someone was bold enough to mention Gideon's name to her, fear-induced adrenaline shot into her bloodstream, kicking her pulse into overdrive.

Rennie checked her watch, then picked up an outdated magazine from a table in the corner and sat down on one of the two upholstered chairs facing the front window. She idly leafed through the magazine, hoping to avoid conversation should the desk clerk wander in, but her thoughts drifted back to the man who would arrive at any minute.

Gideon Lowell. When she'd read his ad for a wife, the wild idea of answering it had occurred to her and she hadn't been able to shake it. Every time she'd pored over the rest of the report prepared by the discreet and expensive private investigator she'd hired to find out about the Lowell family, her mind would jump back to Gideon's ad. She'd read such need in those few, simple words, a need she couldn't help but respond to. So she'd come to Wyoming with the very definite intention of meeting him, and possibly, just possibly, marrying him.

But reading about someone in an impersonal private detective's report is far different from meeting him in person. And nothing she'd felt while reading that report even came close to the impact Gideon had made on her in person.

She really liked him. And despite everything, she was strongly attracted to him. She hadn't counted on that. Would it make the situation easier or harder to deal with?

Tossing the unread magazine on the chair beside her, Rennie rose and began pacing. She had to stop second-guessing herself. Everything Gideon had told her yesterday only reinforced her belief that he and his children needed what she could give them. And she'd already made her decision. What was the use of rehashing it now?

At that moment, a battered tan pickup truck swung into view. It parked, and Gideon got out, slamming the door shut behind him. Rennie hurried outside.

"Hi." She stopped short, smiling hesitantly.

He removed his Stetson and combed his fingers through golden-brown hair that was still damp from a recent shower. "Sorry I'm late." The corner of his mouth twitched into a rueful grin. "I couldn't find a clean shirt, so I had to run a load of laundry through the machine."

"Oh." His honesty made her smile, a real smile this time. "You look fine to me." He looked more than fine, actually, he looked the quintessential cowboy from his scuffed, freshly polished boots to his gray felt cowboy hat.

He was wearing jeans again, less worn than yesterday but just as snug-fitting. A clean white shirt with pearlized snaps and fancy stitching was tucked neatly into his jeans, but the top snap had been left open, revealing a tantalizing glimpse of his throat. And he'd just shaved—the breeze carried the woodsy scent of his after-shave. Had he dressed to impress her, Rennie wondered, or for his children?

"You look nice yourself." The compliment was delivered in Gideon's deep rumble, and though it wasn't much as compliments went, Rennie heard the sincerity behind it.

"I wasn't quite sure what to wear. You said casual on the phone this morning, but I wanted to make a good impression." So she'd worn jeans, not nearly as snug-fitting as his, and had topped them with a bright pink cotton sweater that was soft and comfortable. And she'd worn the brown cowboy boots she'd purchased just that afternoon.

His hazel eyes were openly appreciative of the picture she made, and Rennie felt the oddest sensation in the pit of her stomach. Men had looked at her with admiration before, but somehow this was different. Gideon made it different. And that scared her.

Rennie was the first to turn away, and Gideon's smile faded. "We'd better get moving," he said. "Emily's expecting us for dinner."

During the drive out to the Holden ranch Gideon prepared Rennie for the reception she was likely to receive.

"It'll be tough-going at first, I'm afraid. My daughters don't want a new mother. That is, Nicki doesn't, and her attitude has Trina expecting the worst. I've told them about you, but they don't understand why I'm doing this."

The truck jounced over a bump in the road, and Rennie winced when her elbow hit the door. "And your little boy?"

"Andrew doesn't understand, either, but then, he's only two. And since he doesn't have any memories of his mother, that's one less thing to overcome."

"You're right." But an ache lodged in her heart. It wasn't *right* for a little boy to never know his mother.

"He's gotten pretty attached to Emily, though," Gideon said. "Especially these past few months since I fired the last housekeeper."

"It's understandable. Two's an impressionable age. He probably considers Emily his mother."

Gideon glanced over at her. "It doesn't sound too promising, does it?"

"I don't expect it will be easy."

He hesitated, then added, "I hate to say it, but there's one other problem. Emily doesn't approve, either."

"Since she hasn't met me yet, I won't take it personally." The dry tone in which this was delivered made Gideon laugh.

"It's not you she disapproves of. It's this arrangement. She thinks it's a big mistake to marry without love, and she certainly didn't pull any punches when she told me."

Twenty minutes later Emily Holden was escorting Rennie into her living room while Gideon went in search of his children. Gideon was right, Rennie thought to herself. Emily definitely didn't approve, and her polite manner didn't quite disguise it. When Emily excused herself to check on dinner, leaving Rennie alone, she heaved a sigh of relief.

She wandered nervously around the room, wondering what was taking Gideon so long. To distract herself she studied the framed photographs lining the walls. Some of them were from the previous century, men and women stiff and unsmiling, frozen in a time long gone by. But many of the photos were more recent. One in particular caught her eye and she moved closer for a better look. It was a casual pose of two women standing with their arms around each other, laughing. One of the women was Emily Holden. The other, she decided, noting the strong resemblance, must be Johanna.

Rennie's throat tightened. So this was Johanna Lowell. Blond, achingly beautiful, with a warm, loving smile for the person with the camera. Gideon?

A noise at the door alerted her. Rennie quickly stepped away from the photograph as Gideon shepherded his children into the room. She took a calming breath to quiet her emotions, then tacked a smile firmly into place.

"Rennie, this is Nicki," Gideon said, his hand resting on his oldest daughter's shoulder as he guided her forward. "Nicki, this is Rennie Fortier."

Rennie almost lost her courage in that moment. Even if she'd thought she was ready to meet Gideon's children, nothing could have prepared her for Nicki.

A lovely child of nine, with long blond hair framing a slender face, Nicki clearly resembled her mother far more than she did her father. But her eyes were Gideon's, and those hazel eyes flashed, nakedly hostile. Rennie quailed under the look, but hid it as best she could and held out her hand.

"I'm glad to meet you, Nicki." For a second she thought the girl would refuse to shake her hand, but Nicki finally, though with obvious reluctance, put her hand in Rennie's. She drew it back almost immediately and rubbed it against the side of her leg, as if to remove the contamination of Rennie's touch. Nicki was careful not to let her father see it, though, but her eyes held Rennie's to make sure Rennie knew exactly what she was doing and why.

"And this is Trina," Gideon continued, seeing more than either Rennie or Nicki wanted him to see, but not letting on. He drew Trina forward. She favored her mother, too, a six-year-old version of Nicki. But her face was slightly rounder than her sister's, and where Nicki looked older than her years, Trina looked younger.

Taking her cue from her older sister, Trina refused to smile, but her eyes held no hostility, only confusion and a sadness that made Rennie want to cry.

Rennie bent down and shook Trina's little hand, smiling warmly. "I'm glad to meet you, Trina." Trina started to speak, glanced at Nicki, and fell silent, pulling away from Rennie and moving to stand next to her sister.

"And this is Andrew," Gideon concluded, leaning over to ruffle the hair of the little boy whose baby features held the promise of resembling his father almost exactly.

Ignoring the silent disapproval radiating from Nicki, Rennie knelt in front of Gideon's son and smiled.

"Hey, there, pardner."

Andrew hid against his father's leg.

"He's a little shy," Gideon said.

Rennie concealed her exasperation with her future husband. Obviously the boy was shy, but saying so in front of him only reinforced it.

''It's okay.'' Rennie spoke directly to Andrew and smiled again for his benefit when the little boy stole a glance at her. ''I'm kind of shy, too.'' She dug into her pocket for the quarter she'd put there earlier, and ostentatiously palmed it.

''Abracadabra!'' She blew into her closed fist, then opened it to reveal an empty hand. Feigning amazement and searching the ground at their feet, she asked Andrew, ''Where did it go?''

He shook his head, then watched in wide-eyed wonderment as Rennie reached over and plucked the quarter from his ear.

''Why, Andrew, how did this get there?'' Delighted laughter was her reward, but there was even better to come.

''Do that again.'' The request came, not from Andrew, but from Trina.

Rennie obliged, only this time the quarter reappeared in Trina's shoe. Soon both children were pressing against Rennie, clamoring for more. Nicki, however, hung back, a sullen expression on her face.

As she tirelessly repeated the magic trick and its variations for Andrew and Trina, Rennie was nevertheless aware of Nicki's deepening resentment. Obviously Nicki hadn't wanted her little sister and brother to like Rennie any more than she did, and their defection rankled. But Rennie sensed there was something more behind Nicki's attitude, emotions that went deeper than the natural resentment a child might feel toward a woman who was trying to take her mother's place.

Emily Holden appeared in the doorway. ''Dinner's ready. Nicki, you and Trina take Andrew and help him wash up.''

Nicki was quick to oblige, triumphantly dragging her reluctant siblings away from Rennie. Gideon watched their exit with a thoughtful expression on his face, then escorted Rennie into the kitchen.

On the drive over, Gideon had explained that his sister-in-law was a widow with two children, and in the kitchen Rennie met Emily's boys: Seth, ten, and Matt, seven. And she met Emily's father-in-law, Jim Holden, a brash, plain-spoken rancher, whose weathered face reminded Rennie of men she'd known growing up in Montana.

By the time Gideon's children returned, Rennie and Gideon were already seated together at the table. Nicki slid into the seat on Gideon's right before the two younger children could get there, and a problem quickly arose. Everyone, it seemed, wanted to sit beside Gideon.

Rennie got up and moved over before the problem became a major one. "Trina, why don't you sit here between your Daddy and me?"

The little girl smiled shyly and seated herself. "Thank you."

Which only left Andrew without a place near his father. Gideon solved that by picking up his son and holding him on his lap during the entire meal, totally unconcerned about Andrew's limited abilities with a fork and spoon.

Conversation between the adults was almost impossible with five children at the table. With four of the five children in elementary school, talk centered on school activities. Rennie noticed that Gideon addressed questions to Nicki in a perfectly natural way, even though her answers were silent nods and shakes of her head.

After dinner the children were excused to do chores and homework. Only Andrew remained behind, stubbornly refusing all efforts to coax him from his father's lap.

When Emily began to clear the table, Rennie jumped up to help, stacking the dishes on the counter while Emily rinsed them off. Afterward, Emily served coffee, and the four adults sat around the table. The excitement of the evening had been too much for Andrew, and he soon fell asleep in his father's arms, his mouth making a small, damp patch on Gideon's shirt.

"He didn't have a nap today," Emily explained apologetically to Gideon. "He knew you were coming this evening and he was too wound up to go down."

"That's okay. I'll take him up to bed in a little bit."

The conversation lagged, and it would have been awkward if not for Jim Holden, who kept it going almost by himself. Rennie's reference to her father's ranch in Montana in response to one of Jim's questions brought an unexpected result.

"Fortier. Fortier. I know that name," Jim mused, in a voice made raspy by too many cigarettes. "That wouldn't be Frank Fortier, would it?"

Rennie felt the blood drain from her face, and she stared at the older man. "That's right," she said, forcing the words through stiff lips.

"Now, don't tell me, it'll come to me." He thought for a moment, then said triumphantly, "The Circle F!"

Her throat went dry. "That's right," she repeated.

Jim chuckled and addressed the other two adults at the table. "I may be gettin' on in years, but my mind's still sharp as a tack about some things." He looked at Rennie. "So you're Frank Fortier's daughter." He smiled approvingly, then nodded to Gideon. "Good stock."

Gideon glanced at Rennie, and she could almost hear what he was thinking. He obviously respected the older man's opinion, and Jim's approval of Rennie carried weight.

Then Jim's grin faded as he remembered, and he said with gruff sympathy, "Heard about your father passin' on. Let's see now, must be eight, no, ten years back."

"Yes," she said softly, still feeling a pang of grief even after all these years.

"Heard the Circle F was sold right after he died. Guess Frank had no sons to carry on after him." Jim voiced the chauvinistic thinking still so prevalent in the West, especially among the older generation.

"No," Rennie said quietly. "He had no sons. Only me."

The silence that followed her statement stretched out endlessly, until it was broken by Emily's offer of more coffee.

"Not you, Jim," she said over the older man's growling protests. "Remember what the doctor said."

"Damn doctors, what do they know." Jim appealed to Gideon. "How's a man supposed to function on only two measly cups of coffee a day, I ask you?"

Gideon smiled and shrugged his shoulders. "Beats me."

Jim grumbled, but Emily obviously wasn't going to give in, so he drained the dregs of his cup and turned back to Rennie.

"Come to think of it, I heard the Circle F was sold again a couple years back to one of them big cattle outfits up there." Rennie froze, but no one seemed to notice. Then Jim shook his head and added, "It's a damn shame the way the family ranchers are being driven off, one by one."

The conversation drifted into that vein, and Rennie eventually relaxed enough to put a word or two in. But she was still relieved when Gideon shortly thereafter took Andrew to bed, then returned and announced it was time they left.

Gideon didn't say much on the drive back to Rennie's motel, but his pleased expression told its own story. Rennie, too, was quiet while she contemplated the evening's results. Despite her failure with Nicki, she knew Gideon's opinion of her suitability as a mother and a wife had risen several notches that evening. And her opinion of him had gone up, as well.

Gravel crunched as the truck pulled into the motel's parking lot. Gideon turned off the engine, then shifted on the seat to face her and smiled unexpectedly, a flash of white in the semidarkness.

"You were pretty clever this evening. That magic trick broke the ice. What made you think of it?"

"Children's belief in magic is fairly universal. Look at the most popular Disney movies. There's magic in almost every one."

"Come to think of it, you're right." They sat in silence for a minute, then the conversation took a serious turn. "So. You've met my children. Is your answer still the same?"

She hesitated for only a second. "Yes."

"Good. I was hoping you'd say that. Here's what we need to do, then." Gideon ticked the items off on the fingers of his left hand. "One, the prenuptial agreement I mentioned earlier. My attorney's office is in Sheridan. I called him this afternoon and he'll squeeze us in tomorrow at ten. Two, blood tests. Last time I applied for a marriage license only the female applicant was required to have a blood test. I don't know if the law has changed, but I assume you'll want me to have one, too."

"It would probably be wise."

"I agree, and it shouldn't be a problem. I've known Doc Simms all my life, and he'll rush the blood tests through as a favor to me. He's got a clinic in Sheridan so we can get that done tomorrow, too. Three, marriage license. Cora Mae Kell at the post office is also city clerk. I think all we need to show her is your blood test and our birth certificates. You don't happen to have yours with you, do you?"

Rennie shook her head, hiding a sudden jolt of fear at the mention of her birth certificate.

"Can you get it?"

She nodded. "But I'll have to go back to Los Angeles."

That checked him for a moment. "When will you go?"

"If we're going to Sheridan tomorrow, I'll fly out early Saturday morning. I have to go back, anyway, to pack up my things and ship them out here. I'll come back as soon as I wrap things up there."

"When, exactly?"

Rennie considered everything she needed to do, mentally summing up the time it would take. "I'll need a week, maybe a little less." She could see that her answer wasn't quite the one he wanted, but what did he expect? She was uprooting her entire life for this man and his family. She needed more than just a couple of days.

"Well," he said finally, "we can apply for the license as soon as you return. And maybe it would be a good idea if you spent a little more time with my kids beforehand, anyway." Rennie nodded her agreement, and he added, "Shall we set two weeks from tomorrow as our target date? I'll talk to the local justice of the peace about a civil ceremony. Shouldn't take more than fifteen minutes." Gideon cocked an eyebrow. "Is that okay with you?"

She didn't answer right away, and it must have tipped him off to her true feelings.

"You'd prefer a church service, wouldn't you?" he said slowly. Rennie didn't say anything. "Look, I can talk to the minister at my church. Tom's an old friend of mine. I think I can convince him to marry us even on such short notice." He paused. "Is that...?"

"That's fine." Rennie smiled shyly, touched by his understanding. "Thank you. Even though ours is an arranged marriage, I'd be happier with a church wedding. I doubt I'd feel really married any other way."

* * *

Gideon saw Rennie safely inside her motel room and left her there after arranging to pick her up at eight-thirty the next morning. She locked the door behind him and slipped on the safety chain, then sank onto the bed, drained of energy. The evening had been even more of a strain than she'd expected, and her bad hip ached a little from the tension in her muscles.

It was an effort to get her new boots off, but once she did she stretched out, dragging a corner of the bedspread over her body. At this elevation it got pretty cold at night even in the middle of summer, and it was only the beginning of May. To make matters worse, the heater in her motel room left much to be desired, as she'd learned last night.

The bedside lamp cast a warm glow over the room, softening the stark simplicity. A squat dresser that bowed in the middle, a spindly chair, a rickety end table and the double bed on which she lay took up all the space in the tiny room. But Rennie scarcely noticed. She stared blankly at the wall, her thoughts elsewhere.

Was she really going to do this?

Things were moving faster than she'd realized they would. Part of her was afraid, but part of her, a big part, wanted to let events just take their course.

But could she get away with it?

That scene with Jim Holden tonight had shaken her. She hadn't expected anyone in Wyoming to know her father, especially since he'd been dead for so long. It was a fluke, a coincidence. And even if anyone else recognized her last name and connected it with Frank Fortier as Jim had done, it wasn't very likely that they'd know or remember that his daughter had been named Francesca, after him.

Of course, that bit about her birth certificate had taken her by surprise, too. She'd have to be careful not to let Gideon see it. Francesca was hardly a common name.

Rennie shivered and pulled the covers tighter around her. If Gideon knew who she was…

Don't be silly, she told herself. *There's no way he can find out that Rennie Fortier was once Francesca Renee Fortier Whitney. If he hasn't recognized me by now, he's not going to. And as long as Gideon doesn't see the name Francesca on my birth certificate, I'll be all right. The press in Los Angeles knew me only by my adopted last name, so no one will make the connection between Francesca Whitney and Rennie Fortier.*

But could she go through with it? Could she marry Gideon Lowell?

She liked him even more now than she had before, and that was saying a lot. She'd watched him with his children this evening, had seen the tenderness in his eyes when he looked at them, had seen the flash of pain he'd tried to hide when he hugged and kissed his daughters goodbye. And he'd looked so content earlier, so natural, with Andrew on his lap. He loved his children openly, honestly, and they obviously adored him. So it was easy to understand why he'd taken this drastic step to make their future a little more secure.

But was she strong enough to take that drastic step with him?

She yearned for reassurance, but knew there was no one who would understand. It was her decision to make. Hers alone. "I can do it," she whispered. "I know I can." But she wished she sounded more convincing.

Her gaze fell on the phone beside the bed and she suddenly realized she hadn't called Jess. He didn't know where she was, and he was probably worried sick by now. And she had to tell him what she was planning. He'd go crazy, but she couldn't *not* tell him. Before she could change her mind, she pushed herself into a sitting position, snatched up the receiver and dialed.

The phone rang twice before it was picked up, and the crisp, deep sound of her stepbrother's voice filled her ear. "J. T. Whitney."

"Jess, it's Rennie."

"Rennie, where the hell are you? I've been calling your apartment for the last three days, and I—"

She cut him off. "I'm in Wyoming."

"Wyoming?" Why—" An answer came to him before she had a chance to say anything. "Rennie, you didn't go out there because of what you found out last month, did you?"

"Yes."

"Oh, honey, why?"

She took a deep breath and let it out slowly. "Jess, don't say anything for a minute, please. I have something to tell you, and I know you're going to be upset, but please don't say anything yet. Okay?"

"What is it?"

"I'm getting married." She heard a sharply indrawn breath on the other end of the line, and added, "To Gideon Lowell," then waited for the explosion.

"Are you out of your mind? I turn my back for a moment and the next thing I know you're marrying a stranger! And not just any stranger. Gideon Lowell, for God's sake!"

"I know what you're thinking."

"You do? That's a mighty good trick, Rennie, since *I* don't even know what I'm thinking. I didn't even know you'd left L.A. How can I think anything when you spring this on me with absolutely no warning?"

"If you'd just calm down I can explain."

"Explain? No, I don't think so. You've done some crazy,

impulsive things in your life, but *this,* this goes far beyond anything you've ever done.''

"This isn't a crazy impulse, Jess. I'm serious."

"You're serious. Well, of course, that makes all the difference." The withering sarcasm only strengthened Rennie's resolve and she gripped the phone tighter.

"I'm going to do this, Jess. Please don't try to interfere."

"Rennie, for God's sake, I can't let you make a mistake like this. If you were about to walk into a minefield, would you expect me to just stand there and do nothing?"

"It's not the same thing."

"No? How is it different? If Lowell ever discovers who you really are, what do you think will happen?"

"How can he find out unless you tell him? No one would recognize me the way I look now. And it's perfectly legal to call myself Fortier instead of Whitney. After all, it's the name I was born with, the name on my birth certificate. All I have to do is apply for a Wyoming driver's license in the name of Rennie Fortier, and Francesca Whitney disappears."

"Rennie…"

"Listen to me for once, Jess. For once, just *listen.* If you had listened to me two years ago when I wanted you to lend me the money to buy the Circle F, if we hadn't fought about my moving back to Montana, maybe things would be different. Maybe—"

"I don't believe this! So now it's my fault you're going to screw up your life?"

"No, I didn't say that! You can be so exasperating at times!" She brought herself under control. "Jess, ever since I came out of the coma I've lived in limbo. Now, for the first time in a long time, I have a sense of purpose. I'm not drifting anymore. They need me, Jess, and I…need them."

"Honey, you can't have thought this through. Just take a

minute and think about it now. How can you build a new life based on a lie?''

"It's not a lie. Not exactly."

"Isn't it?" He waited a moment, then said gently, "A loveless marriage can be hell on the soul, Rennie. And haven't you already suffered enough? More than a year in a coma, months of physical therapy learning to walk again, those internal injuries—"

"Don't." Months of heartache and pain condensed into one word.

He pressed on relentlessly. "And what happens down the road if you can't stick it out? You'll only make matters worse than they already are for that family."

"I won't quit." It was a vow. "I won't!"

The telephone line hummed in the ensuing silence. Finally Jess said, "Isn't there anything I can say to make you change your mind?"

Rennie had heard that pleading note in his voice only once before, when she'd struggled to consciousness in the hospital to find him at her bedside. The memory made her try again to explain her motives.

"Jess, you know I've never really been happy in L.A. I was born out here and this land is in my blood. This is the life I've always wanted. God knows I tried to be what everybody wanted me to be, but I can't. I can't. Don't you see? I'm doing this for me as much as for them."

"If the ranch is the only reason you—"

"It's not, and you know it. It's part of it. But the children are the most important part. They're the real reason, Jess. You know I can never have children of my own. But these children need a mother, and that mother can be me. I'm not going to throw this chance away."

"And if Lowell finds out who you are?"

"I'll cross that bridge when I come to it." She sent up a

fervent prayer that she would never have to do so. Then she added the clincher. "This isn't just something I *want* to do, Jess, it's something I *have* to do. Can't you see that?"

He sighed and Rennie knew she'd won, this round at least.

"When is the wedding?"

"Two weeks from tomorrow."

"Good God. Why so soon?"

"Gideon wants his children home with him as soon as possible, and I agreed. They've been living at his sister-in-law's. I'm flying back to Los Angeles on Saturday to pack."

"If you're coming back, why did you tell me all this over the phone?"

"I wanted you to have time to calm down before I saw you."

Silence. "Wise move," Jess said at last. "When does your flight arrive in L.A.? I'll meet your plane."

"I don't know yet. I'll call you when I do. But Jess," she warned, "don't even think of trying to change my mind."

"I can't promise you that, damn it."

Even over the phone Rennie felt his frustration, and her throat swelled with emotion. For seven years Jess had been her only family, and though he'd never understood her, he'd always been there when she needed him. But this time she needed him to let go. It was time he stopped protecting her.

"I love you, Jess," she whispered before he could say anything more.

"I love you, too, honey."

"Wish me luck?"

"With all my heart."

Rennie put down the phone with trembling hands and a sense of finality. It was done. Jess knew, and for the moment, at least, he accepted her decision.

She was committed now.

Chapter 3

The next two weeks passed in a blur, for which Rennie was grateful. If she had had time to think, she might have changed her mind. But the few days she spent wrapping up her life in Los Angeles were so hectic that she tumbled exhausted into bed each night and slept dreamlessly. And when she returned to Wyoming, her days and nights were filled with trips to the Rocking L with Gideon and visiting the Holden ranch to see Gideon's children.

She'd heard nothing but praise of her future husband from the residents of Carter's Junction when she'd first come to town. Now she watched him with the townsfolk and saw that it was true—they liked and respected him. She observed him with his ranch hands, and saw the same. But she saw even more. She saw a man who seemed alone, somehow, even in a crowd, a man who'd forgotten how to laugh. A man who rarely smiled, except around his children.

The children. It all came back to them. Darling Andrew, who loved to be tickled and cuddled. Sweet Trina, whose eagerness to please and mercurial mood swings expressed her underlying insecurity. And Nicki. Troubled, hostile Nicki, who poignantly reminded Rennie of herself so many years ago.

The children needed her. So did Gideon. And as she'd told Jess, she needed them.

On an unusually warm Friday in May, Rennie and Gideon stood side by side before the altar of St. Luke's Church on the Hill. The afternoon sun streaming through the stained glass window above the altar cast jewel-toned shards of light around the sanctuary as they exchanged vows—Rennie in a voice scarcely above a whisper, Gideon in deep, firm tones. Then, as Rennie watched, Gideon slid a slim gold band on the third finger of her left hand.

She stared at the ring for a moment, the symbol of their commitment to each other, and all at once the enormity of what she'd done overwhelmed her. Jess's warnings crept back to haunt her and she trembled slightly, feeling suddenly cold in her short-sleeved lavender dress. *If Gideon should ever find out the truth...*

Gideon's hand closed over hers as if to reassure her, but his touch only added to her fears. Her eyes flickered from his hand, over the gray wool of his suit coat, up to his face, and then away. But that brief look told her enough. Underneath his calm exterior, Gideon was just as nervous as she was, though for far different reasons. After all, he was risking a lot in taking such a momentous step with a woman he scarcely knew. He had no way of knowing that Rennie was determined to do everything in her power to make this arranged marriage a success.

Everything's going to work out, she promised herself. *I'll make it work. There's no reason for Gideon to ever learn the truth. So all I have to do is concentrate on being the best wife and mother I can possibly be from this moment on, and let the future take care of itself.*

But the tiny voice of doubt refused to be silenced.

As Reverend Tom finished the ceremony, Gideon felt a moment of panic. What was he *doing,* for God's sake? How could he think this…arrangement stood a chance? His marriage with Johanna hadn't been nine perfect years. They had fought occasionally, like all couples, but the deep love they shared had carried them through the hard times.

How could a marriage survive without love?

He looked down at Rennie's pale face and realized that she must be experiencing the same last-minute doubts. Gideon knew a brief moment of compassion and comradeship. He caught her eye and smiled encouragingly, as something akin to calm settled over him.

I made the right decision. Rennie's a natural mother. This past week has proved that. Trina and Andrew took to her so quickly it's almost a sign from above that things are going to work out. And God willing, even Nicki will come to accept her, given time. Maybe not as a mother, exactly, but as a friend. God, please let it happen that way. Then Rennie will have what she wants from our marriage: children to love. And she won't expect things from me that I can't give.

Expectations. How different his own expectations this time around. This time he was going into marriage with his eyes open and his heart closed. He knew what he was doing. What you don't love, you can't lose, and he wasn't risking his heart. Never that again.

But he'd take a chance on friendship. Rennie's friendship.

Gideon suddenly became aware of a hushed, waiting silence. He'd been staring blindly in Rennie's general direction for the past few minutes. Now his vision focused on her face. Her lovely eyes were frantically signaling something to him, but Gideon couldn't quite make out the message. He glanced up at Tom, his minister and long-time friend, and raised a questioning eyebrow.

"I said, you may kiss the bride."

Gideon bent down what seemed a long way to brush his lips lightly over Rennie's. Hers were warm, soft, and unexpectedly sweet, tempting him to deepen the kiss. A collective murmur of voices hummed in the background and he pulled back.

Forget it. Now's not the time or place. You've got an audience, remember?

"Congratulations," Reverend Tom said, extending his hand to Gideon.

Gideon straightened and shook his friend's hand. "Thanks, Tom."

The minister had expressed his disapproval over their hasty decision to marry and had tried to convince them to wait. But he'd finally agreed to perform the ceremony when Rennie and Gideon both insisted on going forward as planned, even if it meant not having a church wedding.

Reverend Tom took Rennie's hand in both of his. In a voice pitched to carry no further than the couple in front of him, he said, "If you ever need to talk—" he shot a look at Gideon "—either of you, my door is always open. Remember that. And know that I'll be praying for you."

Rennie smiled tremulously. "Thank you."

Reverend Tom smiled back, then cleared his throat. Stepping to one side, he addressed the congregation. "Folks, may I present Mr. and Mrs. Gideon Lowell."

Hearty applause broke out as Gideon and Rennie turned to face their well-wishers. Thanks to Cora Mae Kell, town clerk, postmistress and inveterate gossip, word of their upcoming wedding had circulated as rapidly as the news three

months ago that Gideon had advertised for a mail-order
bride. Almost everyone in Carter's Junction, as well as a
few of Gideon's friends from Sheridan, had come out to
witness the event. St. Luke's was so crowded there was
scarcely standing room.

The quiet ceremony Gideon had first envisioned had
quickly fallen by the wayside. As news of his impending
wedding spread, he realized he couldn't very well tell his
friends and neighbors, people he'd known all his life, that
they weren't welcome at his second wedding. That would
have caused untold hurt feelings and gossip, gossip neither
he nor Rennie needed.

The church organist, who played forcefully if not accu-
rately, began the newlyweds' recessional music, "Jesu Joy
of Man's Desiring." With Rennie's hand tucked securely
under his arm, Gideon led her down the aisle.

They passed the first pew where his children sat, dressed
in their Sunday best. Trina's solemn face and Nicki's obvious distress sent a shard of pain through his heart. Only
Andrew seemed unaware of what was going on.

Emily Holden was seated there, too, with her two boys
and Jim Holden. Gideon knew Emily had put aside her own
disapproval of the marriage to support him for the sake of
his children, and he was grateful to her for that.

A receiving line of sorts formed in the back of the church.
Gideon's children joined them, Nicki and Trina pressing
close to his side while he held Andrew in his arms. As
Gideon made informal introductions, Rennie accepted the
congratulations of her new neighbors. She was kissed more
times than she could count and desperately tried to fix
names with faces for the future.

"You make a beautiful bride...."

"You've chosen a good man...."

"Hope you'll be very happy...."

"Beautiful wedding, just beautiful..." Tears streamed down the cheeks of a middle-aged woman Rennie didn't know, Alice Something or Other.

"Don't mind my wife, Miz Lowell." Rennie's hand was pumped vigorously by the woman's stocky husband. "She always cries at weddings."

"Such a lovely dress," another woman said, surreptitiously fingering the filmy lavender material, and Rennie recognized the waitress from the café.

"Thank you."

"You didn't buy it around here."

Rennie shook her head, smiling as she confirmed, "No, I didn't. I bought it in Los Angeles."

"Your family couldn't make the wedding?" she asked archly.

Rennie had expected the question, so she was ready with an answer. "My parents both passed away several years ago," she said easily. "And I'm an only child. As for my friends, it's a long way to come on such short notice."

The woman nodded, then looked down at Gideon's daughters and said, "Well, how does it feel to have a new mommy?"

Trina mumbled something that Rennie didn't catch, but Nicki's expression hardened. Nicki obviously wasn't pleased with her sister's answer. Rennie sighed a little, but didn't say anything. There wasn't anything she could do at this point.

She turned to greet the next person in line and found herself face-to-face with Emily. Conscious of the curious eyes all around them, Rennie's heart went out to Emily, whose dilemma was plain on her pretty face. Gideon's sister-in-law might not believe it, but Rennie understood Emily's reservations. She had plenty of her own.

The awkward silence was finally broken by Emily. "Good luck."

"Thank you."

Gideon kissed Emily's cheek and echoed Rennie's thanks. Then Emily moved away and her place was taken by another.

Finally it was all over, and Gideon led his children to one side to say goodbye. Without going into the details, he had already explained to them that he and Rennie were taking a short honeymoon, but that they would be back Sunday night.

Rennie had made the suggestion that they go away for the weekend, and after some discussion Gideon had agreed. They both acknowledged their need for time alone together, however brief, to get their marriage started off on the right foot. If they could get to know each other and become somewhat comfortable in their new relationship, the children would benefit greatly in the long run.

She had left it up to him as to where they should go, however, and he had chosen the picturesque town of Wagon Wheel Gap up in the Bighorn Mountains. It was close enough that they wouldn't have a long way to travel, but far enough away that they wouldn't encounter anyone who knew Gideon. That would insure their privacy.

With Rennie standing quietly a few feet away, Gideon picked up each of his children in turn, hugging and kissing them. Then, with Andrew nestled in one arm, he spoke to Nicki and Trina in a low voice.

"We'll be back day after tomorrow, just like I told you this morning." He brushed Nicki's blond bangs off her forehead with his free hand, then cupped Trina's cheek. The little girl's face quivered ominously. "Don't cry, baby, okay? I promise you I'll come back."

Trina threw her arms around him and burst into tears. Gideon glanced helplessly at Rennie.

Something blossomed in her heart in that moment. Although Emily was nearby, Gideon hadn't turned to her for help. He'd looked to Rennie. She didn't stop to analyze her emotions, just moved to his side.

"Let me take Andrew," she whispered, gently pulling the little boy into her arms. "You deal with Trina."

Gideon nodded when he saw Andrew go willingly to Rennie. He picked Trina up once more, comforting her as she sobbed against his shoulder. Rennie watched his face contort with pain over his daughter's fear of abandonment.

She almost told him to forget their brief honeymoon if it was going to make Trina so unhappy, but bit her lip to keep from blurting out the words. They would be gone only two days. And those two days alone were important, at least to her.

Rennie nuzzled Andrew's neck, kissing him secretly. He smelled so sweet, and his sturdy little body felt so good in her arms. She smiled at him, coaxing a smile in return. Remarkable how much Andrew resembled Gideon, from his sun-streaked brown hair, his hazel eyes, to his solemn little face. As if there were nothing of Johanna in him. Rennie hadn't told anyone—there'd been no one to tell—but she'd lost her heart to Andrew the first time she'd seen him smile.

A prickling sensation along the back of her neck made Rennie look up. Now that Gideon's attention was elsewhere, Nicki's hazel eyes bored into Rennie with unconcealed antagonism. No surprise there. But Rennie sensed other emotions warring within Nicki, emotions she'd experienced herself years ago. She smiled gently at her new stepdaughter, and saw a flash of pain in Nicki's eyes before the girl looked away. Pain, and something else. Something that looked like fear.

Rennie's heart ached for her. *Oh, Nicki. I'm not going to hurt you. I'm going to help you. If you'll let me.*

But she knew this wasn't the right time to say those words out loud. Nicki wasn't ready to hear them. So Rennie turned her attention back to Andrew for now, promising herself that someday she'd find the key to Nicki.

Nicki moved a little ways away from the others, her emotions in turmoil. She knew she was behaving badly, even if Daddy or Aunt Emily didn't say anything. Shame flickered through her, to join the ever-present sense of fear and guilt. Mama would be ashamed of her if she knew.

Dry-eyed, Nicki watched Trina cry, wishing she could cry, too. Tears burned the back of her eyes so badly they ached, and her throat felt scratchy, but she knew the tears wouldn't fall. She hadn't cried the day they buried her mother, nor any day since. She wouldn't cry now.

Daddy had cried. She'd only been seven, but she'd known even then how he'd tried to be strong for her and Trina. But when the men had lowered Mama's coffin into the ground, she'd seen the solitary tear that had defied even Daddy's strength of will to hold it back.

But she hadn't been able to cry. Not then, and not now. Tears were lost to her, just as her voice was lost, just as Mama was lost. And now she was losing Daddy, too.

Trina's sobs finally ceased, and Gideon wiped his daughter's face with his handkerchief. He kissed her once more before handing her to Jim Holden. Rennie reluctantly gave Andrew to Emily.

Gideon grabbed Rennie's hand and tugged. "Let's go."

"But—"

"Come on." He carried her along with him on the tide of his urgency, outside, through the crowd milling around in front of the church and down the steps. Cheers from the crowd followed them. When Rennie attempted to free her hand one last time, he growled, "If we're going to go, let's *go!*"

"But I—"

Gideon opened the passenger door of Rennie's sports car. He seated her and shut the door on her protest. He folded his tall frame into the driver's seat, slammed the door and held out his hand.

"Keys."

"Keys?"

Somewhat impatiently, Gideon explained. "Where are the car keys?"

Rennie licked her dry lips. "They're in my purse."

"So?"

"So, I tried to tell you. My purse is back in the church."

Gideon cursed briefly, a pithy Anglo-Saxon word, and pounded the steering wheel in frustration. "Great. Just great. Why didn't you tell me before?"

"I tried!"

Recognizing the truth of her words, Gideon felt a touch of shame in blaming Rennie for their predicament. She *had* tried, he just hadn't listened. But there was a limit to how much he could take, and that scene with his children in the church vestibule was it.

His head pivoted to the car window. The throng of people was still there, waving and cheering, waiting for them to drive away. Only they couldn't go anywhere without the car keys.

"I can't go back in there," he admitted without turning around.

"I'll go. You stay here." She didn't wait for an answer.

His gaze followed her as she slid out and around the car, gliding gracefully through the crowd. The full skirt of her lavender dress swirled seductively around her slender legs.

She disappeared momentarily inside the church, then reappeared, clutching an enormous purse.

Someone must have made a joke because Rennie laughed. Her reply made everyone around her laugh, too. Then she waved and walked away, toward the car, toward him.

Gideon absently watched her approach, and found himself admiring her as any man would. A stirring in his loins confirmed it.

She's pretty, all right. Not beautiful, like Jo, but there's something about her....

Rennie slipped into her seat and handed him the keys, but when he inserted them into the ignition she put her hand over his to stop him.

"Seat belt, please."

"What?"

"This car doesn't move unless all occupants are wearing seat belts." Rennie buckled hers as she spoke.

Gideon said nothing but did up his own, then started the car. As they drove away from the church and the waving townsfolk, he drew the first easy breath he'd had in days. He looked over at Rennie and cocked a quizzical eyebrow.

"Why the big deal about the seat belt? Don't get me wrong, I usually wear mine and I always make the kids wear theirs, but…"

"I guess I'm a fanatic about it since my accident. I was lucky I was wearing one. If I hadn't, I'd probably be dead."

Gideon's face went blank, all expression wiped clean as he clamped down on memories he thought he'd put behind him.

Instantly Rennie realized what she'd done and mentally berated herself. Why had she brought up the subject? For the past week since she'd returned from Los Angeles she'd made a point of avoiding any mention of her own accident.

And now, in a moment of forgetfulness, she'd opened the door to painful memories for both of them.

She glanced out the window, then back at Gideon. "I'm sorry."

"For what?"

"For what I said. For making you remember your wife."

Gideon's response was slow in coming. "It's okay," he said finally, relaxing the tight control over himself just a little. "To tell you the truth, I was already thinking about her."

"Oh."

"Now *I'm* sorry."

"Why? It's perfectly natural. I should have expected it. I just didn't think, that's all. I know you loved your wife. Still do, for that matter. You don't have to watch everything you say for fear you'll say something that hurts me."

"You mean that?"

"It's not as if we're in love, or anything. To tell you the truth, as you're so fond of saying, I admire you for your honesty."

"Lack of tact, you mean."

Rennie placed her hand on his coat sleeve in an earnest attempt to convince him. She squeezed the taut muscles beneath the gray wool.

"Please believe me, Gideon. I meant what I said."

Their eyes locked for a moment. "Okay," he said in his deepest voice, with just the hint of a smile touching his lips. "I believe you."

Rennie smiled, slowly, sweetly, the first real smile she'd given him all day, and Gideon's body responded with a flush of warmth. Though it might be weeks or even months before he could act on his attraction to Rennie, he felt good about it. Damned good.

He had to force his attention back to the empty road in

front of him. When Rennie removed her hand from his forearm, he wanted to put it back.

"Gideon, can I ask a favor?"

"Sure."

"In the future, would you tell me if something I do or say upsets you? I'll promise to do the same. It's bound to happen, and I'm not very good at reading people's minds."

"You're doing a pretty good job of it so far."

"Please. If we can agree on this one thing, I think we'll have nipped at least a part of our potential problems right in the bud. If our marriage is going to be a success, we have to establish a few ground rules, and this is one of mine."

"A little late for ground rules, isn't it?"

Although his tone was dry and his expression solemn, Rennie saw one corner of his mouth twitch as if he were holding back a smile, and knew he was teasing her. But this was important, too important to joke about.

"No," she said quietly. "I don't think it's too late."

They were fast approaching a slow-moving truck ahead of them on the highway. Gideon flicked on the turn indicator. Although there wasn't another vehicle around for miles, he checked his mirrors, anyway, then passed the truck before responding.

"Okay. Suppose I agree. Any other rules I should know?"

Rennie had given this a lot of thought in the past two weeks. "You've already promised to respect me, never to hurt me deliberately, to be faithful, and never to lie to me. I promise you the same." Rennie shivered inside as her conscience pricked her. Did withholding part of the truth constitute a lie? She hushed her conscience and hurried on.

"In addition, I promise to do my best to be a good mother to your children."

"If I didn't already believe that, I wouldn't be sitting here."

"Thank you."

"Is that all?"

Rennie felt suddenly warm and knew the color in her face betrayed her. If only he would keep his eyes on the road and not look at her! Unfortunately, Gideon ignored her silent plea. His eyes slowly perused the betraying flush and the tightly clasped hands in her lap.

She cleared her throat. "There is one other thing."

"Well?"

She swallowed, the dryness of her throat uncomfortable. What was worse, the flush deepened, but she forged ahead bravely. "I also wanted you to know that I intend to be a good wife to you. Just because we won't sleep...that is...just because we're not...I mean...you promised..." Her voice trailed off miserably, and he took pity on her.

"I promised not to...ah...claim my conjugal rights until we're both ready," he said, not quite smoothly.

Rennie nodded, unable to utter a sound.

He reached over and covered her clenched hands with his large one. "I gave you my word, Rennie," he said very gently. "I don't give that lightly. I meant it."

She found her voice. "I know." Her words were soft but sure. "If I didn't already believe that, *I* wouldn't be sitting here, either."

"Thank you. That means a lot to me."

She turned her hand and slid her fingers through his. "But I do want to be a good wife to you. In other ways." He smiled at her. "I know. You will be." There was assurance in his voice, and something more.

They were silent for a moment, each considering everything the other had said. But when she started to draw her hand away, Gideon retained possession.

"Rennie, I need to ask you something."

For no reason at all, she was suddenly nervous. "Yes?"

"You…you're not a virgin, are you?"

Warmth flooded her face like a tidal wave. Before she could even marshall her thoughts to respond, Gideon hurried to clarify his question.

"I'm not trying to embarrass you, or pry into your past life. It's just, well…hell, if you *are* a virgin, I need to know, so that when…*if* we do…" He stopped, and Rennie detected the faintest tinge of red beneath his tan. His embarrassment mitigated her own.

"No," she said gruffly. "I'm not a virgin." Rennie couldn't leave it at that, however. For some reason she didn't want Gideon to think her promiscuous. "I haven't slept around, if that's what you're wondering. I was seventeen when I… Well, it wasn't such a great experience that I was tempted to do it again."

Gideon digested this in silence. So that explained her extreme shyness in reference to the sexual side of their marriage. He thought back to the coarse suggestion he'd made to her the day they met, and cringed mentally. She was practically a virgin, despite her disclaimer. Once at seventeen and nothing in the intervening years said a lot about the first experience. A sudden distasteful thought occurred to him and his face darkened.

"You weren't ra—"

"No!" Rennie cut him off. "No. I thought he loved me. He didn't. It wasn't rape, but it wasn't very pleasant."

Gideon turned her words over in his mind, realizing how difficult it must be for Rennie to have to tell him these very personal things, even if he was her husband. He decided to honor her confidence with one of his own.

"Johanna was the only woman I've ever slept with." Startled brown eyes rose to meet hazel ones. Gideon smiled ruefully before turning his attention back to the road. "Don't spread that around, okay?"

"I would never..." Her voice trailed off, but he could feel her eyes on his face. "Why?"

"Why am I telling you this, or why was she the only one?"

"A little of both, I guess."

"As for the first, I thought you should know I haven't been parking my boots where I shouldn't," he said whimsically. "I know we passed our blood tests, but a woman's bound to wonder, anyway. I guess I wanted you to know you don't have to worry about that." He cleared his throat. "As for the second, Johanna was the only woman I've ever loved, and I'd known her all my life. I never really wanted anyone else."

Rennie felt her heart turn over. The very simplicity of his words convinced her he was telling the absolute truth. Oh, to be loved like that, to have the single-minded devotion of a man like Gideon. For the first time, Rennie felt a stab of jealousy toward Johanna.

"Thank you for telling me." She couldn't think of anything else to say, and this time when she drew her hand away, Gideon let it go. She moved slightly, tucking her right hand under her cheek against the car window, and stared at the passing scenery.

To some people, northern Wyoming's terrain may have seemed harsh, bleak and unlovely. But for those who cared to look, there was beauty to be found. The folds of the earth, both shallow and steep, the scattered green vegetation among the brown, a lone tree struggling for existence in an arid climate—these things offered a unique, Spartan beauty that refreshed the soul. And after years in a city where smog and skyscrapers choked off her view of the sky, Rennie's eyes drank in the boundless blue overhead.

She sighed softly. If she pretended hard enough, maybe she'd convince herself she was sighing over the scenery, not Gideon's last statement and her unexpected reaction to it. Jealousy wasn't an emotion she had a lot of experience with, especially not jealousy over a man. But Gideon wasn't just any man, she reminded herself. He was her husband.

"Hey."

Startled, Rennie looked up.

"You're awfully quiet. You're not falling asleep, are you?" She shook her head, and he said, "We're coming up to a rest stop. Do you need to use the ladies' room, or anything?"

"No thanks. I'm fine."

He spared her a glance from his concentration on the road, and her faraway expression made him ask, "Is something wrong?"

"No. I'm a little tired, I guess." She searched for a safe topic of conversation. "I didn't expect so many people at our wedding."

"Yeah, well, neither did I."

"But they're your friends. They obviously care about you and want to see you happy."

"I could do with a little less of their attention. You'd think nobody else ever got married in Carter's Junction."

The corners of Rennie's mouth turned up in a tiny smile at his disgruntled expression. "I didn't mind them being there. I thought it was nice, actually."

"You seemed pretty nervous, though."

"Not for that reason." She was skating onto thin ice, and she knew it. Time to change the subject again. "I'm sorry your brother, Caleb, couldn't make it to the wedding. I would have liked to meet him."

"I called, but he was out of town. So I wrote to him."

Then it struck him. "Wait a minute. How did you know I had a brother?"

"You'd be surprised at the things I know about you."

"Oh, yeah?" Gideon was willing to be diverted. "Like what, for instance?"

"Oh, like what you and your twin did the night before your high school graduation."

The look Gideon gave her was full of consternation, and Rennie chuckled. "That's not all I learned about your wicked past," she teased gently. "I know you used to smoke but quit before Nicki was born. You have an interesting scar on your...um...posterior from the time a horse threw you into a fence post. And I heard all about how your father grounded you for a month when you came home from Cheyenne Frontier Days with a tattoo of an eagle on your left arm."

"You've been busy," he said dryly.

Rennie feigned astonishment. "You don't think I *asked* about these things, do you?"

"Then how did you dig up all this ancient history?" Gideon took his eyes off the road again. "You've scarcely been here a week!"

Rennie's brown eyes twinkled. "It's fairly difficult to keep a secret in a small town, Gideon. Once people heard we were getting married, they just came up to me and volunteered all sorts of interesting tidbits."

Knowing his neighbors, Gideon was forced to admit Rennie was telling the truth. There were few secrets in Carter's Junction. And Caleb's name on Rennie's lips reminded Gideon of other teenage escapades better left unmentioned.

"So what else did my *friends* tell you?" His discomfiture was obvious.

"Oh, come on, Gideon, it's not that bad. Everybody has embarrassing incidents in their past."

"Maybe," he conceded. "But no one's going around telling things about you."

"I could tell you my most embarrassing secret."

That got his attention. "Do you have one?"

"Of course."

"Okay, let's have it."

"You're not the only one with a tattoo."

Gideon blinked, then grinned. "I'll be damned! What is it?"

"A butterfly."

"No kidding. Show me." Rennie blushed and Gideon shot her an amused look. "Oh. One of those, huh?"

She cleared her throat. "Yes."

"Will I ever get to see it?"

"I imagine you might. Someday."

"I can't wait."

Chapter 4

It wasn't *what* he said, Rennie decided, it was the *way* he said it that made her breath catch in her throat. And the way he looked at her didn't help matters. Not at all.

A vision of the two of them in the kind of cozily intimate situation where her little butterfly tattoo would be visible floated into her mind, and it took all her self-control to block it out. This certainly wasn't the time to be entertaining fantasies about Gideon, even if he was her husband.

Despite her best efforts, her cheeks barely had time to cool down before they drove into Wagon Wheel Gap.

They had reservations at the Pronghorn, one of the town's two tourist motels. While Gideon checked them in, Rennie looked over the meager supply of postcards the lobby had to offer, then followed him outside when he was done. They drove around the side of the building and parked in front of rooms ten and twelve. Gideon handed her both keys.

"Why don't you open them up and pick out which one you want while I get the luggage."

"Okay."

The adjoining rooms were nearly identical, although mirror images of each other, and almost as utilitarian as Rennie's motel room in Carter's Junction had been. By no stretch of the imagination could the rooms be considered your typical honeymoon suite. But then, she and Gideon weren't your typical honeymoon couple. She sighed just a little before putting that regret where it belonged.

A huge shadow blotted out the light as Gideon entered the open door of room number ten with their unmatched luggage.

"Which one goes where?"

Since it didn't matter, Rennie said, "I'll take this room."

Gideon carefully set her Louis Vuitton case on the luggage rack, then strode into the other room and dumped his battered brown suitcase unceremoniously on the bed.

"Gideon?"

He came back to the connecting doorway. "Yeah?"

As Rennie smiled at him, a shaft of sunlight crept through the partially opened drapes and highlighted her upturned profile. "Are you hungry?"

The sunlight danced over her dark curls and creamy skin, and over the gently curving figure beneath her lavender dress. She looked good enough to eat, Gideon thought distractedly, and tried to remember the question. Hungry? Was he hungry? Their earlier conversation in the car replayed in his mind, followed by the memory of the kiss they'd shared in church, and desire slammed into his gut with shocking swiftness. Before he realized what he was doing, he'd crossed the short distance that separated them.

Almost of its own volition, his right hand caressed her face with a gentleness that belied its size. Her skin was soft, soft as a baby's. With sudden, aching urgency Gideon wondered if it was the same all over. His fingers began the journey of discovery, slipping over the curve of her cheek, down, down, to nestle in the hollow of her throat.

Standing this close to her, he could detect the lingering traces of her delicate perfume, warmed by her body. His heartbeat quickened until blood pounded in his ears, while each breath he drew was painful. Rosy lips beckoned, and his head began to descend.

The sound of raucous laughter just outside the door broke the spell. Gideon jerked himself away from Rennie and temptation. For one shocked moment their eyes met.

"Sorry."

The muttered apology was for convention's sake, but Gideon knew he didn't mean it. Not one bit. What he was really sorry about was that they'd been interrupted before he could finish what he'd started, before he could explore the warm sweetness he'd only had a tantalizing taste of this afternoon. Suddenly needing to put distance between them, he swung around and headed back toward his room. He almost made it.

"Gideon!"

He stopped, one hand clenched around the doorknob. "Yeah?"

"Dinner?"

Her hesitant question made him glance back, and he saw bewilderment on her face. He looked away and uttered a muffled curse of self-derision before meeting her gaze again. "Sorry. I need a shower. Can you give me ten minutes?"

"Sure. No problem." Rennie's smile seemed forced. "Why don't we say half an hour. I'm not really very hungry yet, anyway, and that will give me time to freshen up."

"Sounds good to me," he said, firmly closing the door behind him.

Once inside his room Gideon wasted no time. He shucked his clothes and stood under the shower's icy blast, letting the spray cool his overheated body until goose bumps formed. He stepped out, dripping and shivering. He grabbed a towel and briskly dried himself, running the towel over his body with unwonted force.

Gideon combed his still-damp hair with firm, neat strokes, then looked at himself in the mirror, and laughed softly. Well, he'd known he wanted Rennie from the start. He just hadn't realized how quickly his desire for her could overtake him. Now he would have to apologize, and what could he use as an excuse? Did he dare tell her the absolute truth, that he'd been overcome by unexpected lust for her?

"Oh, yeah, Lowell. *That* will sweep her right off her feet. Tell her you were just about to go off like a rocket. That'll charm her right into your arms." He laughed again, a hearty bellow such as he hadn't given in two years.

Still chuckling, Gideon dressed with his usual economy of motion. As he sat on the edge of the bed to pull his boots on, he muttered, "At least I got my boots off." The image of himself standing in the shower, nude except for his boots, made him choke with helpless laughter.

After quickly unpacking her suitcase, Rennie had nothing left to do, so she rested on the bed while waiting for Gideon. She idly wondered if he knew that the walls were so thin she could almost hear everything going on in his room. While she'd unpacked, she'd heard the shower go on and then off, followed by a faint murmur as if Gideon were talking to himself. Now, a sudden bellow of laughter surprised her. The ensuing silence was broken by more uncontrolled laughter.

I wonder what tickled Gideon's funny bone, she thought. She'd probably never know, she decided, but hoped he wasn't laughing about her, about how pathetically easily she'd responded to him.

Rennie tucked her hand under her cheek, remembering everything with a shiver of fear-laced anticipation. He'd looked at her, touched her, and she'd wanted him. Just like that. She'd stood mesmerized by his mere presence—the size of him, the masculine scent of his body, the gentle touch of his rough hand against her cheek. And his hazel eyes had never seemed more green than in that moment when he had gazed down at her.

And he'd made her want him. It was scary, and not just because of her deception over her identity. Why was she so fascinated by him? And why did his touch make her long for more, even though her one experience with sex had left her gun-shy of men?

She drowsily pondered that thought until sleep stole over her unawares.

A sharp rap on the connecting door between their rooms startled Rennie awake. Disoriented after such a short nap, she didn't realize where she was at first, and it took her another minute to collect herself enough to think about answering the door.

The knocking took on an impatient sound, and Rennie hurriedly slid to the edge of the bed. She felt a twinge of pain in her left hip, and when her feet hit the floor her leg threatened to buckle under her.

"That was stupid," she berated herself as she quickly sat down. "You know better than to try to hurry."

The doorknob rattled. "Rennie! Are you in there?"

"Just a minute," she called as she carefully stood up. It didn't take much for her to realize what had happened. All that standing at her wedding and reception, combined with the inactivity of the car ride, had put an unaccustomed strain on her hip. And the brief nap in an awkward position hadn't helped.

Rennie gritted her teeth and forced herself to walk across

the room with only the slightest limp. She opened the door just as Gideon's knuckles were about to make contact with it.

"You okay? I thought something might have happened."

She leaned her right hip against the doorframe to take the weight off the left one. "I'm sorry. I fell asleep."

Gideon took one look at Rennie's tousled hair, slumberous eyes and slightly rumpled dress, and knew he was in trouble. Big trouble. The cold shower he'd taken earlier hadn't done him one bit of good.

Damn! His mind might counsel patience, but his body wasn't listening. He didn't want to go to dinner. He didn't want to sit in a dimly lit room and make small talk with Rennie. The only thing he wanted to do—and he wanted it badly—was to walk her backward into her room, lay her gently on the bed, and make love to her until his desire was sated.

What he felt was crazy. He'd only known Rennie just over two weeks, for God's sake! And half that time she hadn't even been around. All told, the amount of time he'd spent in her company would scarcely fill one day. He'd known Johanna all his life. His desire for his first wife had grown out of his love for her, had been a natural extension of it.

Rennie wasn't Jo. She wasn't beautiful. She wasn't tall, with ripe curves to tempt a man. She didn't have long, lithe legs to wrap around a man's hips and draw him in.

So why the hell did he want Rennie so much? Why was he going crazy with the absolute conviction of how good it would be between them?

Before temptation made him do what he knew he shouldn't, he said brusquely, "You ready?" He didn't wait for a response. He was across her room, out the door and halfway down the walk before he realized she hadn't followed him. He turned back and saw her framed in the doorway. "Is there a problem?"

"Problem? Problem?" Rennie's voice rose in pitch and intensity, carrying clearly in the crisp evening air. "I don't have a problem, but I'd sure like to know what the heck *your* problem is!"

Two rooms down, a door opened and a curious head emerged. Gideon cursed under his breath before heading for Rennie. He grasped her arms and pushed her gently but firmly into the room, then shut the door.

He distanced himself from her as far as he could, but her room, like his, wasn't all that big. His gaze fell on the double bed looming large in the center of the room. That was a mistake. The imprint of Rennie's body where she'd lain on the coverlet was still visible. Gideon had a vision of the two of them on that same bed, arms and legs entwined, bodies merging, and he shuddered.

Rennie faced him, arms akimbo, dark eyes flashing with indignation as she challenged him. "So what is your problem? You've been acting strange ever since we arrived. At first I let it slide, but I'll be darned if I'll put up with it any longer!"

Gideon removed his Stetson, slapped it against his thigh, and resettled it on his head.

"You want the truth?" he growled. "Well, I'll tell you. I want you, damn it, and I don't know what the hell to do about it."

Hot color stained Rennie's cheeks. Despite her self-acknowledged attraction to him, she wasn't ready for this. The color drained away as she suddenly realized how vulnerable she was, and she backed away from him until she came up sharply against the wall. "You promised."

"I know that!" Gideon threw her a fulminating look. "And damn it, don't cower against the wall as if I'm going to jump on you any second. I gave my word I'd wait until you were ready, and by God I'll do it if it kills me. But you wanted to know what my problem was so I told you. Now, can we get the hell out of your bedroom and go eat?''

The silence vibrated with tension.

''Oh, hell!'' Gideon removed his hat once more, impatiently running his other hand through his hair. Most of it settled back into place, but a couple of strands tufted out, lending his harsh features an oddly endearing, boyish charm.

''Look, Rennie, I'm sorry, okay? I didn't mean to lose my temper like that.'' She said nothing. Gideon tossed his hat on the bed, took a deep breath and expelled it in a rush. The timbre of his voice dropped from baritone to bass. ''Please don't look like that. I'm really sorry.''

Her unreasoning fear dissolved at his earnest plea. Rennie pushed herself away from the wall and limped over to him. ''I believe you.'' She held out her hand. ''I'm sorry, too.''

His brows twitched into a frown. He ignored her hand and her apology, and asked, ''Why are you limping?''

Her hand fell to her side. ''I told you I was involved in an accident,'' she said at last. ''My left hip was badly injured and required surgery.'' Rennie chose her next words carefully. ''Because I was in a coma following the accident, I couldn't begin physical therapy right away. When I finally came out of the coma, I needed a lot of therapy just to walk again. But sometimes I strain my hip, and then I limp.''

''Why didn't you tell me this before?'' he asked curiously. ''Did you think I would change my mind about marrying you?''

''No, not really. It's just that ever since I was a little girl I've had to fight to be taken seriously. No one, not even my father, who understood me better than anyone, believed that all I ever wanted to do was ranch. I was always such a little bit of a thing I had a hard time convincing people I was destined to be anything more than a useless ornament. I didn't want you to think I was going to be a liability, that I wouldn't pull my own weight."

Rennie sighed. "My hip *is* better. A lot better than it used to be. And my doctors assured me that I'll get stronger over time. I'm just too impatient, though." She made a face. "I want to be well *now*."

"I can understand that. I broke my leg in three places playing football in high school. I couldn't wait for it to heal enough to have a walking cast put on." He chuckled at the memory. "You should have seen me trying to get down to the sheep pens on crutches."

She laughed as he'd meant her to, and the shared humor lightened the mood in the room immeasurably.

"So," he said finally, "are you going to accept my apology?"

"Are you going to accept mine?"

"For what? Losing your temper or not telling me about your hip?"

"Both, I guess. And for being so stupidly naive about what was bothering you. I really had no idea that you would want to…so much…so soon. That is…it didn't even occur to me that a man…that you…" She was so hopelessly tangled in half sentences she'd never find her way out. "I didn't think it would be so hard on you to…" Rennie cut herself off and covered her crimson cheeks with her hands.

"Yeah, well, some things are harder than others."

She gasped, choked, then laughed at his dryly stated double entendre.

"And you're an attractive woman, even if you are 'a little bit of a thing,'" he continued, teasing, but smiling to take away the sting of those words. "And you obviously don't know very much about men. Any red-blooded male over the age of fourteen and under the age of eighty would 'want to,' as you so delicately put it.''

"Oh."

"Yeah. Oh."

Rennie's brow wrinkled as she digested what he'd said. An unpleasant thought occurred to her and she raised her eyes to his, seeking reassurance she wasn't sure she'd find.

Gideon read her mind perfectly. "No," he said gently, "that doesn't mean what you're thinking. If all I wanted was a reasonably attractive body, don't you think I'd have found one before now?" She swallowed visibly. "I told you before—there hasn't been anyone since my wife died. I don't lie, Rennie."

His eyes filled with warmth and tenderness, and he whispered huskily, "To tell you the honest-to-God truth, I want you, Rennie. I don't know why, but I do."

The tip of his finger touched her parted lips, then moved to the visible pulse beating in her throat. "But I'm not an animal. I usually keep a pretty tight rein on my desires. And despite my behavior this evening, I'm normally a *very* patient man. I can wait, as long as I have to. But I wouldn't be human if I didn't hope you won't keep me waiting too long."

He was doing it to her again. His eyes held hers willingly captive while his touch caused her heart to race and her lungs to cease functioning. But his voice did the most damage. That deep, husky sound made Rennie's insides quiver with exquisite longing.

Strange yearnings filled her, making her tremble. She was suddenly afraid, but this time she was afraid of herself. If he could do this to her with only a touch, with only a whisper, what then? He could seduce her so easily, make her want things she'd never had, make her dream dreams again.

He could make her love him.

The thought popped into Rennie's head from out of nowhere. She tried to thrust it away, but it wouldn't leave. She didn't want to love him. Love would make her vulnerable to devastating pain should he ever discover who she was, though she would never have married him if she thought there was a chance of that happening. But even if he never found out, he'd already made it plain he would never love again.

No, she didn't want to love him. She'd entered this marriage with her eyes open, with definite goals in mind. She wanted to make a new life for herself here, and she wanted to raise his children in place of the ones she would never have. She had convinced herself these things would be enough. She knew what to expect from Gideon and what he expected of her. Love, her love, was not wanted.

She took a step backward. Gideon's hand fell away from her throat and she could breathe again.

The corners of his mouth twitched into a rueful smile. "Not tonight, I take it?"

Rennie shook her head. She couldn't have spoken at that moment if her life depended on it.

"You can take that worried look off your face. No is no, as far as I'm concerned. I won't try to change your mind. Not tonight, anyway."

Her throat was made of sandpaper, but she managed to say, "Thank you."

Gideon picked up his hat. "So," he said pleasantly as he settled it into place. "How about that dinner?"

Rennie had expected things to be strained between them after that scene in her bedroom, but she was wrong. Gideon went out of his way to put her at ease. Over a good home-style meal, they conversed on a variety of subjects, and she found herself relaxing, even enjoying herself.

His conversation was sprinkled with anecdotes of his children's early years, displaying an unusual knowledge of the details usually reserved for a mother's fond memory. Here was a man not content to take a father's traditional secondary role in his children's lives, and it showed.

Then the conversation took a serious turn over after-dinner coffee, when he began to talk about Nicki.

"I've tried everything I can think of to get her to talk, Rennie. But nothing seems to help. She's seen the best doctors I could find, and they all say the same thing. There's nothing physically wrong with Nicki that prevents her from speaking. The psychiatrists we've seen say it could be the trauma of the accident, that Nicki remembers what happened, that she might have seen Johanna being so badly injured. They talk about security, stability, time and patience. But how can I be patient when my daughter is hurting?"

Guilt jolted through Rennie, as it did every time Gideon talked about the accident that had taken so much from him. She tried her best to ignore it and concentrate on what he was saying.

"The frustrating thing is, the only clue to the cause and the only key to the cure is locked inside Nicki. Only she can tell us, and she's not talking."

He drained the last of his coffee and stared unhappily at the dregs. In a low voice he confided, "Each morning I pray this will be the day Nicki reaches out for help. And every night I pray she won't slip further and further away."

Unbearably moved by Gideon's visible pain, Rennie reached across the table and laid her hand on top of his.

"How can I help?" she asked gently.

Gideon turned his hand over and clasped hers, seeming to draw strength and encouragement from the simple gesture. His reluctant smile softened his whole face.

"You've already done that. It helps just to be able to talk about it."

"I'm glad. Now, tell me what I can do to help Nicki."

"I don't know, Rennie. I just don't know. I was hoping she'd take to you better than she has, the way Andrew and Trina did."

"Oh, Gideon, what did you expect? Nicki's old enough to still have vivid memories of her mother. Then along comes a stranger whom you immediately introduce as your soon-to-be wife. She's bound to resent me for taking her mother's place. She'll probably even hate me at first. I expect nothing less."

His hand tightened, and she felt the desperation in him. She added, "I was seventeen when my mother remarried, and I resented my stepfather terribly, even though he was good to me. I treated both him and my mother very badly as a result, and did some crazy things in rebellion. And Nicki's only nine. It's a lot harder to understand at nine than it is at seventeen." Rennie squeezed his hand in empathy.

"So, *you're* telling me I have to be patient, too?"

She nodded. "I know it's hard, but give it time. Give *me* time." She laughed a little and looked shyly into his hazel eyes. "I want to be a good mother to your children, Gideon. I think I can be, with a little help from you."

Rennie realized that her hand still lay clasped in Gideon's and started to draw it away. He resisted, and her eyes flew to his. Warm admiration shone there, and something more. Her hand remained where it was.

"So what do you need from me?" His voice was husky.

She cleared her throat. "Tell me about each of them, what they like, what they don't like. I feel I've made a start this past week, especially with Andrew and Trina, and I'll probably concentrate on getting to know them first."

"What about Nicki?" Though Gideon loved all his children equally, his troubled oldest child held a special place in his heart.

"I won't ignore Nicki, but I won't focus a lot of attention on her, either. I don't want to back her into a corner she'll have a hard time getting out of later.

"From what you've told me and what I've seen so far, I think one of two things will happen with Nicki. Either she'll be jealous of the attention I give to the younger children and will demand her own share, or she'll resent any affection for me on their part, viewing it as a betrayal of their mother. I'm betting on the latter."

Gideon frowned. "But won't that make things worse?"

She nodded. "At first. She'll probably rebel against any attempt by me to exercise authority over her. I think she'll do her best to put you and me on opposite sides, to cause a rift in our relationship. But her inability to speak will make that difficult."

Dawning understanding broke over Gideon's face. "I'll be damned. You're counting on it, aren't you."

"Sort of. If we can use her anger and resentment of me and her frustration with the situation to make her talk, it will be worth any short-term unpleasantness. But you have to do your part. That's why I needed to discuss this with you. You'll have to give me your support. If this is going to work, you'll have to back me on every major confrontation. It will be hard on you—I'm not saying it won't. But if our goal is to break Nicki out of her shell, you'll have to steel yourself against her tears and silent recriminations."

For the first time in ages Gideon saw a glimmer of hope. Rennie's idea just might work. It just might. At this point he was willing to try anything.

"It won't be easy for you, either," he stated.

"I know." Rennie calmly accepted that fact.

Gideon ran assessing eyes over the woman seated across

from him. Every time he thought he had Rennie pegged, she surprised him. She'd obviously devoted a lot of thought to this. Her insight into the workings of a child's mind were remarkable for a woman who'd never had any children of her own. And her commitment astonished him. She hadn't even lived with his kids yet, but she cared about them already.

How did he ever get this lucky?

"You're really something, you know that?" He surprised her and himself by raising her hand to his lips. The kiss he pressed on it had nothing to do with seduction and everything to do with affection. "Thank you."

She flushed to the roots of her hair. "Those children are going to be the most important thing in my life, Gideon." Her voice was slightly gruff. "They're the reason we married. Is it so surprising that I care about them?"

Although he agreed with her about the reason for their marriage, a small part of him took exception to her statement that the children were going to be the most important thing in her life. As he gazed at her, Gideon realized he wanted to be important to her, too. As important as the children.

The thought shocked him so much he almost blurted it out, but instead he said, "No, not surprising, exactly. I guess I thought it would take longer, somehow. I didn't realize how deeply committed you already are."

It took Rennie a minute to come up with a safe answer. "I wouldn't have married you otherwise." She took a sip from her water glass, and the coolness soothed her suddenly dry throat. She prayed he wouldn't pursue the issue of *why* she was so committed, because she could never tell him, could never explain the combination of yearning and guilt that drove her.

Something must have shown on her face, however, because Gideon asked her what was wrong.

"Nothing."

"You sure?"

His concern was real and somehow touching, but it only added to the burden of guilt she carried. She shifted uneasily in her chair, and forced a smile for his benefit, but it never reached her eyes. "I'm okay. Really."

He seemed unconvinced, but he didn't push it. This time, when she drew her hand away he let it go immediately.

He scrutinized her face intensely as if looking for something he didn't find, then signaled for the check. As they waited, Rennie toyed with her fork, her napkin, her cup of coffee. Anything to keep her eyes from Gideon's. He had the uncanny knack of reading her mind, and she didn't want her eyes to give anything away.

The check came and Gideon paid it, adding a generous tip. He rose, towering over Rennie as he assisted her from her chair.

"How's the hip?"

"Fine," she lied.

His face resolved into stern lines. "The truth, Rennie."

The truth? She could never tell him the truth. Their whole relationship was based on a lie, a lie that could destroy the fragile fabric of trust they'd just begun to weave between them.

"It hurts," she admitted, and only Rennie knew she was referring to more than her hip.

"Can you walk? Or should I carry you?"

Oh, God, she could bear anything but that. She was too vulnerable at this moment, her control too precarious. He'd been so honest with her, and she'd deceived him from the moment they met. If he held her in his arms now, if she felt the strength of him, the warmth, if she laid her head against his heart and heard its lazy thud beating within him, she would confess everything.

"I can walk," she croaked.

He glanced down at her averted face and frowned, obviously sensing something was wrong. She prayed for deliverance, and to her relief Gideon asked no more questions. He tucked her left hand into the crook of his arm, picked up his Stetson and led her out of the restaurant, deliberately matching his strides to hers. He stopped in the entrance to put his hat on before pushing the door open for her. As they slowly made their way back to the motel, he whistled tunelessly under his breath.

Rennie welcomed the silence between them. She didn't think she'd be capable of conversation right now. All she wanted to do was reach the safety of her room so she could regroup her defenses in private.

It seemed like forever, but it actually took only a minute or two to reach their rooms, and Rennie was grateful for the reprieve. Gideon unlocked the door, turned on the light and checked the interior before handing Rennie her key.

"Need any help?"

Rennie shook her head. Words were beyond her.

"I'll say good-night, then. If you need anything, just call. I'll leave my side of the connecting door unlocked. I suggest you do the same. Don't be shy about asking for my help if you need it, okay? And don't forget to lock this door."

She nodded in acknowledgment.

Gideon hesitated, tipped his hat back with one finger, then leaned down and lightly kissed her cheek. "Good night, Rennie."

"Good night."

Chapter 5

Rennie entered her room, slapped a washcloth over her face, brushed her teeth and whipped into her nightshirt in less than three minutes. A flick of the light switch shrouded the room in darkness just before she slid into bed and pulled the covers up to her chin.

Then she lay motionless in the dark, unable to sleep, but doing her best not to think. Too much had happened today. She felt emotionally battered and unable to deal with anything right now. Like the heroine in a famous novel, she firmly told herself, "I'll think about it tomorrow."

Now, as before, Rennie could hear Gideon moving around in his room. The sound of running water in the washbasin meant he was probably brushing his teeth. One thump, then another. His boots were off. A minute later the bedsprings protested under his weight. He was in bed. Creak, creak. He turned over.

Rennie idly wondered what he wore to bed, if anything. Did he wear pajama tops and bottoms? Somehow she didn't think so. He didn't seem the type. Maybe just the bottoms. That sounded more like him, especially since he had young children who might need him in the middle of the night.

But what about tonight, alone in his room? Rennie conjured up a vision of Gideon lying in naked splendor between crisp white sheets. His tanned body would be dusted with the same sun-kissed golden brown hair as was on his head. It would be soft to the touch against the hardness of his muscles. Farther down would be a darker thatch nestling—

Creak, creak, thud. Gideon was out of bed. Rennie blushed in the darkness as if he'd heard her shameful thoughts.

Pad, pad, pad, pad. Water running. The clink of a glass being set down. Silence, followed by an odd sound. What was he…oh. A flushing sound a minute later confirmed it.

Rennie pulled the spare pillow over her head and the covers over that. She felt like a Peeping Tom, or rather, the audio version of a Peeping Tom. She closed her eyes and tried to sleep, but she was suffocating under the pillow. She lifted a corner and propped it so she could breathe, but still keep her ears covered.

Then realization swept over her. If she could hear everything that went on in his room, he must be able to do the same in reverse. She groaned. She'd never be able to use the bathroom again while he was in his room.

She fell asleep trying to devise ways to accomplish that.

Rennie woke to the noise of Gideon singing in the shower. It sounded like a Clint Black song, but she couldn't be sure. Despite her normally less-than-sunny morning self, she had to smile. Her husband seemed oblivious to the fact that he couldn't carry a tune in a bucket. He also had a problem remembering all the lyrics, so he filled in with what passed in his mind for humming. It was rather endearing.

One more tidbit of intimate knowledge to add to her newly hoarded collection.

A glance at the clock conveniently fastened to the night-stand next to the bed informed Rennie that Gideon was a very early riser, as was to be expected from a rancher. Quarter to five. The sun wasn't even up yet, but habits were hard to break. Even though Gideon was on vacation he wasn't the kind of man to lie around in bed wasting time once he was awake.

She reached over and pulled up the pillow which had fallen on the floor during the night, tucking it behind her head and closing her eyes again. She hated mornings. The one thing she hadn't missed about living on a ranch was getting up early. She was going to have to make that supreme sacrifice from now on, and she wasn't looking forward to it.

Rennie heard the shower stop along with Gideon's singing. In her mind's eye she could see him toweling off that powerful body—head, shoulders, arms, legs—then wrapping the towel around the more intimate parts of himself.

Water running in Gideon's washbasin apprised Rennie of what he was doing next. She giggled as he began to sing again, a terrible rendition of a Randy Travis song this time. As if she were in the same room with him, Rennie could see him as he shaved, the frequent pauses indicating he'd reached a difficult patch to maneuver around with his razor. Mindful of the thinness of the walls, Rennie turned and stifled the next giggle in her pillow. Lord, the man must be tone deaf!

The continuing sound of running water was having an unfortunate effect on her. Even more unfortunately, there was no way in hell she was going to use the bathroom while he was right next door and could hear her as clearly as she could hear him.

Desperate needs called for desperate measures. Picking up the phone, she dialed Gideon's room. It rang twice before he answered.

"Yeah?"

"Gideon, it's Rennie. I figured you'd be up and about by this time. I'm awake, but it'll take me a while to get ready. So don't wait for me."

"I don't mind waiting."

"No!" Rennie held her hand over the mouthpiece until her teeth unclenched enough to continue. "No. You go on to the restaurant and order breakfast. I'll meet you there."

"Okay." She could almost see him shrugging. "Whatever you say. How's the hip feel?"

Great. The man wanted to chat at five o'clock in the morning. "It's fine. Look, Gideon, I'm not at my best until I've had a long shower and a cup of coffee."

"Want me to bring you a cup? I can get a take-out."

If it hadn't been such an urgent necessity to get him out of his room, Rennie would have been touched by his consideration. As things stood, she didn't have the time to waste.

"No, thanks."

"Okay. See you there."

While she waited for him to dress and leave, Rennie lay back on the bed, clenched her teeth, and tried to think dry thoughts. The Sahara Desert. The surface of the moon. Death Valley.

As soon as she heard Gideon's door open and close, Rennie was off the bed like a shot.

Later, after a refreshing shower, she slipped on a pair of jeans and another of the loose-fitting cotton sweaters she liked. This one was the color of a ripe plum. Then she sat on the bed combing her damp hair. She preferred to let her curls air-dry rather than use a blow-dryer, so she had time to think about last night.

She had to get a grip on herself. She couldn't possibly go on this way, letting guilt overcome her any time it chose. She'd be a nervous wreck inside of a month. And that wouldn't do the children any good, not to mention herself or Gideon.

No, what she had to do was come to some kind of compromise with her conscience. Then she could get on with the business of building a relationship with Gideon and creating a family with his children.

Gideon thinks his heart is in the grave with his first wife. But it isn't. His heart is with his children, and he married me for their sake, she thought. *He believes in me, trusts me. He's counting on me, and I can't let him down.*

And that's exactly what she'd be doing if she let guilt rule her. If she spent all her time afraid they'd discover who she was, she'd be letting Gideon *and* his children down. And, in a crazy sort of way, herself as well.

"I'm here for a reason," she whispered to herself, pushing a still-damp curl behind her ear. "A good reason. Maybe it was wrong to lie to Gideon about who I really am, but that doesn't mean my motives for coming here were wrong. And if I can make a difference in the children's lives, if I can do some good, then the past doesn't matter. I can't *let* it matter."

Of course, the children, especially Nicki, might never accept her in their lives, but she refused to believe it. She had faith in herself, faith in the love she wanted so desperately to give them.

"I'll make it work," she vowed, even though she knew it would take everything she had in her, every bit of strength and resolution she could muster.

A fainthearted woman might quail at the job ahead of

her. But Rennie was a Fortier. She came from a long line of strong women, like her grandmother, women who had faced adversity and won. A Fortier woman didn't let life dictate her choices; she took life by the scruff of the neck and shook it into what she wanted.

Maybe she'd let life toss her around like a tumbleweed this past year. Maybe she was a bit late in recognizing her own strength of purpose. Maybe the Fortier blood in her veins had lain dormant until this moment. None of that mattered.

She'd made promises to Gideon yesterday. Now she made one to herself. "If I fail, it won't be for lack of trying. From now on I'm going to look ahead, not back. My life will be what I make of it. And I say Francesca Whitney is dead. I'm Rennie Fortier. Rennie Fortier *Lowell*," she amended, tossing the comb she held onto the bed beside her.

She ran her hand up under the back of her hair and found it almost dry, then stood up and checked her appearance in the dresser mirror. A different woman looked back at her than the one who'd entered this room last night. More confident. More assured.

The doubts weren't completely gone, nor the guilt, but she'd locked them away where they couldn't hurt her. Or Gideon. Or his children. And that's where they were going to stay.

At first Gideon waited for Rennie in the restaurant despite what she'd told him. He read the local newspaper and drank a cup of black coffee, expecting her to arrive at any moment. But at last he gave in to the rumblings in his stomach. After a quick perusal of the menu, he ordered the Early Bird Special—two eggs, bacon, hash browns, toast, juice and coffee. He also requested a side order of ham, a large glass of milk and a bowl of oatmeal.

When breakfast arrived before Rennie did, Gideon folded the newspaper and devoted himself to the serious business of eating. He was just finishing the oatmeal when something made him look up.

Rennie had entered the restaurant. Gideon watched her speak to the hostess then turn to where he sat in the far corner, slightly screened from view by a large plant. As she walked toward him he noted that the limp was gone, but that wasn't the only thing different about her this morning. He couldn't quite figure out what it was. Her hair was the same riot of curls. She hadn't added any more makeup than she usually wore so far as he could see. And her clothes weren't anything out of the ordinary, just jeans and a soft sweater. But the reddish-purple color set off her creamy skin, and matched the warm tint of her lips.

Still, there was something else about her. Maybe it was her expression. She looked more determined, somehow. And jaunty. Yeah, that was it. There was a liveliness to her that hadn't been there before.

He stood up when she reached his table, and waited for her to be seated before sitting down again.

"Good morning." Rennie's smile lit up her entire face.

"Mornin'."

A waitress appeared with a coffeepot, filled Rennie's cup and topped off Gideon's, then asked Rennie if she was ready to order.

"I'll have a bowl of fruit and a slice of wheat bread," Rennie said. "Cracked wheat, if you have it. Toasted, no butter."

Gideon waited until the waitress left before asking, "Is that all you're having?"

Rennie made a face at him. "I'm puny, remember? It doesn't take much to keep me going."

"Guess that rankled," Gideon said as he started on his bacon and eggs.

"What rankled?"

"Calling you puny that first day."

She wrinkled her nose in consideration. "Yes," she said finally. "It did. But I called you a mountain, so I guess we're even. How's the bacon?"

"Good."

"Hickory-smoked?" Her tone was wistful.

His lips curled up at the edges but he controlled himself. "No, sugar-cured."

"Oh." There was a wealth of meaning in that little word.

The eyes Gideon raised to Rennie's were dancing. "Would you like a piece?"

"No, thank you." But she gazed longingly at the bacon on his plate when she thought he wasn't looking.

Gideon forked a bite and chewed with gusto. Rennie's eyes followed his every move. He cut another piece.

"Sure you don't want any?"

"Oh, no," she assured him. "My breakfast should be here soon." But she swallowed when Gideon did and her stomach growled audibly.

Gideon finished his eggs and bacon with the last of his toast, then made serious inroads into his hash browns. He washed that down with a gulp of coffee and started on the ham.

Rennie fiddled with her napkin, stirred artificial sweetener into her black coffee, then placed the spoon just so on the saucer. "How's the ham?"

He choked and swallowed. "Good."

"Sugar-cured?"

"No." He bit his lip to keep from laughing. "Hickory-smoked."

"Oh."

Gideon chuckled. He couldn't help it. "Would you like some?"

"Oh, no. I'm sure my breakfast will be here any minute." Rennie glanced anxiously at the kitchen door. "I don't know what's taking so long."

Gideon's body shook with repressed laughter. He speared a bite and held it to her lips. "Rennie, eat the damn ham."

She started to shake her head, then chuckled. "Since you put it that way, how can I refuse?" She took his offering.

The kitchen door swung open and their waitress came out. She deposited Rennie's toast and fruit in front of her and left.

As he sipped his juice Gideon watched Rennie cut her plain piece of toast into four neat triangles, which she then proceeded to daintily gobble down.

"Explain something to me."

"Hmm?"

"If you wanted ham or bacon, why didn't you just order it?"

Rennie spooned a bite of cantaloupe and ate it before responding. "Would you believe I'm a vegetarian?"

Gideon distinctly remembered Rennie ordering chicken the night before. "No."

"Well, how about this. I gave them up for Lent."

That took a moment, then Gideon shook his head. "Lent is in February and March. 'Fess up, Rennie. What's the real reason?"

Rennie considered the question for a moment, then her eyes turned soulful. "When I was Trina's age, I won a shoat in a contest at the county fair. He was so little and cute and cuddly, I named him Squeaker. He was the first animal that belonged to me alone, and I was responsible for taking care of him." She smiled as if at fond memories. "Squeaker was so tame and so attached to me he followed me around like a little puppy. Even when he grew to be bigger than I was he still thought himself small enough to sit on my lap.''

"What happened?" Gideon was pretty sure he knew where this story was leading and his throat tightened just a bit.

"The next year my mother took me into Billings one Saturday in October. When we came home, I raced down to Squeaker's pen to see him. He was gone. My parents told me Squeaker must have gotten out somehow. I didn't believe them, but what could I do? I cried myself to sleep that night. I moped around the ranch for weeks afterward, waiting for Squeaker to come home, but he never did.''

She sighed dramatically. "I never found out what happened to Squeaker, but—'' Rennie's eyes narrowed as she added darkly "—it sure looked suspicious to me that we had a lot of ham and bacon around our house that winter.''

Gideon's throat ached for that younger Rennie. He looked at the remains of the ham on the platter, then pushed it away. His eyes were on Rennie's downturned face as he reached across the table and patted her hand consolingly as if she were still as young as Trina.

Her mouth quivered and Rennie raised her napkin to cover her face, but not before he'd seen her eyes. Suddenly Gideon knew he'd been had.

"Damn!" He jerked his hand away, feeling foolish.

Rennie convulsed into giggles that she muffled behind her napkin. Her eyes peeped at him, inviting Gideon to share the humor, and he laughed reluctantly.

"You never had a hog named Squeaker, did you?"

She shook her head, her eyes twinkling. She replaced her napkin in her lap. "And if I had, my father never would have butchered it. He doted on me.''

"I should have known. Did he ever put you over his knee and give you the spankings you undoubtedly deserved?''

"No. He left that to my mother. Are you going to finish that ham?"

Gideon glanced down at the platter he'd pushed to one side. "Yeah, I guess I am," he said, suiting his actions to his words. "And no, you can't have any more."

"I wasn't asking."

"Like you didn't ask before?" He polished off the last bite. "So, are you going to tell me the real reason, or not?"

Rennie smiled. "I don't want to get fat."

Gideon ran his eyes over her slender frame. "And you're so dangerously close to the edge already," he teased.

She laughed again, delighted with his teasing. "No, but I'm so short I do have to watch what I eat." Rennie leaned toward him slightly and her voice dropped a notch as if she were sharing a secret. "The thing is, Gideon," she confided, "if it's not on my plate, it doesn't count."

"Is that how it works?"

Rennie nodded solemnly. "That's one of the basic laws of dieting. That, and crumbs."

"Crumbs?"

"It's a scientific fact that crumbs have no calories. I can crumb my way through an entire bag of chocolate chip cookies."

Laughter rumbled out of Gideon's chest in an uncontrollable rush as he envisioned her doing just that. Damn, but Rennie was good for him! He'd laughed more in the last twenty-four hours than in the past twenty-four months.

Rennie leaned back. "So you see, as long as I watch what I eat and follow those basic rules I'm okay. But if I ate everything I'd like to have, I'd soon be—"

"As big as Squeaker?"

"Exactly." She beamed at him.

He grinned. "You sure had me going there for a while."

"Sorry. I never thought you'd actually believe me or I never would have spun you that tale."

"That's okay."

Rennie giggled as she remembered his expression. She couldn't help it. "If you could have seen your face! I never thought a rancher would get so sentimental over the death of an animal, and a hog at that."

Gideon chuckled. "Pretty silly, I guess." He shook his head at her. "You sure can tell a convincing tale."

Rennie finished the last of her fruit. "I've had a lot of practice. I used to tell stories to the children in the hospital while I was there. That and magic tricks were my big draw."

He eyed her suspiciously over his coffee cup. "Is that the truth or just another tall tale?"

"No, that's the truth. I spent a lot of time with the kids in the hospital." She smiled at him and changed the subject. "What would you like to do today?"

Gideon wiped his mouth with his napkin and leaned back in his chair, hooking an elbow over the back. "How's your hip this morning?"

"Fine."

"How long has it been since you were on a horse?"

"About two years." Rennie tilted her head. "Why?"

"Do you feel up to taking a little ride? I checked with the desk clerk. She said there's a place we can rent horses about fifteen miles outside of town. We can pick up a few things at the grocery store to take along for a picnic lunch."

"Sounds like fun. Where will we go?"

"The desk clerk told me about a trail leading to a deserted mining town farther up the mountain."

Rennie's eyes lit up. "A ghost town?"

Gideon smiled. "Something like that."

"Let's do it!"

"If you haven't been on a horse in two years you'll probably be sore tomorrow."

"I don't care. It'll be worth it."

"Okay, but don't say I didn't warn you."

Outside, Gideon checked the sky. The clouds he saw held no threat of rain or snow, the last being something that was still a possibility even though it was May. Instead, it looked to be a perfect day for horseback riding. The sun would dissipate the chilliness in the air by mid-morning, but the clouds would keep them from getting too hot.

The sun had risen while they were in the restaurant, coloring the sky peach and palest blue. Gideon had never told anyone, but Wyoming sunrises always made him think of babies. Soft, fragile and innocent. Of all the things he'd seen in his life there were three things he never tired of: the sight of his children sleeping, Wyoming sunrises and Wyoming sunsets. If forced, he could *exist* elsewhere; he could only *live* in Wyoming.

They stopped to pick up jackets they might need later, and Rennie changed her tennis shoes for boots while Gideon called the horse ranch for exact directions. On the way out of town they also stopped at the convenience store for some ready-made sandwiches, fruit, a bag of cookies and a six-pack of soda.

As he was paying, Gideon glanced over at Rennie browsing through the paperback books on a rack by the door.

"Just a second," he told the salesclerk, and moved to the stack of inexpensive straw hats in the aisle next to the counter. He picked out the smallest one he could find, then strode to Rennie's side and clapped it on her head.

Startled, she turned around.

"You need a hat," he told her by way of explanation. "How does that one fit?"

Rennie adjusted it, then nodded and smiled. "It's fine."

She had no idea what a captivating picture she made, almost as appealing to Gideon in her casual clothes as she had been yesterday in a fancy dress. Her eyes were sparkling in anticipation, and once again Gideon felt that tug of attraction.

She made him feel good. Damn good. He'd risen this morning more cheerful than he'd felt in a long time, despite waking in the same half-aroused state he'd gone to sleep in. Maybe his dreams of Rennie last night had something to do with it.

Gideon smiled at the memory and dragged his eyes away from Rennie. "Add that on," he told the salesclerk.

They headed out of town.

Behind the wheel again, Gideon drove for a couple of minutes, enjoying the power and responsiveness of Rennie's little sports car. "This is a nice car," he said.

"Yes, but it's not very practical for a family. I'm thinking about trading it in for something more suitable."

"Don't." The word slipped out before Gideon could prevent it. Rennie looked over at him and he confessed, "I've always dreamed of driving a car like this. Completely impractical, totally unsuitable for a rancher." He grinned like a sixteen-year-old. "But I'll bet it could do one-seventy on the open road."

Rennie shook her head at him but smiled. Another chink in Gideon's armor revealed the boy inside the man and Rennie was charmed yet again.

"If you'll keep this car and let me drive it sometimes, I'll buy you another one for everyday use. The Blazer the housekeepers used is on its last legs, anyway, so I'll get you a new one. Deal?"

"Deal."

"That reminds me. When we get back home we need to sit down and discuss finances. The ranch has charge accounts at a couple of the stores in Carter's Junction and in Sheridan, but we'll need to get you added as a signer on my personal checking account for grocery shopping and such.''

''Where do you do your shopping?''

''For groceries we usually go to Sheridan. The selection in Carter's Junction isn't very big. For the rest, it depends. Some things we just have to order, and we have those shipped to Carter's Junction.''

Having exhausted that topic, they drove in silence for a couple of minutes. They almost missed the battered sign indicating the turnoff for their destination. Gideon braked sharply, his right arm instinctively thrust out to keep Rennie from being thrown forward. She gave him an odd look but refrained from saying anything.

He turned the wheel and they exited the highway. A cattle guard rattled beneath the small car as they drove over it and down a slight incline. The dirt road they were now on was in surprisingly good shape, with no deep ruts, but was still rough enough to jostle the car's occupants, though Gideon reduced their speed even further. Low-slung sports cars just weren't made to handle dirt roads. A plume of dust followed them as they wound their way through the hilly terrain.

A short distance later they came to a gate across the road and Gideon pulled up in front of it. Before he could open his door, Rennie was out of the car. He watched her unlatch the gate and push it open, enjoying the way her jeans molded to her body. Her sweater was a different matter. Loose-fitting, it only hinted at the delicate curves beneath, but he had a good imagination. Too good. He wondered how long she would make him wait before consummating their marriage. Not long, he hoped. Not long.

He drove through the opened gate, and she closed it behind him, carefully securing the gate latch, then got back in the car.

"Thanks." It was the passenger's job to open and close gates on a ranch and Rennie seemed to know it as well as he did, but the little courtesy came naturally to him.

She ran her fingers through her hair, which had been blown awry by the wind. He watched her for a few seconds, then reached across and brushed an errant curl away from her cheek. The desire to kiss her came out of nowhere. A memory teased him as it had last evening—the softness of her lips under his when he'd kissed her at their wedding. He wondered what she'd do if he kissed her now.

Instead of finding out, he turned away from temptation and put the car into gear.

Chapter 6

A few minutes later they spotted the outbuildings of the ranch. When Gideon pulled up and parked in front of the ranch house, he said, "Wait here. I'll be right back."

So Rennie waited in the car while Gideon stood on the porch and dickered with the owner. At one point Gideon gestured toward her, and she gave the two men a smile and a little wave. Then the men headed for the barn closest to the house and disappeared inside.

Rennie sorted through her purse for a comb and a few other things that she thought she might need, and tucked them into the pockets of her jacket. After a moment she undid her seat belt and reached over to the back seat, digging into the grocery bag there. She found an apple and slid it into her jacket pocket, too.

She impatiently tapped her fingers against the window, but Gideon didn't reappear, so her thoughts wandered. Even though she was really looking forward to this ride, and to sharing with Gideon something they both loved, part of her was already thinking ahead, worrying about tomorrow and what would happen when they went home.

Home.

It was funny in a way, but Rennie truly had felt as if she'd come home the first time she'd driven onto the Rocking L. The sights, the sounds, even the smells—they'd all given her a sense of déjà vu. Even though the animals dotting the countryside were sheep and not the cattle she was used to, even though the semimountainous terrain was not the more familiar, flatter expanse of her beloved Circle F, Rennie had known she'd come home. This was where she belonged. This was the life she'd hungered for all those years in Los Angeles.

And it was certainly worth a few sacrifices. She would miss Jess, of course, and those few friends who had remained so during the time she was in a coma and through her long recovery. Especially Bethany Kent, the only person besides Jess whom Rennie had confided in.

Rennie smiled to herself. Dear Bethany. It wasn't until after the accident that Rennie had realized just how good a friend Bethany was. And unlike Jess, Bethany had surprisingly and wholeheartedly supported Rennie's decision to marry Gideon when the whole story had been explained to her.

"Marry him," Bethany had said as she helped Rennie pack. "If this is truly what you want, then don't let Jess talk you out of it. Don't let anyone talk you out of it. Follow your heart. You can't go wrong that way."

Oh, yes, she'd miss Bethany almost as much as she'd miss Jess. But they could always write to each other, and telephone. She'd made the right choice. She knew it in her heart. Now all she needed was the courage to be herself with Gideon and his children, and her new life would make up for what she'd lost.

When Gideon returned a couple of minutes later, he was smiling. "It's all set," he said, putting the car into reverse, then parking it behind the barn. He pocketed the keys and grabbed his jeans jacket and the bag with their lunch. "Let's go."

She slid her arms into her own jacket and followed him into the barn. The dusky interior was a stark contrast to the bright sunlight, and it took Rennie's eyes a moment to adjust. She paused near the doorway. The familiar aroma of horses, leather, hay and manure assaulted her nose, bringing a smile to her lips. Although she'd ridden as often as she could in Los Angeles, she hadn't been allowed inside a barn since she was fifteen. Funny how people assumed that having wealth meant that you wanted to be spared any contact with reality. Horse manure was as real as you could get.

The soft clip-clop of hooves drew her attention to the center of the barn, where Gideon and the owner were leading two glossy-coated quarter horses on rope leads. Rennie assumed the smaller of the two, a compact chestnut mare, was hers.

She ignored the two men and approached the mare. She was careful to make no sudden moves, letting the animal adjust to her presence before stroking the shining nose.

"You're a beauty, aren't you," she crooned, running her hand under the horse's neck and over the withers.

The mare smelled what was in Rennie's jacket pocket and nudged her. Rennie removed the apple she'd secreted there and held it out. As the horse munched contentedly, she stared at Rennie out of one big brown eye. Rennie stared right back, rubbing a hand along the side of the mare's neck and whispering a few more compliments. By the time the apple was finished, the horse and Rennie were friends.

Rennie glanced over at Gideon and the other man, and

realized they'd been watching her all this time. She flushed slightly.

"I guess I don't have to ask if she'll do," the owner stated.

Rennie smiled shyly at him. "No, you don't. What's her name?"

"Sweetwater. Want me to saddle her up?"

"I can do it," Rennie said.

Gideon opened his mouth to protest, but closed it without uttering a sound. He was curious to see if Rennie was really as capable as she'd claimed the day they'd met.

As he took care of his own horse, a big, buckskin gelding, Gideon watched her every move without seeming to do so. Quietly, efficiently, she bridled and saddled the mare, double-checking the cinch and adjusting the stirrups with the assurance that could only come from long experience.

Gideon carefully went over the borrowed rifle and satisfied himself with its condition, slid it into the sheath attached to his saddle, and stowed their lunch and the spare ammunition in his saddlebags. When he was done they led the horses outside. Gideon turned to give Rennie a leg up, but she was too quick for him. She was already seated, leaning in the saddle to make some minor adjustment. When she straightened, he thought he saw a twinge of pain flash across her face, but it was gone before he could be sure it was ever really there.

He swung into the saddle, pulled his hat low across his face and looked down at the owner. "We'll be taking the trail up to the old mining town, like I told you," he said. "We should be back well before dark."

"Sure you don't need a guide?"

"I think we can handle it. Your directions are pretty clear. Thanks for the loan of the rifle, though."

''No problem. Just in case you need to use it, you should know it pulls a shade to the left.''

''Thanks for the warning.'' Gideon looked at Rennie. ''Ready?''

She nodded, the excitement she'd felt earlier returning in full force.

''Then, let's go.''

Gideon took the lead, following the directions he'd been given, spotting the landmarks with an unerring eye. He rode easily, with a light hand on the reins, controlling the strange horse with only a word, a touch. For such a big man he looked remarkably graceful in the saddle, seeming one with his horse.

From her vantage point a few paces behind him, Rennie was in a perfect position to admire the very male picture he made, like something out of the Old West.

She'd been startled at first when he'd casually brought out the rifle, but realized her years in L.A. had made her forget how very untamed this land still was. Anything could cross their path, a bear or a rattlesnake or a cougar. Gideon had handled the rifle with comfortable assurance. She had no doubt he'd handle any trouble they encountered along the way with the same ease.

They made their way in silence through the sagebrush and scrub pine, which filled the air with their pungent odor. Soon the last traces of human habitation were left behind. They forded two streams, one so small it was scarcely more than a wet spot between the rocks, even though the spring thaw had already begun, and picked up the old trail.

A raucous sound drew both their gazes skyward. A red-tailed hawk wheeled and dipped in the distance against the clear blue, then dived toward the earth for a target only he could see. They waited, but the hawk didn't reappear, and they pressed on.

The trail wound its way up the side of the mountain, and at one point it widened enough to ride two abreast. Gideon reined in, signaling for Rennie to come up beside him.

"How are you doing?"

"Fine."

"How's the hip?"

Rennie let him see her exasperation. Concern was one thing. Coddling was another. She hated to be coddled. "The hip is fine, thank you very much. Sweetwater is doing all the work."

Gideon hid a smile, but not very well. She gave him a level look and he nodded, then clicked to his horse and started off without another word to her.

They came upon another mountain stream, this one wide and rapid enough that he made her wait on the near side while he crossed. It was deep, deeper than it seemed, and at one point the buckskin stumbled. Rennie's heart leapt into her throat, but Gideon caught his horse up with a sure hand on the reins.

Once she'd made it safely across, she asked, "How much farther?"

"I'm not sure."

The last part of the trail was much steeper than before and less winding. Sweat flecked their horses' coats, and Rennie told herself that if it got any worse, she and Gideon would have to get down and lead them.

Then, without any warning, they topped a rise. The ground leveled out for about ten yards, then sloped away into a tiny, hidden valley.

Gideon pulled up and waited for her. They rested their mounts while they surveyed the deserted mining town. The valley below was dotted with weathered buildings, which Rennie thought a good stiff breeze would knock over. And from here they could see the gaping hole in the side of the mountain, only partially boarded up, the played-out mine that had been both the birth and death of the town.

Rennie was suddenly overcome with a sense of the sadness of it all. People had lived here once, had built this town—houses, stores, saloons and everything else—and sought to fulfill their ambitions in that mine. Then the winds of fortune had blown, taking away their livelihood and driving them away one by one.

Gideon leaned one arm on the pommel of his saddle, watching the expressions flitting over her face. Finally he said, "There are places like this all over the West, Rennie."

"It's so sad."

He shook his head. "It's not sad. It's just the way of things. People come and go, following their dreams. That's the way life is."

Rennie looked at him, really looked at him then.

"You know," he said softly, looking out over the valley, "that's a problem with many small towns these days. There aren't always enough opportunities to go around for the younger generation, so they're forced to seek employment elsewhere. And of course, a lot of kids get restless and bored with small-town life and head for the bright lights of the big cities. I guess they think they'll find what they're looking for—excitement, action, the fast-track life-style."

She thought about that for a moment, then said, "I wonder how many discover that no matter how far and how fast you run, you can't escape who you are. I wonder how many wish they could come home again, but are too afraid to try or too proud to admit they were wrong."

A long silence followed her words, broken only by the creaking of saddle leather and the snorts of their horses. Then Gideon said, "My brother was one of those who ran."

She stared at him. "I wondered about that. When you

said you had to write him about our wedding, I figured he didn't live around here.''

"I don't see Caleb very often.'' Gideon's face reflected only a hint of the conflicting emotions he felt whenever he thought about his brother. "He runs an air charter service in Las Vegas. He drops in every now and then, usually unannounced, but it's a long time between visits.''

"Were you close? Growing up, I mean.''

"Yeah, though I never really understood him. I was the older twin, the steady one. He was the wild one, always getting into trouble and expecting me to pull him out of it.'' Gideon smiled a little. "And he was always daring me, pushing me to be as wild as he was. That tattoo I have, well, that was Caleb's doing. He dared me once too often and like a fool I let him goad me into having it done.''

"You miss him, don't you?''

"Yeah, sometimes. But not so much as I did at first.''

Rennie didn't say anything, as if she sensed his need for silence. After a moment Gideon shook off his contemplative mood. "Enough about that. Do you want to go down there and have a look around?''

She threw him an incredulous look. "Are you kidding? After coming all this way? Of course!''

Gideon laughed, and side by side they rode easily down into the valley.

They tied their horses up near the old livery stable on the outskirts of the town and loosened the cinches. Rennie was a little stiff and sore, but it wasn't too bad, and she hid it from Gideon.

"Come on,'' she said quickly. "Let's see what there is to see.''

They walked down the center of the town's one street. There were a few weeds growing in it, but for the most part the packed-down dirt was bare.

"Kind of odd, don't you think?" Rennie said. "I would have thought it would all be grown over by now."

Gideon shook his head. "That just goes to show you how fragile the ecosystem is out here. Did you know that in parts of Wyoming you can still see the wagon tracks of the Oregon Trail? Even after a hundred years the land hasn't recovered."

They passed several structures partially or completely collapsed from age and neglect. They didn't stop, just headed for the first intact building they could find. They tried the door, but it was warped tightly into place. Rennie wanted Gideon to force it open, but he told her the whole building might come down on them if he did, so they peered in the small windows. The glass that had once been there was gone, leaving them with an easy view of the Spartan interior. An empty gun rack, a fortified inside door and tattered remnants of wanted posters, which still clung to the walls, bore testimony that this was the old jail.

Two buildings down from the jail was one identified by a large sign over the swinging doors as the Silver Lady Saloon. "That's certainly convenient," Gideon said. "The sheriff wouldn't have far to go to round up any trouble-makers."

The walls appeared sturdy enough, so they decided to chance entering it. But once inside, they both stopped short. Over the bar was a larger-than-life-size painting of a voluptuous woman. Faded as the woman was after years of exposure to the harsh elements, they could still clearly make her out.

She reclined on a red divan, scantily clad in a silvery wrapper, her bountiful breasts barely covered. Her dark tresses were elaborately curled but arranged in charming disarray on her lily-white shoulders. One shapely leg was thrust forward, artfully concealing her other feminine attributes while at the same time giving an unmistakable invitation. But if you somehow missed the invitation in her pose, the sloe eyes in her painted face left no doubt as to what she had in mind.

Rennie's eyes widened and she cleared her throat.

"I guess we know where the Silver Lady Saloon got its name."

Gideon's eyes didn't even flicker. "Yep."

"She's…uh…certainly…um…well endowed."

"Yep. She is that."

"And she's beautiful," Rennie added, unaware of the touch of wistfulness in her tone.

Gideon noted it, however, and turned to eye Rennie with the same concentration he'd given the Silver Lady's portrait. "If you like that sort of artificial, painted beauty. I prefer the natural look myself."

"Really?" Rennie couldn't conceal her pleasure in his comment.

Gideon smiled slowly. "Really." Without even glancing back at the painting, he said, "Have you seen enough?"

Rennie nodded and Gideon headed for the door. She followed him in silence, but at the last moment turned back for one last look at the Silver Lady. Those half-closed eyes seemed to mock Rennie, and she couldn't resist the childish temptation to say "So there!" under her breath, before walking out into the sunshine.

Next to the saloon was the only other two-story building in town, the Blackstone Hotel. A once-gilded sign, now badly deteriorated, was nailed to the front of the hotel, listing the various amenities offered by Gilbert Blackstone, Proprietor, to his patrons. Gideon's eyes locked onto the line that read Baths, 75c. French Baths, $2.00.

He began to chuckle. The chuckle turned into a guffaw, which in turn became helpless gusts of hearty laughter.

"What's so funny?"

Still laughing, he pointed to the sign.

Rennie read it through twice, out loud. Each time, Gideon laughed harder.

Her hands came out, palms up. "I don't get it. What's a French bath?"

Gideon struggled to regain his composure. When he finally had himself under control, he wiped the tears from the corners of his eyes and said, "I'm not quite sure. I've never seen it before." His eyes danced with merriment. "But considering the other phrases containing the word *French* and what they mean, I could hazard a guess."

She waited for him to continue, and when he didn't, she said a little impatiently, "So? Let's hear it."

"Well," he drawled, enjoying this, "I think it might include 'assistance' from one of the…uh…'ladies' from the Silver Lady Saloon next door."

"Oh." Then she added, "Oh!" The last word was drawn out as comprehension dawned on her. A vision appeared in her mind. A hotel room in a dusty western town. A gun belt hanging over the back of a wooden chair and a man's clothes scattered across the floor. Gideon's golden body ensconced in a hip bath, steam rising from the water swirling around him. And herself in a damp and disheveled silk negligee "assisting" him with his ablutions.

Rennie blushed again.

Gideon grinned wickedly, then took pity on her. "Come on." He shifted the rifle to his left hand and put his right arm around Rennie's waist. "I don't know about you, but I'm starving. Let's eat."

Contact with Gideon's very masculine body sent shivers of awareness surging through Rennie. As they strolled back in the direction they came, she let herself enjoy the feel of his arm around her, the fluid movement of his firmly muscled body next to hers. She loved the way he smelled of horses, leather and man. It did funny things to her insides.

When they reached the livery stable, Rennie stopped to answer nature's call while Gideon walked on to check on the horses. Satisfied with their condition, he sheathed the rifle, then threw his saddlebags over one shoulder, slung the bedroll he'd had the foresight to bring along over the other, and went looking for a likely spot for their picnic.

They made short work of the food. Afterward, replete, Gideon stretched out on his side and lazily watched Rennie methodically pack away the luncheon remains and the trash in the saddlebags. He felt a little guilty letting her do all the cleanup work, but when was the last time he'd been able to laze around on a sunny afternoon in spring? He couldn't remember.

The sun brought out glints of red in Rennie's dark hair, which the slight breeze kept tousling. She kept pushing the curls out of the way, the movements causing her sweater to dip and swell over her gentle curves. When his body responded, Gideon wasn't surprised. By now he'd come to expect this reaction to her. She turned him on so fast it was almost pathetic.

He laughed softly to himself and willed that part of his anatomy to simmer down. After all, despite his own feelings on the matter, it wasn't very likely that Rennie would suddenly decide that this was the moment to consummate their marriage. But he still let his gaze follow her as she walked down the hill toward the horses.

When she returned, Rennie stood self-consciously beside the blanket for a moment, unsure of what to do next. Her hip was bothering her a bit, and her thigh muscles were complaining as well at the workout they'd endured. She wanted to lie down next to Gideon and rest, maybe take a little nap, but wasn't sure if that was a wise thing to do. She knew all too well how her body reacted to his.

He solved the dilemma for her. His arm snaked out and snagged her knee, exerting just enough pressure to pull her down beside him.

"What..."

"You look tired. So am I" was all he said as he removed her hat and his. Then he shifted onto his back, pillowing his head on one arm, and stared at the sky. He sighed, a deep, contented sound, and Rennie relaxed, turning onto her back as well.

They were silent for the space of a few heartbeats, watching the clouds scudding across the sky. Then Rennie said, "Montana may be called Big Sky Country, but Wyoming has its share, too."

"Yeah. I know what you mean."

"I guess I appreciate the open spaces a lot more now than when I was younger. I thought I remembered what it was like, but I was wrong. Living for so many years in a place where even a small piece of sky is a luxury, you forget how vast it is out here. So much blue."

"The nights are even better. You can see the stars out here like nowhere else."

"I know. The first night I stayed in Carter's Junction, I went outside and just stared at the stars for almost an hour. Diamonds on blue velvet, that's what they looked like to me. So different from what I'd become used to in L.A. I'd forgotten just how breathtaking the night sky can be."

Rennie was silent for a moment, then added, "Kind of makes you feel that your problems aren't that important in the grand scheme of things, doesn't it."

"Yeah."

Gideon turned his head slightly, smiling, and Rennie

smiled back. His hazel eyes were green again, she noticed, and wondered why.

A sudden windy gust of cooler air made her shiver, and Gideon pulled her gently closer. "Come here," he said, curling his body to shield her.

After only a slight hesitation she snuggled next to his warmth, not at all unnerved by his nearness. Surprisingly, it seemed natural.

Gideon watched sleep overcome Rennie, watched the darkly lashed eyelids flutter and close, saw the gentle rise and fall of her chest slow. In sleep she looked impossibly young. He wondered if she'd lose that gentle, innocent look someday, if somehow life with him, a life without love, would erase that soft, vulnerable expression.

He frowned at the thought. He didn't want Rennie to change.

Had he ever met a woman like her? So open and trusting in some ways, so shy and inhibited in others. Gideon smiled, thinking about how much fun it was to tease her, to watch her blush. It made him feel young again, and it was wonderful.

I'm only thirty-three, not fifty-three. Why shouldn't I feel young? I haven't had this much fun since the last time Johanna and I went to the Wyoming State Fair and Rodeo the summer before she got pregnant with Andrew.

Johanna. The name was like a cold rain shower shocking Gideon into awareness. Johanna. He'd scarcely thought of her since yesterday afternoon. Not even last night in his dreams had the memory of her come to him. And this morning, instead of his usual realization of Johanna's absence from his bed, he'd awakened with a song on his lips.

Rennie had replaced Jo in his thoughts.

No. It's been too long for me since Jo died, that's all. It's sex. Just sex. Rennie's attractive, convenient and avail-

*able, and as my wife she's acceptable to my conscience.
That's all it is.*

But he knew it was a lie. He'd told Rennie the truth last
night in her motel room. His desire was for *her,* not just for
a reasonably attractive body. Hell, he could have had plenty
of women by this time from Carter's Junction and the surrounding area if that was all he wanted.

He'd had offers, but he'd turned them all down. He'd
been tempted a couple of times, but had only come close
once: after he'd gotten rid of the last housekeeper and he'd
had to take his kids to Emily's place again.

Everything had reached a crisis point then. Jo had been
dead for a year and a half, and he'd finally accepted she
wasn't ever coming back. He'd just brought Nicki home
from another round of doctor visits, this time at the medical
center in Casper, defeated once more. They'd arrived at the
Rocking L a day earlier than expected and he'd walked in
on his housekeeper, Mrs. Marsh, whipping five-year-old
Trina with one of his leather belts. He'd come damn close
to murder at that moment. Fortunately for Mrs. Marsh, she'd
read her probable fate on his face and resigned on the spot,
saving herself and him. He'd held a sobbing Trina on his
lap until she fell asleep. When he'd carried her to bed and
slipped her into her nightgown, he'd seen the welts on the
backs of her legs.

He'd cried that night. He'd tucked the covers around
Trina and kissed her, checked on his baby son, and helped
Nicki unpack and get ready for bed. Then he'd gone to his
own room, closed the door, and wept. He hadn't cried when
he heard about Jo's death, and the few tears he'd shed when
he buried her had scarcely touched his deep well of grief.
But he'd wept that night for everything. For Jo, who was
gone. For Nicki, who was lost. For Trina, for Andrew, and
for himself.

The next day he'd told his foreman not to expect him back for a few days, took his children to Emily and went off to Casper again, where nobody knew him, to get quietly drunk.

That weekend was lost in a haze. He had vague memories of a number of women coming on to him in the bars. One in particular, tall and full-figured with long blond hair, had attached herself to his side Saturday night, and he'd let her stay. Then when he was drunk enough, he'd taken her back to his motel room.

She hadn't really looked like Johanna, except in the most superficial way. But to his alcohol-fogged brain, she was Jo come back to him. He'd kissed her and caressed her, told her what he wanted to do to her in coaxing whispers as he'd done with Johanna, but then the woman spoke and the illusion was shattered. He couldn't get it back. Desire faded and reality returned. Jo was lost to him forever.

He had apologized to the woman. She'd let him call a cab for her and give her money for the fare.

He never even knew her name.

He'd spent Sunday morning drying out, and then had headed home. On the long drive north he'd taken a good, hard look at himself, hating what he'd almost done, and then made himself a promise. He'd never take another woman to his bed unless he could desire her for herself.

He'd reached a hard decision, too, as his truck ate up the empty miles. He'd decided to advertise, not for a new housekeeper this time, but for a wife. The decision had brought Rennie into his life.

And now he wanted her, not just because she was attractive and available. He wanted her because she was *Rennie*. Bright and sassy, shy and forthright. And sexy. Damned sexy.

He wanted her in his bed, blushes and all. He wanted to

tease her with words and tantalize her with kisses. He wanted to taste those firm, round breasts and coax them into arousal with his tongue. He wanted to part those silky legs and caress her there until she melted for him. Then he wanted to slide into her body and lose himself in her, taking both of them to the peak and beyond. And he wanted to lie in her arms afterward. He'd been so cold for so long. He needed the fire that he'd found in her to warm him through the long, lonely nights.

He needed it badly. Needed her badly.

As she slept, Rennie moved closer to him. He shifted and carefully slid one arm under her head, curving the other across her slight frame. Predictably, his body reacted with a surge of desire as he pressed against her, but he didn't care anymore. It felt good to hold a woman again, even if only in sleep. Then he corrected himself. It felt good to hold Rennie. In any way.

His last coherent thought before he drifted to sleep himself was that a little over two weeks ago he hadn't even known she existed.

Chapter 7

An hour passed. The air turned colder and the sky darkened. Gideon stirred, but neither he nor Rennie woke.

Then the heavens opened, deluging them with icy rain.

"Damn!"

Gideon instantly reached for his hat and jumped to his feet. Rennie followed suit only a second later, grabbing the blanket as she scrambled up. His eyes judged the distance to the nearest shelter, then he faced her and jerked his head toward the open door of the livery stable. She nodded her acknowledgment.

"Can you make it okay? I have to get the horses," he shouted above the hiss of the rain, pulling the Stetson low over his eyes to shield his face.

"Go on," she urged, throwing the wet and unwieldy bedroll over her shoulder. "I'll be fine."

They separated, Rennie dashing for the dubious protection of the barn and Gideon making his way to the split-rail fence where they'd tethered their horses.

Soaked and shivering, she stood in the doorway and watched him unhitch both horses and lead them toward the stable. The rain was coming down in sheets, and neither horse was happy about it. When lightning forked down from the sky close by and thunder boomed, the buckskin took exception. He reared and fought the reins. The chestnut mare caught the buckskin's snorting terror and suddenly Gideon had more than he could handle.

Almost before he realized he needed an extra pair of hands they were there. Rennie took Sweetwater's reins from him, leaving him to deal with the much larger gelding.

Even though most of Gideon's attention was focused on avoiding the buckskin's flailing hooves and bringing him under control, he was aware of how competently Rennie was dealing with the mare.

"Get her under cover," he shouted over his shoulder. "Don't wait for me."

She nodded, though she knew he couldn't see her. "Come on, girl," she coaxed over the pounding rain. "Come on, Sweetwater."

Once separated from the other horse, Sweetwater became docile and easily led. Rennie brought her into the livery stable, sparing a backward glance to see how Gideon was faring.

Man and horse were locked in a struggle that appeared to be an unequal match—twelve hundred pounds of terrified horseflesh against two-hundred-twenty pounds of determined man. But Gideon was no stranger to this situation and he knew exactly how to use whatever leverage he could, both verbal and physical, to its best advantage. His boot heels planted deep in what was rapidly becoming mud, the muscles of his arms distended, and his voice pitched in its most soothing tones, Gideon battled the big buckskin. Although she couldn't hear his exact words over the rain, Rennie could imagine what he was saying to the horse to re-assure him.

She turned away and twined Sweetwater's reins around the closest post, then busied herself with unsaddling the mare. In the absence of anything better, she used the saddle blanket to wipe down her horse. By the time Gideon finally brought the gelding inside and tied him down, she was almost finished.

Like Rennie, Gideon saw to the comfort of his horse before he gave a thought to his own condition. Rennie gave Sweetwater one last pat, then moved to help Gideon. They worked side by side in silence for a minute, then he spoke.

"I'm sorry about this."

She threw him a startled glance. "About what?" He motioned to the rain visible through the open door of the stable, and she said, "It's not your fault. No one can control the weather."

"Yeah. But I should have checked the forecast and not relied only on the sky. I know better than that. Weather around here can be pretty damn unpredictable, especially at this time of year."

Rennie shivered. She couldn't help it, now that the initial rush of adrenaline had subsided. Nor could she prevent her teeth from chattering. She was drenched and the air was so cold that steam was rising from the horses' coats. Gideon saw her shake uncontrollably, and he took the blanket from her hands and led her away from the open door.

"Hey, you're soaked to the skin. I'll finish up the horses. You've got to get out of those clothes."

Rennie waited for the latest bout of shivers to pass before she answered him. Then she said, "But what will I wear?" She ground her teeth to stop them from chattering. "I can't walk around here naked."

He grabbed up the other saddle blanket, which was still

fairly dry, having been mostly shielded from the rain by the saddle. He shook it out and thrust it at her.

"Here, put this on. It might not be the sweetest-smelling thing you've ever worn, but it'll be better than those wet clothes you're wearing now."

He turned to give her some privacy, and kept his back to her while he finished wiping down his horse. But he could hear the little sounds she made as she undressed, and his imagination filled in the rest. Despite the cold, despite his rain-drenched clothes, Gideon's body filled with heat at the thought of Rennie's soft curves bare.

He tried to shake off the thought by telling himself this was hardly the time to be thinking about sex. His body didn't want to listen.

Impatiently he shrugged off his own thoroughly wet jacket and hung it on a rusty nail. His shirt was damp, but not too bad, so he left it on. His jeans were the worst, but he figured if he couldn't keep his heated thoughts off Rennie his jeans would be dry in no time.

He concentrated again on the buckskin, rubbing with forceful strokes that pleased the horse but only relieved a fraction of the tension in Gideon's body. When he was done, he untied the horse and led him into one of the stalls that was still in fairly decent condition, then did the same with the mare.

·When he came out, his eyes were drawn to the corner where Rennie stood. Her jacket, jeans and sweater had been wrung out and slung over a stall railing. The straw hat he'd bought her that morning hung from a nail. And her boots stood neatly underneath them all. But none of those things held his attention.

The saddle blanket was wrapped around her body sarong-style, leaving her shoulders and legs uncovered. Even in the gloomy interior of the stable her skin gleamed softly, inviting him to imagine what lay hidden from view. In his mind's eye he saw the blanket fall away, inch by inch, teasing him as it slowly revealed the woman he wanted so badly.

From there it didn't take much to picture those slender legs wrapped around his hips. His eyes followed her legs upward as his hands wanted to do, past the blanket's hem, past the concealing folds and bare shoulders, up to Rennie's face.

She'd done her best to comb out the wet tangle of her hair, but there was nothing she could do to tame the curls that clustered damply, sexily, around her face, curls that begged for a man's hand to stroke them. And there'd be similar curls elsewhere for a man to play with.

Damn! He'd done it again. He'd let his imagination run wild, and now he had no one to blame but himself that his entire body throbbed for the release that only sex could give.

Sex with Rennie. Lusty and quick or deep and slow; at this moment he didn't give a damn which way as long as it happened *now*. How easy it would be to take those few steps that separated them and pull her body against his. How easy to slide his hands between the blanket's folds to the woman underneath. And how temptingly easy it would be to lift her, part her legs, and let her heat cradle him intimately. Very intimately.

His promise to her chafed his conscience just as his damp clothes chafed his body. God, he wished he'd never made her that promise, never more so than at this moment when his body desperately craved contact with hers.

But a promise had been made. And Gideon kept his promises.

Rennie shivered slightly, more from the intensity of Gideon's brooding gaze than from the cold. Her mouth went dry. The look of naked longing in his eyes seared her, igniting a fire that coursed into her veins, warming every part of her.

She was tempted. Oh, she was tempted! She wanted to brazenly drop the coarse blanket and stand naked before him. She wanted to cross the short distance that separated them and slide her arms around his neck. And more than anything in the world she wanted him to lift her in his powerful arms and crush her against him with the strength of his passion.

But before she could take that step toward him, he turned away. He picked up the sopping wet bedroll from where she'd left it by the doorway and began wringing it out.

"Gideon, I..."

He swung around and she took one step forward, her hand outstretched, when reality crashed in. Pain stabbed without warning, and she stumbled. Gideon dropped the bedroll and caught her.

"It's your hip, isn't it," he rumbled, correctly identifying the problem.

He lifted her, not in a passionate embrace, but in a gentle one, and Rennie whimpered, as much from frustration as from pain. He didn't understand and he shifted her carefully, thinking he'd hurt her. Which he had, but not in the way he thought.

He braced his back against a pole and slid down into a sitting position, Rennie cradled gently in his arms. He settled her next to him, her head against his shoulder. Then he removed his hat and sighed.

When he slid his hand underneath the blanket, Rennie gasped, but his touch was meant to soothe, not to arouse. His hand sought her hip, rubbing it firmly, and the warmth and the pressure eased the ache there. The ache elsewhere went unappeased.

"Is that better?"

She nodded, and Gideon removed his hand, much to her disappointment. But then she realized maybe it was for the best that things had turned out this way. After all, these were hardly the proper surroundings in which to make love with Gideon for the first time. When she had imagined the two of them together, she hadn't pictured them rolling around on the dirt floor of a stable, or herself wearing nothing but an old blanket that distinctly smelled of horses. It wasn't exactly a romantic setting.

But she'd wanted him so much in those few seconds that nothing else had mattered—not their surroundings, not the past, not even her physical scars from the accident, about which she was still self-conscious. She had wanted him to make love to her. She still did.

Outside, the rain continued to pour down, pounding on the livery stable's roof and hissing into the ground. In his stall, the buckskin gelding snorted his displeasure.

"Sorry, boy," Gideon said over his shoulder. "Nothing I can do about the rain." He looked down at Rennie. "And I'm sorry I dragged you out here and got you into this mess."

"I already told you it's not your fault. And you didn't drag me anywhere. I wanted to come."

"Yeah, but—"

"But nothing," she said firmly. "If anyone is to blame, it's me."

"How do you figure that?"

"I was the one who fell asleep first. If I hadn't, you probably wouldn't have, either. And we'd have started back long before the rain started."

He smiled. "Okay. Let's just agree that it's no one's fault, and leave it at that."

"Sounds good to me."

He was silent for a moment, then said, "You realize we might be stranded up here tonight."

"What do you mean?" From her expression it was obvious that the thought hadn't occurred to her.

"If the rain doesn't let up shortly, it'll be too late to start back. It'll be dark soon, for one thing, and the trail will be slippery. I don't want to chance it unless I have to."

"Oh. You're right. It wouldn't be safe."

"How much food is left from our picnic lunch?"

She thought about it, then said, "One sandwich, a couple of apples and three cans of pop. Oh, and I think there are a few cookies left in the bag."

"That's better than I hoped. We should probably eat the sandwich tonight before it goes bad, and save the rest for tomorrow morning."

"What about the horses?"

"When and if the rain lets up, I'll take them out and let them graze for an hour or so. They'll be okay as long as I don't let them eat too much grass this early in the year."

"That's good." Rennie shivered a little and rubbed her hands up and down her arms. She smiled wryly at Gideon. "It's getting colder."

"Yep." He stood up suddenly and walked over to a broken-down stall, where he began to pull apart the nailed slats.

She slipped to her feet and followed him, with only a slight limp. "What are you doing?"

"Getting wood for a fire."

"Can I help?"

He threw her an amused look. "Yeah. You can go back and sit down."

"But I want to do something to help."

"Your hip has had enough strain for one day."

"I'm not an invalid, you know."

"I know it, and thanks for offering, but I can handle this."

As she opened her mouth to argue, he picked up another board and said, "If you really want something to do, check out the forge's hearth and see what condition it's in. I want to build the fire there, if possible. There'll be less chance of an accident that way."

"Okay."

He broke the board across his knee and tossed the pieces on the pile beside him. "And could you throw the other blanket and the bedroll over one of the stall walls? I'd like to get them dry as soon as possible."

"Sure."

"Oh, and Rennie?"

"What?"

"Your blanket's slipping."

She wildly clutched at the front of the blanket, only to find it still securely fastened. She hitched it higher and tightened the tuck, anyway, throwing him an accusing look. He laughed.

Despite the awkward circumstances, despite the discomfort of their surroundings, Rennie enjoyed being stranded on the mountain with Gideon. After they started a cozy fire with the matches he'd carried in his saddlebags, the two of them checked out the livery stable to make sure they didn't have any unwelcome company. Eventually the rain slowed to a drizzle, then stopped altogether. But the sun had already set by then, and they agreed they were better off staying where they were for the night.

While Gideon took the horses out to graze, Rennie brought her clothes to warm by the fire. She hoped they'd dry quickly—she was already sick of wearing the blanket. The coarse wool chafed her sensitive skin, and when Gideon

was near she was all too aware that she was completely
naked underneath it.

*So I'm attracted to him. Why shouldn't I be? The way he
looks at me reminds me that I'm definitely a woman. And
he's all man. Every beautiful inch of him.*

Shame on you! Rennie's conscience told her. *It's character that counts, not how a man looks in a pair of jeans.*

Or out of them.

You haven't seen him out of them, her conscience chided.

Only in my dreams.

Despite the cold, Rennie suddenly felt warm. All over.

To distract herself, she made a quick trip outside, around
back. Gideon still hadn't returned by the time she was finished, so Rennie dug into his saddlebags for the food she'd
packed away. It didn't look like much when she spread it
out, especially for a man as big as Gideon, not when the
food had to cover both dinner and breakfast. Well, she
wasn't all that hungry, anyway.

She checked her clothes. Her scrap of a bra and her cotton
undies were almost dry, so she turned her back to the door
and slipped them on. She flipped the rest of her things over
and waited by the fire for Gideon.

She heard them coming, heard her husband's low, coaxing tones as he and the horses squished through the mud.
He led them in and stabled them, then pulled off his boots
and joined her by the fire. He held his hands out to the
warmth, glancing at the food she'd laid out.

"That looks good."

"It's all yours. I've already eaten," she fibbed.

"Um-hm." The look he gave her said he knew she'd lied.

"I'm not very hungry," she told him. "Really."

He didn't say anything, merely picked up half the sandwich and held it out to her. Rennie accepted it reluctantly,
and they ate their meager shares in silence.

When she was done, she wiped her hands and checked her clothes once more. They were fairly dry, so she took them into the corner and dressed quickly. It was cold away from the fire. Gideon glanced at her when she came back and sat next to him. She offered him the blanket.

"No, thanks. You keep it. It's going to get colder before the night is over."

"Don't you want to let your clothes dry by the fire?"

"They're pretty dry already. I'll be okay." He rose and placed another board on the fire, then sat down a little distance away from her.

Without anything better to do, Rennie watched the dancing flames, stealing glances at Gideon whenever she thought he wasn't looking. A few times he caught her at it, and their eyes held for breathless seconds before one or the other would look away. The silence was heavy with their unspoken thoughts.

This won't do, Gideon finally decided. His body had settled into a permanent state of semiarousal, and he knew he'd better get his mind thinking of something else before he did something he'd be sorry for.

With his eyes on the fire, he said, "You never told me how things went in Los Angeles."

"Fine."

"To tell you the truth, I half expected that you wouldn't come back." He turned toward her in time to catch a strange expression on her face.

"I gave you my word," she said.

"Yeah, but promises don't always mean the same thing to different people. I thought you might change your mind once you were back home. Didn't anyone try to talk you out of it?"

"Jess did, but it didn't make any difference. I'd already made my decision."

He stiffened as possessiveness exploded through him unexpectedly, and his next words came out as a growl. "Who is Jess?"

Rennie caught her breath and her eyes widened, as if he'd taken her by surprise, but she said calmly, "Jess is my stepbrother. I thought I mentioned him before."

Some of the tension left Gideon, but not all. "Yeah, you did, but never by name."

"Who did you think he was?"

He was hard-pressed to say. The affectionate way she spoke Jess's name told him she cared about the other man more than a little. But it was his own possessive reaction that bothered him the most.

Possessive? About Rennie?

It didn't make sense. Rennie was his wife and he desired her, but she wasn't his love, nor yet his lover. So why had he felt almost threatened, as if Jess had invaded his boundaries? And worst of all, why had his body tightened fiercely with the urge to mark Rennie as his territory, to brand her as his?

But he couldn't tell Rennie any of those things. "I don't know what I thought," he said for lack of a better response.

"I love him, but I'm not *in* love with him," she said, as if she knew what he'd been thinking. "Jess is the older brother I never had. My mother married his father when I was seventeen, and they died in a plane crash six months later. Jess became my guardian."

"Are you close?" He couldn't hold back the question, nor keep his unreasonable jealousy at bay.

She smiled a little. "I would have to say yes, but would you believe me if I said he doesn't understand me?"

"In what way?"

"In a lot of ways. For one thing, he thinks I'm crazy to be here."

He held her gaze. "And what do you think?"

"This is my home now, Gideon. This is where I want to be, where I belong."

Something about the way she said it touched a chord in Gideon. He thought of the Rocking L. Home. Or rather, it would be home again for him, once his children were there.

Neither of them spoke for a while, both lost in thought. When the fire began to die down, Gideon judiciously added more of the tinder-dry wood.

"You're good at that," Rennie said quietly.

"What? Keeping a fire going?"

"Um-hmm. Did you camp out a lot when you were young?"

"Yeah. I did. Mostly with Caleb."

She wrapped her arms around her knees and tilted her head to look at him. "Tell me about it."

"That's old history."

"Please."

He sprawled on one side, leaning his head on his hand. "What do you want to know?"

Her heart thudded. *What do I want to know? I want to know everything about you, and not just the things everyone else knows. I want to see inside your heart, to understand how you came to be the man you are.*

She stared at him, noting the fluid movement of muscle beneath his shirt as he settled his body into place beside the fire. The flames cast a warm glow over his features, and for a crazy, slow-motion moment Rennie felt as if she were falling. Her voice trembled a little as she said, "Tell me about camping with your brother."

"I haven't thought about that in years." He chuckled softly as old memories, good memories, came back to him. "Caleb didn't care for ranching, but he loved roughing it. There's this one place—I haven't been there in ages—where we made camp a lot. It's nothing but a tiny meadow, really, about halfway up the mountain. It's a rugged climb to reach it, but the view is fantastic once you get there. And there's a stream running through one corner.''

Rennie chanced a glance at him. She had never seen that particular expression on Gideon's face before, and at first she didn't recognize it. Then she knew. Happiness. For the first time since she'd known him, Gideon looked happy. Happy, and at peace with himself.

''Lord, but that water was cold, even on the hottest days,'' he continued. ''Caleb and I used to challenge each other to see who could take it the longest.''

''Who usually won?''

He gave her a smile of pure, male machismo. ''Who do you think?''

''I think it was probably a tie.''

He laughed. ''Yeah, you're right. We'd stay in that water until our lips, not to mention various other parts of our bodies, were blue. Neither of us wanted to give in.''

''What else did the two of you do?''

''I don't know. All the usual things kids on a ranch do, I guess, on and off horses.'' He breathed deeply and exhaled, a reminiscent smile softening his angled features. ''When I think back on it now, as a parent myself, I shudder at the chances we took. Although I have to admit my brother was a bit more reckless than I was, it's still a wonder one of us wasn't killed.''

He raised his eyes from contemplation of the fire to Rennie's face. ''How about you? What was your childhood like?''

Suddenly she wanted to share as much of her past as she could with him. ''Much like yours, I guess, even though I was an only child. From the time I could walk I trailed after my dad, always asking questions, always trying to help. I was probably more of a hindrance than a help at first, but my dad never made me feel that way. He was always patient and encouraging. Gram was just like him.''

He raised a questioning eyebrow, and she explained, ''Gram was my grandmother on my father's side. Everyone says I take after her.''

''In what way?''

''Just about every way, I guess. She was small, like me, and I have her coloring and her temperament. She taught me a lot, and I loved her dearly. She died when I was twelve. I still miss her.''

In the silence that followed, Gideon got up to tend the fire. This time he sat down near Rennie, close enough for his body warmth to reach her.

''What about your mother? You haven't said much about her.''

She sighed and shifted uncomfortably, extending her legs to relieve the strain. ''My mother loved me. I know that. But she wanted different things for me than I did. She hated the ranch, even though she loved my dad enough to stay there with him. But when he died, she couldn't wait to escape. Unfortunately, she took me with her.'' Rennie shivered.

''Cold?''

She looked at him. ''Not really,'' she admitted. ''I just don't like to think about that time in my life.''

He put a comforting arm around her, and she let him draw her close. ''I guess everyone has bad times that they don't want to remember. I know I do. Why don't you try to get some sleep. It's going to be a long night.''

''What about you?''

''Somebody has to tend the fire.''

''I can do it.''

"I'll take the first watch and wake you in a few hours. How's that?"

"Okay." Reluctantly she slid away from his embrace and stretched out on the dirt floor, drawing the saddle blanket over her and pillowing her head on her arms. She squirmed a little, trying to get comfortable, and soon realized it was impossible. But she was exhausted, so she closed her eyes and willed herself to sleep. She was floating toward oblivion when Gideon spoke.

"Rennie?"

"Hmm?"

"Do you really have a tattoo?"

"Um-hmm."

"Where is it?"

"I'll never tell. Why?"

"No reason. I just wondered."

She was smiling as sleep claimed her.

Miles away, in much different surroundings, Nicki restlessly turned over in her comfortable bed. She stared enviously through the darkness at Trina sleeping so peacefully in the twin bed next to hers, and wished she could sleep, too.

Daddy didn't call tonight, she thought miserably. He always called whenever he couldn't be there in person to wish them good-night. *Did he forget? Maybe he just doesn't want to remember. Maybe he's so interested in* her, *that woman who thinks she can take Mama's place, that he doesn't care about us anymore.* Well, she was a big girl, but Andrew and Trina were just little kids. They wouldn't understand even if she could explain it to them.

Nicki swallowed hard, but the lump in her throat wouldn't go down. And the coldness inside her congealed into a solid chunk of ice around her heart. She shivered and pulled the bedclothes tighter around her, but no amount of warmth could dispel the fear that Daddy wasn't coming back.

Chapter 8

Rennie woke in Gideon's arms. When she realized she was draped all over him, she rolled away, stifling a groan as her aching muscles protested. Gideon sleepily watched her for a moment, then rose, towering over her.

"Good morning." He reached down and helped her to her feet.

"Morning," she mumbled, pushing her hair out of her eyes, conscious of her dishevelment as well as a grungy taste in her mouth. Where, oh where, were her hairbrush and toothbrush when she needed them?

Gideon yawned and stretched, then ran a hand through his hair. Rennie noted ruefully that except for the stubble of his beard, no one would know he'd spent the night in a stable. Whereas she looked like something that had been dragged through a bush.

On the defensive, she said the first thing that came into her head. "Why didn't you wake me last night?"

"I tried. You told me you were awake, then turned over and went back to sleep."

"Oh." Nonplussed, she said, "I'm sorry. Did you get any sleep at all?"

"I dozed for a couple of hours at the end there."

"I'm sorry," she repeated.

"That's okay. You obviously needed the rest more than I did."

"How did I end up in…"

"In my arms?" he finished for her, and she nodded. "At about two this morning you started shivering, so I picked you up and carried you a little closer to the fire to get warm. I didn't have the heart to put you back on the cold ground afterward, so I held you on my lap. Then I dozed off. How do you feel?"

"Like yesterday's leftovers. I need a cup of coffee, a toothbrush and a bathroom, in that order."

He laughed. "No coffee and no toothbrush, I'm afraid, but I can substitute a can of soda and an apple." He motioned toward the open door leading outside. "And your bathroom awaits you."

Half an hour later they started down the mountain trail. It was a soft, beautiful morning, and the sun was just rising over the far horizon. The rain had washed away the nearly ever-present layer of dust, leaving the landscape with a fresh-scrubbed look. And the air smelled early-morning wonderful.

They had no troubles on the trip, as if Mother Nature had decided they'd already suffered their share of hardships the night before. The trail was passable, though a little slick in spots. Rennie was stiff and sore at first, but it wore off eventually.

When they finally reached the horse ranch, they turned

over the horses and made their explanations to the owner. He had been concerned but not unduly so, correctly assuming they'd been stranded by the storm and had wisely decided not to return in the dark.

Rennie said goodbye to Sweetwater while Gideon took care of the financial end of things. Throwing her arms around the mare's neck, she pressed her cheek against the horse's warm skin.

Sweetwater whinnied softly and nuzzled Rennie's shoulder. In the span of twenty-four hours Rennie had become attached to the little mare, the way it sometimes happens, and it seemed as if the horse felt the same.

"Goodbye, girl. Take care of yourself." Sweetwater nickered her response.

"You ready?" Gideon slid his wallet into the back pocket of his jeans. Rennie stroked the mare's soft nose one last time, then nodded. "You want to drive?"

"No. You drive. I know how much you enjoy it. Unless you're too tired?"

His grin flashed. "The day I'm too tired to drive that car you can wheel me into the old folks' home."

It seemed no time at all before they were back in Wagon Wheel Gap. Gideon pulled into the motel parking lot and parked in front of the office. He turned to Rennie, hesitated, then spoke.

"What would you say if I suggested we stay over another day?" Before she could answer, he added, "I need food and a few hours of sleep, but afterward we could do something in town and have a nice, quiet dinner. If we turn in early we can leave by sunup tomorrow morning. How does that sound?"

Rennie could scarcely contain her smile. "I think it sounds wonderful."

"Fine. I'm sure Emily won't mind having the kids one

more night, but I'll call to make sure and to talk to my kids, since I didn't have the chance last night. And I'll check in with my foreman. If everything's okay, I'll arrange to keep our motel rooms for one more day.''

Ten hours later Rennie closed the door, kicked off her shoes and threw herself on the bed in her motel room. She pressed her fingers to her lips, reliving the last precious hours of her honeymoon, culminating with the kiss she'd just received. Gideon's kiss.

They'd spent a wonderful day together, laughing and joking with ease as if they'd known each other for years. He'd teased her when she browsed for an hour in a tourist shop made up to look turn of the century, before deciding on gifts for his children. Then he'd bought her the lovely and expensive cameo brooch she'd admired when she thought he wasn't looking.

He'd laughingly protested when she dragged him into the souvenir photograph store to have their picture taken in authentic costumes from the Old West. But he was the one who'd picked through the racks to find just the right dress for her to wear.

And dinner had been quietly romantic. The night they'd spent on the mountain had drawn them closer, creating an intimacy between them that went beyond the physical. They'd talked little, letting their eyes say what was in their hearts. The crowning moment came when Gideon toasted her with his wineglass.

''To the only woman I wouldn't mind being stranded with again.''

She loved the way his gorgeous eyes smiled and twinkled at her while he kept a straight face. She loved the way his lips tilted up slightly when he was amused and trying not to show it. And she loved his nose, uncompromisingly straight and just right for his lean, tanned face with its harsh angles. In fact, she was increasingly aware that she was terribly, wonderfully attracted to everything about him.

They'd walked back to their motel hand in hand as twilight stole over them. He'd kissed her, one of those kisses that melted her insides and curled her toes. Then he'd touched her cheek and left her.

That wasn't how Rennie wanted the day to end. Not this time. Not this last night of her honeymoon. But Gideon had made her a promise, and being the man he was he wouldn't break it. So it was up to her to make the next move. She knew what he wanted, what *she* wanted. She just didn't quite know how to go about it.

Her mind teeming with various approaches, she stripped off her clothes and took a quick shower, rehearsing opening lines under her breath. She got out and dried off, then dusted herself with lilac talc. Her body felt like a stranger's.

Naked, she padded into the bedroom and took out the one and only nightgown she possessed, bought for this very purpose. Usually she slept in an oversize cotton T-shirt, but tonight she needed the confidence of something truly feminine. On the hanger in the store the nightgown hadn't seemed like much—a sleeveless, full-length froth of diaphanous white layers. But when she'd tried it on she'd known it was perfect for her. The draped material curved gently above the soft swell of her breasts and delicately cupped them, then fell to the floor in a filmy cloud that swirled around her legs as she walked. And though the gown was designed to entice, it hinted rather than revealed.

She slipped it on, the silky folds caressing her skin and sending pleasurable shivers through her. Gideon had done this, had awakened her body to sensual awareness. A fine trembling seized her, and she drew on the long-sleeved matching peignoir to distract herself. She had to tie the ribbons at the throat three times before she got them right.

In the bathroom she brushed her teeth, then peered at herself in the small mirror. She looked pale, even more so than usual, so she applied a little lipstick, then blotted most of it off so it wouldn't be obvious. There wasn't much she could do with her hair—her dark curls refused to be styled—so she brushed out the tangles and left it at that.

Finally there was nothing left to do, but still she hesitated.

"I'm scared," Rennie told her reflection.

But that wasn't quite true. Not scared, exactly. She was nervous. That was more like it. She wanted this, wanted Gideon. But so many things could go wrong, snapping the fragile threads of trust they'd just begun to weave between them.

There was her inexperience. Her one previous sexual encounter years ago had been a disaster. Rennie knew the mechanics of sex, but she didn't want to have sex with Gideon. She wanted to make love with him. Would desire guided by instinct be enough?

And what about her scars from the car crash? They probably weren't as bad as she thought, but would Gideon be turned off by them? Or would he pity her? She'd almost rather see rejection or indifference in his hazel eyes. Anything but pity.

Maybe we could make love in the dark. Maybe I'll just keep my nightgown on.

"Maybe this is a bad idea." The spoken words startled her.

No! I want this one night alone with Gideon. I may never have the chance again. Once we're home there'll be so many distractions and demands on both of us. Lovemaking may be limited to stolen minutes at the end of an exhausting day or brief morning interludes before the children wake up. Now's the time to do this. Now, when we have privacy and all night long to get it right.

Getting it right. That raised another question. Gideon was a big man. Big in *every* way? And she was small, especially compared to him. Would he...fit?

Rennie's laugh held a touch of hysteria. She could just picture Gideon's expression if she walked up to him and asked, "Oh, by the way, would you mind terribly if I measured you before we start to see if we're physically compatible?"

This is silly. Gideon isn't going to hurt me. On the contrary, he'll be a wonderful lover. All that power and passion. He'll woo me with teasing words and sweet, drugging kisses. Dark and sweet. Deep and sweet. Then he'll touch me with those hard yet gentle hands, and...

Warmth invaded Rennie's body as she imagined the two of them intimately entwined. Gideon moving with her, within her, in the oldest dance.

Her heartbeat quickened. Was she ready to play with fire? *Tonight. It has to be tonight.*

Before she could change her mind, Rennie moved swiftly to the connecting door between their motel rooms. She pressed her ear against the wood panel. Silence. Was he already in bed?

She took a deep, steadying breath, then knocked. There was no answer, so she knocked again, harder this time.

"Yeah, just a minute." Interrupted in the act of removing his shirt, Gideon shrugged it back on but didn't bother to button it before opening the door.

He stopped dead at the sight of Rennie in the kind of silky, not-quite-there-but-not-quite-bare thing that was the stuff male fantasies thrived on. He exhaled suddenly and looked away, then focused on her face.

"What's up?"

She opened her mouth to speak, but she couldn't remember a single one of the lines she'd practiced. They all flew out of her head at the sight of Gideon, barefoot, with his shirt hanging open, revealing a golden thatch of hair that arrowed down and disappeared into the front opening of his jeans. The top button of his jeans was undone, and her eyes rested on it. Her mouth went dry and she swallowed.

"Rennie? Is something wrong?"

She forced her gaze upward and shook her head. "May I come in?" She hated the breathy way her words came out, but she couldn't do anything about it.

"If nothing's wrong," he said slowly, "then maybe this isn't the best time."

"Please."

"Rennie, I…"

She placed her hand on his arm. "Please. I'm not very good at this. I don't know the procedure."

Understanding dawned, and his body hardened in one wild rush. He pushed the door wide. She entered and closed the door behind her, then braced her back against it. He took one step toward her, close enough to smell the perfumed warmth of her skin, close enough to see the barely discernible tremors that shook her. But he didn't touch her. He didn't dare. Before this got out of hand he had to know for sure.

"Does this mean what I think it means?"

Soft brown eyes met warm hazel ones. "You said…you said it was my decision." Her fingers tugged loose the ribbons at her throat and the peignoir slid open. A slight shrug of her shoulders and it fell in a gossamer pool at her feet. "I'm saying yes."

"Oh, God." He curled one hand around her waist possessively, pulling her toward him, and caressed her cheek with the other, tilting her chin up with his thumb. His lips brushed hers, warm and firm, yet gentle. And then not so gentle.

"I want you, Rennie. God knows I've been going crazy with it." His voice was hoarse as he struggled to keep himself under control. "But you have to know how it is with me. It's been a long time, maybe too long. If you change your mind even a few minutes from now, I don't know if I'll be able to stop."

If he was trying to discourage her, he was going about it all the wrong way. Her breasts ached from just the simple contact with his bare chest, the thin fabric of her nightgown rubbing against her skin as he moved slightly, adding to the exquisite pleasure.

"I won't change my—" She caught her breath sharply, shivering when his tongue discovered the delicate shell of her ear.

"Be very sure," he whispered just before his teeth tugged gently at her earlobe.

"I am sure." She wrapped her arms around Gideon's neck as she'd longed to do the night before, and pressed her body all along the length of his.

He made an incoherent sound and swung her effortlessly into his arms, then caught her mouth with his own in a rough claiming. She clung to him as he carried her the short distance to his bed. He laid her on top of the bedspread and followed her down, unwilling to let her go even long enough to pull down the covers. This time his kiss plundered, his tongue sliding deftly through parted lips to the moist warmth within. Again and again he took her mouth. She could scarcely breathe but she didn't care. Here was the fire, the passion she'd dreamed of. Nothing else mattered.

When he finally released her mouth, her lips were swollen and throbbing, and her lungs gasped for air. But the respite was brief. He sought the fragile hollow of her throat, nuzzling, tasting. She moaned when his lips trailed down, seeking and finding one hardened nipple through the silky material of her gown.

Her hands clutched his shoulders and her back arched, giving him greater access. He immediately took advantage, wetting the fabric with his tongue and lightly nipping her with his teeth before drawing her nipple into his mouth. Liquid warmth blossomed deep inside her, and her legs tightened involuntarily. Electric pulses flickered through her body as he suckled, tiny shock waves radiating from the point of contact to her core, arousing her unbearably. When he sought her other breast she whimpered. The velvet torture went on and on, and she clung to sanity by her fingertips.

Gideon's hands shifted from her waist to her hips, pulling her farther beneath his powerful body. The hardness of him only emphasized her yielding softness. He lifted his mouth and their eyes met in open acknowledgment of what was happening between them. Without conscious thought she ran her hands down the column of his neck and over his chest, loving the feel of him. She inhaled deeply. His musky male smell, overlaid with plain soap and water, mingled with the scent of lilacs that came from her—a potent combination that aroused her even further. With a daring she never knew she possessed, she slid her arms underneath his and urged his body closer, then planted a string of kisses along his jaw.

Gideon almost lost control in that moment. He rained savage kisses over her face, her neck, everywhere he could reach. Desire pounded through his body, his arousal straining against confining denim. He groaned and settled his jeans-clad hips firmly on hers, using his knee to part her legs, then ground his aching fullness against her loins. But it wasn't enough. He needed her naked. He needed to be naked himself. Impatiently he tugged at the neckline of her nightgown, desperate for the feel and taste of her bare skin. When the material refused to give, he growled his frustration.

"Wait." Rennie's hands closed over his, then pushed lightly against his chest.

He froze. For one terrible moment he didn't know if he'd be able to stop. He'd wanted her forever, it seemed, and now, when he was this close to having her, he didn't know if he was strong enough not to take her by force, if necessary. His mind wrestled with his body for endless seconds, then he cursed and rolled off her.

He threw one arm over his eyes against the brightness of the overhead light. His chest heaved as he fought the primitive urge to coerce her. Damn it, he'd warned her!

He heard a soft rustle and felt the bed shift as Rennie left it. A clicking sound puzzled him, then the overhead light flicked off. With a muttered oath he sat up, then stopped abruptly.

Rennie stood beside the bed, her face in shadow. The light from the bathroom, the only light in the room, outlined her body through the filmy gown. As he watched, she reached down to the gown's hem and slowly pulled it over her head. She was naked beneath it.

"I thought…" He swallowed thickly. "I thought you'd changed your mind."

She knelt on the bed and touched his face. "I'm sorry," she whispered. "I didn't realize." Then she kissed him, a passionate, wanton, yet strangely innocent kiss.

Eons later he broke the embrace and stood up, but only to tear off his clothes. Sudden shyness made her avert her face at the rasp of his zipper, so she rolled down the covers and slipped between the sheets, pulling them up to her chin. She looked at him then. Naked, he was even more magnificent than he was clothed. Even the dim light couldn't hide the taut muscles that corded his arms, thighs, abdomen. And his manhood rose strongly, proudly, in readiness.

Her nervousness returned. He was so perfect, while she was so flawed. She'd turned off the light before removing her nightgown so he wouldn't see her scars, but she knew they were there and the knowledge added to her nervousness. As if he understood, he gently removed the sheet from her hand and pulled it down, exposing all of her to his gaze.

"You are so beautiful," he said hoarsely, as he joined her on the bed. His eyes confirmed his words, and suddenly her shyness melted away. Then his mouth found hers, and passion flared between them again.

He couldn't seem to get enough of her. His hands roamed her body at will, caressing, enticing, teasing her to fever pitch. His lips held hers captive, his tongue stroking in and out of her mouth in imitation of what was to come.

He reminded himself he had to go slow as he parted her thighs. When his fingers slipped through the folds of her womanhood she gasped. He rubbed the tiny nub there gently, firmly, feeling her surrender in degrees. He loved the sounds she made, breathy little moans of pleasure that came from deep within her and raised his own level of arousal another notch. And when he slid one finger carefully inside, she cried out in sweet agony and tore her mouth from his.

"Please…"

She was already wet for him, but he needed more. She was tight around his finger, almost virginal. And he knew it had been a long time for her. He wanted her so ready that she wouldn't even notice the pain of his entry, so aroused that she would welcome his possession to assuage that ache. He shuddered and gritted his teeth, praying that his tenuous control would hold long enough.

Rennie couldn't bear it. The things he was doing to her, the sensations that flooded her body, were so incredibly exquisite as to be close to pain. She thought she'd known desire, thought she'd understood what her body was capable of feeling. She hadn't even come close.

Words to describe what she was feeling eluded her, but if she couldn't tell him, she could show him. She could give him the same pleasure he was giving her. No shyness now. It seemed the most natural thing in the world for her hands to seek him out, wrapping around his sex and caressing him instinctively as he trembled and groaned his pleasure.

Then he caught her hands and held them still. "No more."

"But I..."

His voice was harsh with strain. "If you don't stop it'll all be over."

"Oh."

He kissed her, a blazing kiss of masculine hunger, then he poised himself between her thighs, holding his weight on his arms. She clung to him, wanting him, unwilling to wait any longer to belong to him in the most elemental way. He began to enter her, slowly but inexorably, a steady pressure that forced her body to accept his. And it hurt. She tried not to let her expression show just how bad the pain was, but it was impossible. She turned her face away to hide the tears leaking out of the corners of her eyes.

"God, Rennie. Don't." A tremor shook him. He kissed her eyes closed, catching her tears with his tongue. Though it cost him every ounce of willpower he had, he started to withdraw.

"No!" She was fierce in her denial. She tightened her slender thighs around his hips, holding him in place. "Please, Gideon. Don't stop." He hesitated, and she reached down between their bodies to touch him where they were joined.

The last shreds of his control vanished into oblivion. A

groan rumbled out of him and the muscles in his buttocks flexed, completing his possession of her in one stroke. She cried out, a small sound that escaped despite her best efforts to hold it back. He heard it, a whiplash against his conscience, and he flinched.

But she felt so good, so tight and wet and soft. It had been so long he'd almost forgotten how good a woman's body felt as it closed around him, had almost forgotten the waves of pleasure generated from being held within those warm depths. He almost came in that moment, buried so deep in Rennie that he touched her womb. Only that small cry of pain held him back. He had to make it good for her. He *had* to.

So instead of beginning the driving rhythm his body craved, he rolled over on his back, bringing her with him. His move was so unexpected that she sat up, straddling his hips. Exactly what he wanted. Freed of the need to support his weight, his hands cupped her breasts, flicking his thumbs over her nipples. Then his fingers trailed down and found that tiny button of flesh, and he caressed it until he felt her involuntary response.

The pain receded as her body began to accept his invasion. Rennie felt new ripples of lightning shiver through her at his touch. She began to rock against him, compelled by a need that had swiftly rebuilt to explosive proportions. He helped, lifting her partway off him, then sliding her back down over him as they found their tempo.

Her heart hammered inside her breast and her breath came in pants. Her hair clung in wisps around her damp face. She gazed down at Gideon, the savage expression on his face matching the wildness inside her. The pace quickened as she reached for something just out of her grasp, and she sobbed, wanting this to be over, yet never wanting it to end.

The crest caught her unprepared. It tore through her, endless spasms of such violent pleasure that she collapsed on his chest, weeping and crying out his name over and over.

Her climax triggered his. He made a guttural sound and rolled them over once more, pulling up her legs and driving into her soft depths, riding her hard. She tightened her legs around him and arched to meet his thrusts as he came, hot jets that filled her and emptied him.

He sagged against her, all strength gone. Just breathing seemed almost too much effort, and his chest heaved as he tried to drag in enough air. Rennie made a tiny sound, and he realized he must be crushing her. His arms trembled as he attempted to free her.

"No." She pulled at his hips, anchoring him where he was.

"But I'm too heavy for you."

She rubbed her cheek against his chest. "No," she whispered. "Please stay."

He compromised by moving to one side and shifting most of his weight, but remaining inside her. She made a contented sound and snuggled as close to him as possible, hooking one leg over his to retain the connection. When their breathing eventually slowed and their heartbeats returned to normal, she murmured something he didn't catch. He brushed his lips against her forehead.

"You okay?"

"Um-hmm." She took a deep breath and let it out slowly, then smiled. "Are you?"

"Yeah." Satisfaction, rich and dark, colored his voice. "Oh, yeah." His arms tightened around her.

Though the silence between them was warm with the echoes of the passion they'd just shared, the room became chilly as their bodies cooled. When she shivered and huddled closer to his warmth, he gently disengaged their bodies, then reached down and dragged the covers over them.

Sleep beckoned. Gideon dozed off and Rennie watched him, savoring these quiet moments in his arms. She kissed him, a butterfly kiss that didn't disturb his slumber.

No woman could have had a better lover, she thought. Her only regret was that he hadn't been the first. But in a way he had been. He'd been the first man to show her what her body was capable of experiencing, the first to tap the depths of passion she'd never even suspected she possessed. She'd never even imagined some of the things he'd done. Even the pain of their joining had been welcome because of him. Feeling him so intimately, seeing the pleasure he derived from her body, had fueled her desire to the point where nothing else mattered but loving him.

Remembering brought a blush to her cheeks, and her body flushed with heat. Of their own volition her hands stroked his chest, tangling in the soft covering of hair, then sliding downward over the incredibly taut muscles of his stomach and abdomen. She found what she sought, and her fingers closed over him.

"You're gonna be in trouble if you don't stop." The deep, raspy sound startled her, but she recovered quickly.

"Oh?" Her wide-eyed look of innocence was belied by the way her hands continued to caress him.

"Full of sass, aren't you. What happened to that shy woman who came to my room?"

"She went for coffee. I'm taking her place." His deep chuckle turned into a groan of pleasure as she reached farther and cupped him. "Do you want me to stop?"

His "no!" was emphatic enough to warm any woman's heart. He turned fully onto his back, pulling her on top of him, and spread his legs. Then his hands caught hers and taught them a better rhythm. Soon they were both aroused, hearts pumping in irregular fashion. Mouths met, tongues entwined, and arms and legs meshed inextricably.

The shrill of the telephone shocked them into immobility. They stared at each other for endless seconds, panting slightly, while the phone continued to ring. Then Gideon fumbled for the receiver.

"Yeah?"

The change that came over him was almost frightening. He jackknifed into a sitting position, instantly alert. He asked only two questions, "How long?" and "Where have you looked?" He listened intently to the answers he received, and his sudden emotional retreat from her as the caller spoke was almost a tangible thing. Then he said, "We'll be home as soon as possible," and hung up.

He sat on the edge of the bed for a moment, his shoulders hunched in a way she'd never seen. Then he stood up, grabbed his jeans from the floor and began pulling them on. He avoided her gaze, or so it seemed to her.

"Gideon? What is it?"

He tugged his shirt on and buttoned it hastily, then tucked it in and zipped his jeans. "How long will it take you to pack? We've got to get back to Carter's Junction right away."

He hauled his suitcase from the corner and flipped it open, throwing his things in haphazardly. She scrambled from the bed, dragging the sheet with her.

"What's happened? What's wrong?"

He picked up one boot and stared at it for a second, then dropped it and looked at her. His expression held equal parts anger and pain. "It's Nicki. She's run away."

Chapter 9

Nicki rubbed the back of her hand across her eyes. Darkness surrounded her like a blanket, and she was tired, cold and scared. But the tears still wouldn't fall, even though she desperately wanted to cry, *needed* to cry. And the ache in her chest wouldn't go away, either. The hurt inside was so big it almost choked her.

Daddy wasn't coming back. Nobody knew it yet, except her. And she knew why, too. It was because of her, because of what she'd done.

She straightened in the saddle and nudged her heels into Cheyenne's sides. The horse tossed his head, balking at the trail ahead of them. Nicki dug her heels in harder. She didn't care if Cheyenne didn't want to take her where she wanted to go. He had to. He just had to.

Cheyenne snorted his disapproval, but the third time she kicked him he finally gave in and started slowly upward.

It wasn't even midnight when Rennie and Gideon checked out of the motel. So much had happened tonight that Rennie thought somehow it should be later.

The drive back to Carter's Junction took much less time than the trip out. She said nothing when Gideon pressed the accelerator to the floor and told her curtly to watch for wild-life on the road. And when he took the dark mountain curves at terrifying speeds, she gripped her hands in her lap, trust-ing in God, Gideon and her little sports car to get them safely home.

The dark, brooding silence of the stranger beside her tore at her heart. She sensed the unspoken self-recriminations weighing heavy on his conscience. She ached to comfort him, but he'd withdrawn from her so completely she didn't know how to bridge the chasm. Still, she had to try.

"It's not your fault," she said softly.

"Then whose fault is it?" His tone was bitter. "I broke my promise. I told my children we'd be home tonight. I *promised* them. I've *never* broken a promise to them."

"But that doesn't mean—"

His anger at himself splashed over onto her. "A promise may not mean much to you, but it's damned important to me!"

Stung, Rennie fired back, "Promises are important to me, too!"

He ignored her as if she hadn't spoken. "But I was so caught up in having a good time, I forgot my promise to my kids. Damn it, I didn't even get a chance to talk with them when I called Emily this morning!"

"Why not?"

"They were getting dressed for church. Emily said they were already running late, so I told her I'd call them after dinner to explain why I wouldn't be home till tomorrow." He threw an accusing look in her direction that seared her even in the darkness. "Then you came to my room."

"So it's my fault?"

When she put it into words he realized how unfair it was to blame her, but his guilty conscience made him lash out. "You've had me so hot this entire weekend that when you finally said yes, I forgot everything else."

"I never meant—"

"Hell, it doesn't matter what you meant." He laughed harshly as he downshifted, slowing slightly to round a blind curve. "It doesn't change what happened."

"But it wasn't like that!"

"Maybe. Maybe not. All I know is what I see." He increased pressure on the accelerator and the car responded with a spurt of speed. Something more than his guilt over Nicki drove him to add, "Didn't take you long, though, did it? For someone who claimed to have almost no sexual experience, you certainly learned fast. Makes a man wonder."

"Don't. Please don't."

Pain ripped through his gut when he heard the tears in her voice, and he despised himself for putting them there. He was a bastard for taking this out on her, but damn it, couldn't she see that he didn't mean it? And he didn't have time right now to apologize.

Dark silence pulsed around them. When they reached the bottom of the mountain, Gideon turned onto the highway and unleashed all the power Rennie's car was justly famous for. The speedometer needle leapt upward, and Rennie remembered with a pang how he'd grinned like a kid—was it only the day before yesterday?—and said he'd bet her car could do one-seventy on the open road. He'd sounded so carefree that morning, almost happy. Now he had the opportunity to find out if he'd win his bet, but she knew he wouldn't even remember.

He was happy that day. We were happy. But none of it

means a thing unless Nicki's all right. It will destroy him if anything happens to her.

Rennie couldn't let her thoughts continue in that vein. The consequences were too devastating to think about. Abruptly she asked, "Would you tell me what Emily said on the phone?"

At first she thought he wasn't going to answer, but then he said brusquely, "She said Nicki's been brooding all weekend, hanging around the house, not even wanting to go out riding, which she usually loves. But Emily wasn't really worried about it until tonight, when I didn't call. She said Nicki scarcely ate any dinner, then hovered over the phone till way past her bedtime. Emily said when she finally made Nicki go to bed, Nicki looked stricken. That was the word she used. Stricken. An hour later, when Emily checked on the kids, Nicki was gone."

"Oh, Gideon, I'm so sorry." She wanted to touch him, to comfort him somehow, but she knew her touch wouldn't be welcome now. "Where do you think she might have gone?"

His breath expelled in a rush and he shook his head. "No idea. Emily's already started the search, but since Nicki's horse is also missing, there's no telling how far she may have gotten. We have to assume she could be anywhere. And tracking at night is chancy at best."

"So what are you going to do?"

"Damned if I know. But I've got to do something. I can't just wait around and hope she comes home." He glanced at her. "She's only nine, Rennie." His words came out husky with pain and urgency. "It's killing me to think of her all alone out there in the dark. She might be lost, or hurt, or just cold and frightened. Not knowing is the worst of it." His voice dropped to a whisper. "Not knowing..."

"We'll find her. I know we will."

He continued as if he hadn't even heard her. "I can't lose her, too. Not Nicki, God, not my baby. Watch over her, Jo. Don't let anything happen to her."

Rennie was certain Gideon didn't even realize what he was saying. It was so obviously second nature for him to speak his beloved first wife's name in times of stress. She averted her face from his and stared out at the star-studded midnight sky.

Well, you knew from the first that he loved Johanna, she reminded herself. *But that didn't stop you from marrying him. That didn't stop you from trying to make things up to him. So you can't let this get to you. You can't let yourself feel rejected.*

But it still hurt. Especially after the beauty of their love-making only a few hours ago. She'd felt so close to him, sharing her body with him the way she wanted to share the growing emotions in her heart.

Lovemaking on your part, maybe. But just sex for Gideon. Good sex, passionate sex, but sex all the same. His heart still belongs to Johanna. And why do you care, anyway? It's not as if you love him. So why does it hurt so much?

But she shied away from answering her own question, and gave herself a mental shake. She shouldn't be thinking about herself right now. She should be trying to figure out where a confused nine-year-old girl would go to nurse her pain and sense of betrayal.

Rennie was still puzzling over that thought when Gideon pulled her car up in front of the Holden's sprawling ranch house.

It seemed as if every light in the house, the bunkhouse and the barns was on, and the stableyard bustled with activity. Half a dozen men on horseback with lanterns congregated around an older man standing in the bed of a pickup truck, and Rennie recognized Jim Holden. He was shouting out instructions, but when Gideon unfolded himself from the driver's seat of the sports car, Jim jumped down and hurried over.

"You made good time."

"Have you found her?"

Jim darted a glance at Rennie, who had come to stand at Gideon's side. He grimaced, then looked back at Gideon. "No, and it doesn't look good," he said gruffly. "We been searchin' everywhere, but nobody's found Nicki. Just haven't had much luck trackin'."

Gideon didn't flinch, but Rennie almost felt his muscles clench against the pain and fear she knew must be tearing him apart.

Jim continued. "Already got two search parties out right now, and the third's just formin' up." His grizzled head gestured at the group behind him.

"Got a horse for me?" Rennie scarcely recognized the harsh voice as Gideon's.

Jim nodded. "Take mine. She's in the barn, saddled up and ready to go. I'll get another and join you soon as I can."

"Thanks."

"Least I could do. I'm real sorry about this. Emily and I shoulda seen it comin'."

Gideon clasped the older man's shoulder and squeezed it. "Not your fault, Jim. Mine. Only mine."

Jim shook his head in sympathy, then headed for the barn without a word. Gideon turned and almost bumped into Rennie. By his startled look he'd obviously not even known she was there.

"Rennie, I..."

"I'll be okay. You go do what you have to do." He looked at her strangely, almost beseechingly, and without even thinking about it she slid her arms around her husband's waist and held him tight. After a second his arms closed around her. "She'll be fine," Rennie reassured him. "I know she will. You'll find her. You'll see."

They remained like that for only a moment before Gideon tore himself away. Rennie stood where she was and watched him mount the horse Jim brought out of the barn, then ride away with the other men.

"Oh, God, let me be right. Let Nicki be okay," she whispered to the night.

A movement at the corner of her eye made her swing around. Emily stood a few feet away, the bemused expression on her face changing to wonderment.

"You care about him."

Rennie didn't even try to prevaricate. "Yes," she said softly, simply. "I do. Very much."

"You hurt for him."

"Yes."

"You'd take his pain if you could."

"Yes," Rennie answered for the third time.

"I once felt like that." Emily looked suddenly older and very, very tired.

"Not…not about Gideon?"

"Oh, no." Emily's laugh was the saddest thing Rennie had ever heard. "Not Gideon. Someone else. A long, long time ago. A lifetime ago." She stared past Rennie into the darkness as if seeing something only she could see.

"Emily…"

The other woman blinked, then shook her head as if shaking off memories too painful to bear. She looked at Rennie again, this time with remorse. "I'm sorry I had to bring you back like this, sorry I didn't take better care of Nicki."

"It's not your fault. Gideon doesn't blame you and neither do I."

"If anything happens to her, he won't be able to bear it."

"I know. That's why I have to find her."

"You?" Emily's confusion was obvious.

"Me." Rennie put her hand on Emily's arm. "Where would she go? Think, Emily. Nicki was hurting. Where would she go?"

"I don't know." But there was a flicker of something in Emily's face.

"I think you do. It's someplace special to her, isn't it? Someplace where she went with her father or her mother. That's it, isn't it?"

"She wouldn't," Emily whispered. "Not in the dark."

"Where?" A sense of urgency came to her out of nowhere, and she grasped the other woman's arms tightly. "Where wouldn't she go?"

Emily's frightened eyes focused on Rennie's. "The Top of the World."

"What?"

"It's a place…oh, I can't explain. It doesn't have a real name, but that's what Jo always called it. Jo loved it. Gideon…Gideon proposed to her there."

"Does Nicki know that?"

"Yes. And she's been there before. But, Rennie, it's almost twenty miles from here! Nicki couldn't possibly find her way in the dark."

"Maybe not, but I'll bet that's where she headed." Rennie was already running toward the barn before she'd even finished the sentence. Emily was right behind her.

Jim Holden was just leading out a freshly saddled horse when the two women reached the barn door. They both spoke at once.

"Mr. Holden!"

"Jim!"

The women stopped and looked at each other, then Emily signaled for Rennie to go first.

"Mr. Holden, we have to bring Gideon back. We know where Nicki went."

"We think we know," qualified Emily. "But it's worth a try, Jim. Where's the phone? I have to reach Gideon."

Jim didn't hesitate. He reached into his saddlebag and pulled out one of the cellular telephone units they used on his ranch. He punched in a series of numbers, then handed the phone to Emily.

Anxious seconds ticked by. Emily held the phone so that Rennie could hear the unanswered rings with her. Their eyes met over the receiver, and Emily shook her head.

"The phone doesn't always work in these mountains. Sometimes the signals get lost. Where was Gideon's search party heading?" This last was directed at Jim.

"Blackridge Wash."

"Damn! That explains it, then." Emily let the phone ring futilely a few more times, then disconnected it and handed it back to her father-in-law.

"You mean we can't get through to Gideon?" Rennie looked from Emily to Jim.

"Looks that way. When the phones are carried into narrow ravines like Blackridge Wash," he explained, "the steep walls prevent the signals in or out from gettin' through. As long as they stay in Blackridge Wash, the only way to reach Gideon and the others is to go after 'em."

"I can't wait for that." Rennie's gaze returned to Emily. "I can't, Emily. *We* can't."

Emily nodded. "I know. Jim, can you ride after Gideon? Tell him we think Nicki's gone to the Top of the World, and we're going after her. He'll know the place."

"The top of the world? Where's that?"

"You know the ridge that runs along northwest of Carter's Junction, just this side of Drover's Creek?"

"Yeah."

"There's a lookout spot near the top of the southernmost peak. My sister called it the Top of the World. Gideon will remember." She turned to Rennie. "You used to be able to drive right up to it on the old logging road that winds around the mountain, until a landslide wiped out a couple of miles or so of the road. The only way to reach it now is on horseback."

Jim looked dubious. "That's a far piece to go and not easy to get to. What makes you think she went there?"

Rennie answered. "It was her parents' special place, and Nicki knows it. Emily says Nicki's been there before."

"Jo and Gideon used to take the kids up there for picnics sometimes," Emily confirmed. Then she turned to Rennie, her eyes suddenly alight. "And I just remembered something. There's another way to reach that ridge, and Nicki might know it. If she followed the new highway toward Carter's Junction and turned off just past the K-Bar-H Ranch road, she'd save at least five miles. She could pick up the old logging road from there because the highway cuts right across it at the bottom of the ridge. That would take her at least halfway up the mountain. She probably thought she could find her way from that point by using the old hiking trail."

She gripped Rennie's arm and added, "The more I think of it, the more I'm sure you're right. That's where Nicki went."

"But damn it all to hell and back," Jim said, "why would she do such a damn fool thing, anyway?"

"Gideon broke a promise," Rennie said softly.

"Well, hell, men have broke promises before."

"Not Gideon."

Emily cut in. "Jim, it doesn't matter *why* she did it. All that matters right now is finding her. Can you hook up the double horse trailer to the truck before you go after Gideon?

It'll be faster if Rennie and I drive as far as we can before switching to horseback.'' She glanced at Rennie for confirmation.

"Sounds good to me."

"Then let's do it."

"What about them kids sleepin' in the house?" Jim interjected. "Who's gonna watch 'em?"

"Call Reba. She phoned earlier and asked if there was anything she could do. She's only ten minutes away."

"Okay. And I'll try to raise Gideon on the phone once more while I'm at it. Maybe they're outta Blackridge Wash by now and the signal will get through."

"Right. Come on, Rennie. Let's get the horses."

They drove out of the barnyard eleven minutes later. Beyond the circle of light surrounding the ranch house and the outbuildings, the night enveloped them. The pickup truck's headlights cut a swath, bisecting the darkness as the truck jounced over the gravel road.

Emily flicked on the heater switch. "It'll warm up in a minute or so."

"I'm fine." Rennie huddled inside the sheepskin jacket Emily had loaned her. It was two sizes too big for Rennie's size seven figure, but she wasn't complaining. The temperature outside couldn't be much above freezing, and the fleece-lined jacket's protection was welcome.

"I keep thinking of Nicki out there in this cold," Emily said. "Lost. Maybe hurt."

"Me, too."

"I should have kept a closer eye on her. I knew she was terribly upset about Gideon not coming home when he said he would. And I saw the look on her face when he didn't call, either. I should have suspected something like this might happen." Emily sighed. "Gideon trusted me to watch over his children, and I let him down."

"Gideon blames himself," Rennie said quietly, "because he broke a promise. You blame yourself because you think you betrayed his trust. And I..." She paused for a moment before continuing.

"Of the three of us, I guess I'm the most to blame. I should have predicted how Nicki would react, because I went through the same thing myself. When my mother remarried after my father died, I felt the same sense of betrayal that Nicki's probably feeling now."

"Did you run away, too?"

"In my own way I did." The memory flashed briefly through Rennie's mind, and her next words came straight from the heart. "There've been so many changes in Nicki's life in the past two years, and she's particularly vulnerable right now. Gideon was the one constant in her life. When he abandoned her, as she saw it, she needed her mother desperately. So she went searching for her in the only place she knew to look."

Silence followed, the silence of shared thoughts. The tenuous bond forged earlier tonight between Rennie and Emily with the recognition of kindred emotions was rapidly developing into something stronger. And despite their relationship's strange beginnings, they both realized how easily they could become friends.

Emily slowed the truck at the entrance to the highway, but didn't stop before pulling onto it. The darkness within the truck's cab stripped away the usual boundaries between relative strangers, and she found herself asking, "Did you know you cared about Gideon when you married him?"

"No."

"Why did you marry him, then?"

Rennie hated to lie to Emily. She searched for an answer

that would be truthful without revealing her past. "I wanted a certain kind of life," she said finally. "I wanted children, which I can't have myself. And I truly believed I could win the children's love, given time. I thought that would be enough."

A sad little laugh preceded Emily's response. "I could have told you that it wouldn't be." Suddenly she braked sharply and turned off the highway. The truck bounced over a cattle guard, and the horse trailer rattled behind. "Hang on," she advised.

Hang on was about all Rennie could do. The noise in the cab as they drove over bone-jarring ruts in the winding, uphill road precluded conversation. And Emily had all she could handle just keeping the truck on the road and avoiding the worst potholes.

By the time the truck finally stopped, Rennie felt as if every bone in her body had been rearranged. She peered out the windshield and saw a barricade across the road. The headlights didn't carry much beyond that point.

"This is it," Emily said, jumping out of the truck. "Let's get the horses."

Emily and Rennie let down the back of the trailer, then Emily slipped inside and backed the horses out one at a time, tying them to the trailer. Rennie fetched the saddles and horse blankets from the back of the truck.

As they saddled up, Emily asked, "You ever done any night riding?"

"Some." Rennie hooked the left stirrup over the saddle-horn and tightened the cinches, then pulled the stirrup back down and adjusted the strap a couple of notches. She ducked under the horse's neck and checked the right stirrup leather.

"How long has it been since you've ridden?"

Rennie laughed wryly. "This morning."

"On your honeymoon?"

"Um-hmm. It's quite a story." Satisfied with the condition of the pinto mustang called Barnum, who belonged to
Emily's son, Seth, Rennie untied the reins and came back
around to the left side again. "Ask me about it when we
have more time and I'll tell you what happened."

"It's a deal." Emily finished saddling Mariah, her roan
mare, and glanced over at Rennie. "Do you need a leg up?"

"Thanks, but I don't think so." To prove her statement,
Rennie fitted her foot into the stirrup and swung into the
saddle, ignoring the stab of pain in her hip.

Emily returned to the truck and came back juggling an
armful of gear—a couple of battery-powered flashlights, two
coils of rope, a cellular phone and a rifle. She dropped the
ropes on the ground and handed both flashlights to Rennie.
"Hold these for a minute."

Emily fitted the rifle into place, tucked the phone in her
saddlebag, then picked up the ropes. She looped one of them
around her saddlehorn, the other around Rennie's. She
mounted up, then brought her horse over to Rennie and
retrieved one of the flashlights. "Let's go."

They started out side by side, but the trail they took was
too narrow to ride abreast, so Rennie fell back, letting Emily
take the lead. When the trail split into two, Emily stopped
for a moment to get her bearings, then chose the left fork.
Rennie followed. The trail led upward at first, then veered
down into a ravine.

Rennie lost count of the ups and downs on the steep
mountain trail. The sparse undergrowth and overforested
pine trees gave mute testimony to the cause of the landslide
that had wiped out the logging road they'd left behind.

Night riding in the mountains, she soon discovered, was
different from night riding anywhere else. There were times
when the trail was so narrow she didn't dare look down.
She wasn't afraid of heights, she reminded herself. Not re-

ally. She was just afraid of falling. Somehow the distinction was cold comfort.

Jagged peaks loomed above them, snow still clinging to their tips. As they made their way up the mountain, the moon played hide-and-seek with the clouds, occasionally casting a ghostly glow to guide their way. But they mostly relied on the powerful flashlights they carried in their left hands. They made slow progress for that reason, and because they frequently paused to call Nicki's name, casting their flashlight beams to each side, searching for some sign of her.

Forty-five minutes later they stopped in a tiny clearing to rest their horses. Leather creaked as Rennie shifted in the saddle, uncomfortably aware that her body had been subjected to a great deal of physical strain in the past forty-eight hours. Her hip ached. Her thighs ached. And she ached in private places, as well. She adjusted her position as best she could, and tried to put her various aches out of her mind.

"How far have we come?"

Emily looked over at her. "I'm not sure. A couple of miles, maybe."

"Is this the only way to get there? I mean, is this the way Nicki would take?"

"I don't know. There are a couple of other routes, but this is the shortest way I know. I haven't seen anything to confirm that she came this way, though. Have you?"

"No. But it'd be easy to miss something in the dark."

"Yes, I know."

"How much farther is it?"

"A mile. Maybe less. But the hardest part is ahead of us. You ready to go on?"

"I'm ready." Rennie started to gather up the reins when the pinto's head came up suddenly. His ears pricked back, then he snorted nervously and danced sideways. Rennie controlled him and looked over at Emily, who reached for her rifle.

"What—"

"Shh!"

They both heard it at the same time. Hoofbeats. Coming down the trail in front of them, fast. Then a riderless horse burst into the clearing.

Emily recognized the gelding. "Whoa, Cheyenne!" she yelled as she tried to stop him, but she was hampered by the rifle she held.

Rennie reached for the horse's reins as he bolted past, and just missed. "Damn!" She watched in frustration as the horse disappeared into the darkness beyond the clearing. "Was that Nicki's horse?"

Emily nodded. "Something sure spooked him. It doesn't look good, but at least now we know we're on the right trail. Come on."

They left the clearing single file, with renewed urgency. Almost immediately the path narrowed and the incline steepened, making passage difficult and footing unstable. Emily's mare stumbled once, hooves slipping. Rennie held Barnum up and waited. Absently she turned her flashlight to the left and glanced in that direction.

She almost missed it. Her eyes passed over it at first, then swung abruptly back as something registered. It wasn't much as clues went, just a shallow depression where a rock had once lain. But the dark, moist patch it left behind was out of place in the seemingly undisturbed area.

Rennie urged the pinto closer to it and saw the indentation of fresh hoofprints all around. Her eyes widened. She kicked free of the stirrups and slid out of the saddle, clutching the reins tightly. She inched closer to the dangerous edge and shone the flashlight beam downward. Her breath caught in her throat. The powerful beam picked out a narrow ledge about thirty feet below. And precariously positioned on that ledge lay the body of a child. Nicki.

Chapter 10

"Oh my God!" The fervent whisper was torn from Rennie as she frantically swept the flashlight beam over Nicki's body, praying for some sign that Gideon's daughter was still alive. The slight figure never stirred.

A horse snorted, and suddenly Emily was dismounting to come to her side. "Rennie, what—oh, no! Nicki!"

Rennie thrust her horse's reins into the other woman's hands, and laid herself flat on her stomach, disregarding the dangerously crumbling cliff edge. "Nicki! Nicki, can you hear me? Nicki!" She dropped the flashlight and cupped her hands around her mouth for added carrying power. Emily's voice joined hers as they called Nicki's name repeatedly. But there was no response.

Rennie picked up the flashlight and again played it over the little girl's body as it lay facedown on the narrow ledge. Nothing. No movement, not even the tiniest indication of life.

She stood up. "I'm going down there."

"But I should be the one—"

"I'm smaller than you. There's no telling how stable that ledge is—it could give way under any more weight. We can't chance it." She grabbed the coils of rope slung around her saddlehorn and began unlooping them. "Besides, it'll be easier for you to lower me than the other way around."

Emily hesitated only for a second. "You're right. Here, you hold the horses. I'll do that. I've climbed in these mountains before." She stripped off her leather gloves and tucked them in her back pocket, then took the rope from Rennie. She retrieved the other coil of rope from her own horse and fastened the two ropes together. "One won't be long enough," she said by way of explanation. When she was done, she tied one end to her saddlehorn and quickly fashioned the other end into a sling.

While she was doing that, Rennie led the pinto out of the way and tied him to a scrub pine. She stole a few seconds to bury her face against his neck, uttering a prayer for courage. The thought of going down the cliff in the dark, dangling on the end of a rope, terrified her.

"I don't have a choice," she whispered. "Nicki needs me."

Emily was finished by the time Rennie returned, and was tugging her gloves back on. She efficiently fitted the sling around Rennie, then, with coaxing words, she backed her big roan mare up the trail a few steps and ground-tied her. She took hold of the rope, positioned herself a safe distance from the edge of the cliff and pulled the rope taut.

Emily looked at Rennie. "Have you ever done this before?" Rennie shook her head. "Well, I have. Hold the rope with both hands. Keep your toes pressed against the cliff face if you can, and lean out. But don't look down. You have to trust me—I won't let you fall. I'll walk you down nice and easy. Okay?" Rennie nodded. "Are you ready?"

"Ready." Rennie slid her flashlight in her belt. "Just one thing. When I reach the ledge, I'll call for you to stop. I don't want to put my full weight on it without testing it first."

"Okay. And be careful."

"I will." Rennie took a deep breath and exhaled, the warm air escaping in a small cloud, then braced herself, and stepped backward off the cliff.

With Emily skillfully playing out the rope in measured increments, Rennie descended the thirty feet to the ledge where Nicki lay in less than a minute. She told herself she didn't have time to be afraid, but each second stretched interminably.

Her heart pounding, she clutched the rope like the lifeline it was, and did exactly as Emily had instructed. She didn't dare look down, but she didn't need to. Her destination was burned into her memory. The ledge below was eight, maybe ten feet long, and scarcely five feet wide at its widest point. Other than the ledge, there appeared to be nothing but a vertical drop all the way to the bottom.

Can't think about that. Can't think about falling. Can't think about Emily losing her grip on the rope and—

She squelched that thought and focused instead on how lucky they were to have found Nicki at all. Emily's horse stumbling in the same spot where Nicki's horse must have stumbled, spotting where Nicki had gone over the edge— both things were luck, sheer luck.

Or was it divine providence? She didn't know. But Rennie hoped it would apply to her, as well. One small ledge had stood between Nicki and certain death when she fell. The same ledge would be the only thing that might break her own fall should anything hap—

Damn! Don't think about falling. You're almost there. Think about Nicki. Dear Lord, please let her be okay.

At that moment her feet touched something horizontal, and she quickly yelled up to Emily. "Stop!"

Emily responded as they'd planned, and Rennie felt herself being lifted slightly. She glanced down. Nicki was on her right, but too close for the test Rennie wanted to do. She pushed off from the wall and maneuvered herself over a couple of feet, away from the little girl, her toes reaching for the ledge. "Down a little," she called. Inch by inch now, the rope lowered her, until her full weight had been accepted. The ledge remained firm.

"Give me some slack." Emily's affirmative floated down, and several feet of rope followed.

Rennie hurried to Nicki and knelt beside her, hands reaching for a pulse. There! Yes, it was there! A little weak, but steady. "She's alive!" she shouted, then bent her head and whispered through sudden tears of thankfulness, "She's alive. Thank you, God."

Very gently she placed a hand on Nicki's back and felt the shallow rise and fall of breathing. Good. At least that was one less worry. She pulled out her flashlight and shone it on Nicki's face, shaking the girl's shoulder slightly at the same time.

"Nicki? Wake up, Nicki." No response. She tried again, louder this time. "Nicki, it's time to wake up." Did her eyelashes flutter? Rennie couldn't be sure. She tried a third time. "Nicki! Wake up!" Still no response.

She sat back on her heels for a moment, considering her options. Deciding she'd better see how badly Nicki was injured, Rennie ran her hands carefully over the little girl's body. Her first aid training, learned years ago on her father's ranch and never forgotten, came in good stead right now. Other than a nasty gash and a sizable lump on Nicki's forehead, which obviously were the cause of her unconsciousness, there didn't seem to be anything else seriously wrong. She couldn't be sure, though.

Nicki's proximity to the far side of the ledge worried Rennie. If she wakened, the little girl could easily roll right over the edge before Rennie could react. She thought about pulling Nicki farther away from the edge, but decided against it. Spinal injuries were dicey things, and Rennie wasn't going to chance moving her any more than she absolutely had to.

A memory from her time in the hospital came back to her, and she carefully worked one of Nicki's boots off, then removed her sock. She ran her fingernail along the sole of the little girl's foot, and was relieved when the toes splayed reflexively. No paralysis, thank God, and probably no damage to her spinal column.

But she still didn't want to risk moving Nicki, just in case, so she put the girl's sock back on, then untied the rope sling, her fingers fumbling a bit from cold and impatience. When she finally worked the knots loose she slid the rope under Nicki. It wasn't easy to do without shifting her, but eventually she was able to secure the rope beneath the little girl's arms.

Then she removed Emily's jacket and spread it lengthwise over Nicki. Although her stepdaughter was dressed warmly, Rennie knew that the cold night air was especially dangerous in Nicki's unconscious state.

Tiny clods of dirt tumbled down from above, prefacing Emily's voice. "Rennie? Can you hear me?"

She cupped her hands and called up. "Yes."

"I've tied off the rope. How is she?"

Rennie spaced her words carefully. "She's still unconscious, but she seems okay otherwise. I can't find anything broken, and her reflexes are good. I don't want to move her, though."

"So what do we do?"

"I'll stay down here with her. Can you try to get Gideon or Jim on the phone? We need a stretcher."

"Okay. I'll try."

Rennie shifted, settling herself as close as she could to Nicki, but keeping her back to the wall. Now that the urgency to reach Gideon's daughter had passed, fear returned in waves. She was more than ever aware of the precariousness of her position, especially now that she'd given her lifeline to Nicki. From this angle, with the flashlight slicing through the darkness, they seemed to be perched on the edge of a bottomless abyss. One wrong move...

She shivered, cold and fear combining to make her tremble uncontrollably. She turned off the flashlight, pulled up her knees and wrapped her arms around them. Now the night was illuminated only by the moon. Rennie kept her gaze elevated. As long as she didn't look down, she'd be all right.

But she couldn't keep herself from sneaking peeks at Nicki's inert form every few seconds. A couple of times she leaned over and checked Nicki's pulse and breathing. Both times she was reassured. Still, the wait seemed endless.

"Rennie?"

More dirt fell, and Rennie ducked her head to avoid it. "What?"

"I couldn't reach Gideon. But I did contact one of the other search parties back at the ranch. They're on their way with a stretcher. And a med-evac chopper is standing by."

"Good."

"How's Nicki doing?"

She's doing better than I am, Rennie thought wryly, but only answered, "Fine."

"That's good. Rennie?"

"What?"

"There's only one problem."

"What is it?"

"They don't know the way up here. I'll have to go back and meet them at the truck."

Momentary panic washed over Rennie. *I can't stay here on this ledge all that time! I can't! At least when Emily is here I have someone to talk to, someone to keep my mind off the possibility of falling.*

But she knew they had no choice. Even if Emily traded places with her, Rennie didn't know the way back down the mountain. And it was inconceivable to leave Nicki on the ledge by herself.

She struggled with her unreasonable fear, telling herself not to be such a coward, and when she finally trusted herself to speak, she responded. "I understand."

"I'm taking your horse. Barnum is more surefooted than my Mariah, and I'll make better time."

"Okay."

"I'll be as quick as I can. Will you be all right?"

"I'll be fine."

"Okay, then. I'll be back in a flash." And she was gone.

The sound of hoofbeats faded away. Terror circled her, like a pack of hungry wolves closing in for the kill. She fought it off, checked on Nicki once more, then wrapped her arms around her knees again. She closed her eyes and rested her forehead against her knees. It didn't help much.

Gideon galloped into the clearing where Rennie and Emily had stopped to rest their horses. When he and his men had come upon Cheyenne a few minutes past, nothing could hold him back. He had outdistanced the rest of his search party in his urgency to find Nicki.

The familiar clearing seemed strange by moonlight. He'd followed the trail through this small clearing to the place Jo had called the Top of the World many times in his life, but never like this—with fear stalking him. When Jim had found him and relayed Emily's message, he'd quickly realized that she could be right. His daughter just might have come to this mountain searching for reminders of happier days, when her mother was alive.

His eyes darted around, seeking some sign of his daughter. Nothing. He swore in frustration. Then guilt surged up in him again.

I failed you, Jo, you and Nicki both. I didn't mean to, but it happened. Don't you fail us. Watch over her, Jo. I'm counting on you to keep our daughter safe until I can reach her.

The rest of the search party came up behind him amid a jingle of metal and the thud of hooves.

"Any sign of her?" Mike, his ranch foreman, asked the question.

Gideon shook his head, then spurred forward. Suddenly he heard something from the opposite direction and pulled up sharply, silencing the men behind him with a word. Then they all heard it, hoofbeats coming down the trail at a fairly steady clip.

Emily entered the clearing from the other side and reined in when she caught sight of Gideon and the other men. "Gideon! Thank God! Jim must have found you."

"Yeah, he did." He rode over to her. "Where's Rennie?"

"Back up the trail a little way. She's with Nicki."

Relief coursed through his veins. "You found her? Is she all right?"

Emily bit her lip. "I don't know. She's unconscious. I tried to phone you, but the signal wouldn't go through. So I called the ranch and they're bringing up a stretcher. I have to meet them at my truck."

"A stretcher? Oh, God. What's wrong?"

She touched his arm in sympathy before breaking the news to him in a rush. "She fell, Gideon. About thirty feet. She went over the side of the cliff and landed on a small ledge." Emily felt the flinching in him and tightened her hold on his arm. "But Rennie thinks Nicki will be all right. Nothing seems to be broken. The stretcher is just a precaution."

Gideon shook his head, trying to clear it. "What do you mean, Rennie thinks Nicki will be all right? How does she know?"

"Rennie went down the cliff to check on her."

"What the hell?" A new fear sank its fangs into Gideon. His worry about Nicki was momentarily shouldered aside as he thought of Rennie deliberately endangering herself for his daughter. He knew from experience she was stronger than she looked, but that hip of hers wasn't up to the kind of stress it had endured in the past forty-eight hours. He went cold just thinking about what could happen if it gave way without warning.

"She insisted she be the one to go down," Emily said, "and I had to agree. She's smaller than I am, and we were concerned about the stability of the ledge. So I made a rope sling and belayed her."

"Where are they?"

"Not far. Just follow the trail. But be careful—the footing is pretty bad. And watch out for the rope I lowered Rennie with. It's strung across the trail. I tied it to a tree so I could fetch the men with the stretcher and lead them back up. They don't know the way."

"Joe and Charlie can do that." He looked at the two men in question and they nodded, immediately turning around and heading back the way they came. Gideon returned his gaze to his sister-in-law. "Let's go."

* * *

Rennie turned off the flashlight once more. She'd needed it to check on Nicki and to read her watch. A shaky sigh escaped her. Only ten minutes had passed since the last time she looked, and only eighteen minutes since Emily had left. By Rennie's reckoning, Emily still had a long way to go just to reach the truck, and then they had to come back up that winding trail. At best she had to endure a couple of hours on this ledge. At worst...

She scrunched herself tightly against the wall, but her thigh muscles and her bad hip protested. Sitting here with nothing much else to do, each ache was magnified. She tried to shut out the pain, just as she tried not to think about how far down the bottom was from this ledge. But the only other thing that came to mind was that all this was her fault in the first place.

"I should never have come here," Rennie whispered to herself. "I should never have married Gideon. If I hadn't, Nicki wouldn't have been so unhappy, she wouldn't have run away, and she wouldn't have fallen." She lay her head against her knees again. "It's all my fault."

Despair washed over her, and for a moment she was too tired to fight it off. Just as she had done when she'd first learned about Johanna Lowell's death months ago, she let guilt ravage her.

Guilty. God, she'd felt so damned guilty when she read the private detective's report, she'd cried herself to sleep. Two little girls left motherless and a baby boy who would never even know his mother because of Rennie.

Her mind slid back to what little she remembered of that fateful night. She'd fought with Jess that evening about her returning to Montana. She'd kept in touch with her father's old foreman for years, and when he'd written that her beloved Circle F was up for sale again, she'd approached Jess about lending her the money to buy it.

He'd turned her down flat, so sure that he knew what was best for her, and they'd fought. But she hadn't convinced him, and at the end she'd stormed out in tears. She remembered the rain-slick roads, remembered the heartbreaking disappointment that had distracted her, remembered dashing tears from her eyes as she drove. But the rest of her memory was gone, swallowed up by gray blankness.

So although she hadn't been driving under the influence of alcohol or drugs, she knew in her heart that she'd been driving in an unfit state emotionally. That's why she blamed herself for the accident. That's why she felt responsible. And that's why she was here.

"You've been all through this before," she told herself, wiping the corners of her eyes on her sleeve. "Don't do this to yourself."

But it isn't fair, her heart cried.

No, none of it was fair. It wasn't fair that Johanna died. It wasn't fair that Gideon lost the wife he loved so deeply. It wasn't fair that Johanna's children lost their mother so young.

And it wasn't fair that she, who loved children and who had always planned on having a house full of kids someday, would wake from a coma to find herself denied even the possibility of having children of her own.

Was it any wonder she'd devised this…this…scheme? When she'd read Gideon's ad, it almost seemed fated. Gideon needed a mother for his children, and Rennie needed children to love. The rest of it was unimportant, she'd told herself. She'd work it out, somehow.

And now Nicki lay hurt and unconscious just a few feet away, because Rennie's conscience had brought her to Wyoming.

Thinking about Nicki made Rennie get up and check on her again. Satisfied that the girl's condition was no worse than before, she knelt beside her for a moment, stroking the tangle of golden hair. "I'm sorry, Nicki," she whispered. "I'm sorry."

The echo of her grandmother's voice came to her from over the years. "What's done is done—you can't change the past. You can only go on from here."

Rennie didn't remember the occasion that had prompted the words, but it didn't matter. A kind of peace stole over her then, giving her the strength and courage she needed, and a renewed hope. She went back to her spot by the wall, and folded herself down.

Thinking about Gram, Rennie began to sing softly to herself, a song her grandmother had sung to her a hundred times, and one that had always comforted her over the years. At first her voice was wobbly, a pitiful sound that could scarcely be called a tune. But by the time she reached the end the song had done its job. That song reminded her of another, and this time the notes came out sure and true. In the stillness her voice carried clearly, a sweet soprano that floated on the air like a bird in flight.

She stopped in mid-song, startled, when she heard unexpected sounds above her. Then a bright light fell upon the ledge, accompanied by a shower of dirt, and a deep voice carried down to her.

"Rennie?"

"Gideon!" She brushed the dirt out of her hair and started scrambling to her feet before she realized what she was doing. She quickly sat down again, then glanced up, shielding her uplifted face as more dirt rattled down the cliff. "Gideon, be careful! That edge up there is crumbling."

"Yeah, I see that. Are you okay?"

The concern in his voice warmed a small place in her heart, and she tucked the memory away for safekeeping.

"I'm fine. Nicki's here. She's unconscious, but I don't think anything's broken."

"I know. I met Emily on the way up." He spoke to someone behind him, something Rennie didn't catch. Two more flashlights played over the ledge. Then he said, "Watch out. I'm coming down."

"No, Gideon, don't! It's not safe."

"I'm coming down," he insisted.

Rennie flattened herself against the wall. Less than a minute later a length of rope tumbled down beside her. She continued to look upward, watching fearfully as Gideon swung over the edge and rappeled down the cliff face. She couldn't bear to watch, but she couldn't look away, either. Each second lasted a heart-pounding eternity, as she expected disaster to strike at any moment, but he finally reached the ledge safe and sound.

He knelt immediately beside Nicki, his glance taking in the jacket laid across her to keep off the cold, and the rope tied around her body to protect her from falling. Rennie's jacket. Rennie's rope. A tiny part of him wondered at that, then he pushed the thought aside.

He pulled off one glove to check his daughter's pulse and breathing. He heaved a great sigh of relief when he discovered both were steady. He looked over his shoulder at Rennie.

She crept to his side on hands and knees, then sat back on her heels. She touched him comfortingly, feeling the tense muscles beneath his jacket. "I've been checking her every few minutes," she said softly. "I went over her carefully earlier, and I did a reflex test. But if you want to see for yourself, go ahead."

He hesitated. "It's not that I don't trust your judgment, but..."

"I understand, Gideon. I'd want to check for myself, too."

He was quick about it, but thorough. Then he stood and helped Rennie to her feet. "You're right. I can't find any broken bones, and I don't see any sign of swelling or internal bleeding, either. My guess is concussion is the only thing we have to worry about. But that's bad enough."

"I asked Emily to call for a stretcher."

He nodded. "I know, and I think you did the right thing. The stretcher's on its way here."

"So now we just wait?"

Gideon glanced up at the sky, then eastward toward the horizon. "Sun'll be up soon." He turned back toward Rennie. "When the stretcher arrives, we'll take Nicki up the trail, not down. There's a place not far from here where a helicopter can land—barely. Before I came down I told Emily to have the chopper meet us there in about an hour."

He grasped the rope he'd come down the cliff on and started tying it around Rennie's waist. "In the meantime," he said brusquely, "I want you safely off this ledge, and I want you and Emily to go back to the Holden ranch."

"But—"

"There's not a lot of room to maneuver on that trail up there, and I've got four men with me. There isn't anything you can do for Nicki right now."

"But I—"

"Damn it, don't argue!" Pent-up fear, relief and frustration combined to make his tone harsher than he intended.

"All right," she said, her voice shaking slightly as despair bit into her soul again. What she desperately needed right now was for him to hold her and tell her how brave she was, instead of looking as if he couldn't wait to get rid of her.

She shivered, only partly from the cold, then rubbed her

arms to warm herself. Gideon shrugged out of his jacket. "Here. Take this."

She shook her head. "No, you keep it. You'll need it." She glanced down at her borrowed jacket tucked around his daughter. Her eyes widened and fear coursed through her as all at once she realized how close they were to the edge. She began to inch toward the wall. She swallowed dryly and croaked, "It's way too big for me, anyway."

"Then take this one back," He leaned over, removed the jacket that covered Nicki, and replaced it with his own. When he straightened, he saw that Rennie had backed all the way to the wall. Then he noticed her expression.

"You're terrified," he said softly, wonderingly. Then with dawning understanding his eyes followed hers to the edge. "You're scared to death being on this ledge, and yet you still..."

Rennie didn't say anything, averting her face from his, ashamed of her fear. Gideon took the half step that brought him to her. He dressed her in Emily's warm sheepskin jacket, buttoned it up to the neck, then tilted her chin up and stood looking down at her for several heartbeats.

"You are one hell of a lady, you know that?" His lips claimed hers, a gentle kiss that somehow made up for his earlier behavior.

A voice from above intruded. "Hey, down there! Gideon! Hey!"

She was shaking when he let her go. He whispered, "You okay?" and waited for her nod before his voice rumbled upward. "Yeah, Mike. What is it?"

"We're ready any time you are."

Gideon checked the rope around Rennie, then said, "I'll call you from the hospital to let you know how Nicki's doing."

"Thanks."

"Be careful going back."

"I will."

He turned her around to face the cliff, bracing her against his body. "Don't look down," he murmured in her ear, his warm breath sending tingles up and down her spine. He dropped a quick kiss on her cheek. "See you back at the ranch." Then he raised his head and hollered, "Ready!"

Rennie clung to the rope and felt herself being pulled up, slowly, steadily. Despite Gideon's warning, halfway up she stole one downward glance at him, but he was kneeling beside Nicki and he didn't look up.

When Rennie reached the top, several strong hands grasped her and pulled her carefully to safety. The four men of the search party helped her stand. No one said anything, but their warm, approving glances told Rennie she'd measured up to Wyoming standards and won their respect.

Their admiration was balm for her wounded heart and restored her spirit. She stiffened her wobbly legs, refusing to let herself be embarrassed in front of these men by collapsing on the ground. But it wasn't easy. She brushed herself off, then untied the rope around her waist.

She limped over to where Emily stood by the horses. If the men hadn't been around, she would have hugged her. But it was too awkward with them there, so she contented herself with grasping both of Emily's hands in hers and squeezing firmly.

"Thanks, Emily."

Emily cleared her throat, obviously feeling the same emotional tug that Rennie did. She busied herself with tying off a loose leather thong on her saddle. "The helicopter is on its way, just like Gideon asked. Did he say what he wants us to do now?"

"He wants the men to wait here for the stretcher while

you and I go back to the ranch. He'll call us from the hospital.''

Emily's "Humph!" brought a wry smile to Rennie's face.

"I know. I felt the same way, as if we're being brushed aside now that the men are here. But he's right. There's only so much room on this trail, and the men *are* stronger. So it's only reasonable for us to be the ones to make way. Since Gideon's with Nicki now, and since I'm sure he'll be riding to the hospital in the helicopter with her, there really isn't anything else for us to do.''

"Except worry and wait."

Rennie nodded. "Except that."

"Well, I've had my share and more of that this past week. Why should tonight be any different?" Emily untied Barnum and Mariah, handing Barnum's reins to Rennie. She swung onto her horse and Rennie followed suit, her aching body protesting.

"I don't know about you," Emily said, leather creaking as she settled into the saddle, "but I won't be able to sleep until we hear how Nicki is. So what do you say we head on back, break out Jim's twelve-year-old sippin' whiskey, and you can tell me that long story about your honeymoon you promised to tell me sometime."

Despite the concern she still felt about Gideon's daughter, concern she knew Emily shared, Rennie found herself relaxing just a little. "Sounds good to me."

"So what are we waiting for?"

Chapter 11

Gideon hated hospitals.

He knew why, of course, but that didn't make it any easier to bear. And just as he couldn't escape the unmistakable antiseptic smell, he couldn't avoid the memories they conjured up. Memories he'd just as soon stayed buried.

Buried. Like Jo, lying so peacefully in her hillside grave, and all his happiness buried with her.

Don't think about that now.

While the emergency room doctors examined Nicki, Gideon paced the floor in the waiting room, counting floor tiles and hating every minute. He longed for a cigarette. Although he'd given them up years ago and hadn't smoked since, he really could have used the distraction and calming effect of just one coffin nail.

Damn it, Lowell, can't you think of anything except death? Nicki's going to be fine. The doctor will be out soon to confirm that nothing's broken, there's no internal bleed-

ing, and all we have to worry about is a concussion, just like you told Rennie.

Rennie. On the heels of this thought came the picture of her standing on the ledge in the moonlight—hair tangled and windblown, her inexplicably dear face streaked with dirt, so scared and brave at the same time—she'd looked so damned beautiful he ached just thinking about it. The memory had danced in and out of his mind at will while he waited for the stretcher and during the helicopter ride to Casper, teasing and tormenting him.

He stopped pacing, tucked one hand in the back pocket of his jeans, and propped a shoulder against the wall as he considered everything that had happened.

You were a real bastard tonight, Lowell. Again. You didn't even thank Rennie for finding your daughter, or for staying with her even though she was terrified. No, you just ignored everything she'd done as if it were nothing, and told her to go back home like a good little girl. And when she wanted to speak you cut her off and yelled at her. Nice going.

His self-recriminations were cut short by the entrance of the doctor into the waiting room.

"Mr. Lowell?"

Gideon straightened. "That's me."

"I'm Dr. Forbes, the resident on duty." The woman offered her hand and Gideon shook it. "Your daughter is one lucky little girl, considering what happened. As you suspected, she suffered a mild concussion, but that's the worst of it. Her X rays were negative. She's got some bad scrapes and she'll be bruised and sore for a while, but nothing to be concerned about. She regained consciousness before we brought her down for X rays. She was alert and responsive to stimuli, which is a good sign, but she didn't answer any questions."

"I told the woman who admitted her that—"

"She doesn't speak. Yes, I know. But I checked your daughter's medical records. Since her original loss of speech was diagnosed as hysterical in nature, that is, caused by shock, there's always the chance that another shock to the system would break down the mental barrier."

"But it didn't." Gideon's disappointment was obvious.

"No, I'm sorry. It did not."

"So what happens now?"

"We'll keep her overnight for observation. And they'll probably want to run some tests tomorrow, just to be on the safe side. But I think she'll be ready to go home the day after that."

"Can I see her?"

"Of course. They're taking her up to her room right now, so give the nurses a few minutes to get her settled, then check with the clerk over there. She'll direct you." Dr. Forbes smiled. "Now, if you'll excuse me, I have other patients waiting."

She left. Gideon stood there for a moment, letting everything sink in. Nicki was going to be all right. She really was. He'd told himself that ever since he'd examined her on the ledge, but he'd been afraid to believe it. Now a great weight lifted off his shoulders, and he wanted to share his profound relief with someone who would understand. Rennie. He needed to talk to Rennie. Gideon looked around, then headed for the nearest pay phone.

Nicki lay in her hospital bed and gazed listlessly out the window. The smell of the freshly laundered sheets reminded her of the time two years ago when she'd woken up in the hospital and learned that her mother was dead. She'd hated the smell ever since.

The door to her room opened, but she didn't turn her

head. Out of the corner of her eye she saw her father come around the curtain and stop for an instant. Then he sat in the chair between her bed and the window. He didn't say anything, just took her hand in his much larger one and looked at her with tired, sad eyes, the same way he'd looked at her in the hospital two years ago. She hated that look, too. And this time, just like last time, she was the one who put that look on his face.

"I'm sorry, Nicki. Sorry I broke my promise," he said finally. "But why did you run away?"

She wanted to tell him. Oh, how she wanted to tell him. But she couldn't. Not now, not ever. Because if she did, he wouldn't love her anymore. And then he'd go away with Rennie again, just like before, only this time he'd never come back. So she closed her eyes and hardened her heart.

Two and a half days later, Gideon drove up the last hundred yards of the dirt road leading to the Rocking L. At his side sat Nicki—pale, bruised and sporting a two-inch scrape across one cheek, but otherwise completely recovered from her ordeal.

He parked the brand-new Chevy Blazer in front of the house and glanced over at his daughter, who resolutely kept her face turned away from him. He reached over and tucked her shoulder-length blond hair behind her ear as he so often did, but this time Nicki shrugged away from his touch.

Gideon sighed deeply. He'd talked to Nicki again this morning about what she'd done. He'd told her how badly she'd hurt everyone, including herself, and he'd explained the danger, the risks she'd taken, not only with her life but with the life of her beloved horse. There had been a flash of remorse in her eyes when he mentioned Cheyenne, but beyond that he knew he hadn't reached her.

He made a sound of frustration and jerked the keys out

of the ignition, then got out and came around to open
Nicki's door. But she hadn't waited for him, and was already halfway up the porch stairs.

"Nicki!" She paused, then turned, a stony expression on
her face. "Your Aunt Emily said she was coming over this
afternoon to see you, and to help Rennie settle in."

Nicki stiffened, but no other response was forthcoming.

"No matter what else, you owe your aunt an apology for
running away and frightening her. She loves you very much
and she's done a lot for you. Especially since your moth—"
Gideon stopped in mid-sentence at the stricken look on his
daughter's face. He shifted his stance and recovered his own
composure. "Anyway, I expect you to apologize first thing.
Do you understand?"

For a minute he thought she was going to be stubborn,
but then she nodded. Obviously her anger didn't extend to
her aunt.

"Good girl." He smiled, hoping to coax a smile from
Nicki in return, but without any luck. She just looked at
him, then turned and went into the house.

He cursed under his breath, several choice words he usually reserved for stubborn horses and sheep. Then he
grabbed the small duffel bag he'd gotten the day before
when he'd bought clothes for himself and Nicki to wear,
and followed Nicki into the house.

Inside, he hung his Stetson on the coatrack by the front
door and dropped the duffel bag beside the hall table. The
sound of voices led him to the kitchen. He pushed the door
open.

"Gideon!"

"Daddy!"

"Daddy's home!"

Trina reached him first, scrambling down from her chair
and running across the room. She threw her arms around

his leg. Gideon bent and lifted her into his arms, hugging her tightly, kissing her hair as she burrowed against him.

"Daddy, Daddy, you came back! I missed you!"

"I missed you, too, sweetheart. Have you been a good girl?" Before she could answer, Andrew was there, tugging at Gideon's jeans.

"Daddy, Daddy, pick me up! Pick me up!"

Without putting Trina down, Gideon grasped Andrew and swung him up, settling him against his hip. Andrew snuggled his head in the crook of Gideon's shoulder, smearing peanut butter and grape jam on his father's new shirt.

His younger children's ecstatic reaction to his return was just the balm Gideon sorely needed. He ducked his head and kissed his son, not minding in the least the stickiness that transferred itself to his lips. "Hey, champ! Have you been good, too?"

The little boy nodded, his head bobbing up and down several times for emphasis. "And I dint cwy."

Gideon swallowed the lump in his throat and said heartily, "Of course not."

Jealous of the attention Andrew was receiving, Trina placed her hand on her father's cheek and pulled his face around to look at her. "Daddy, guess what?"

"What?"

"I drew you a picture. Want to see it? It's a horse. Rennie put it on the refrigerator with tape. And guess what? Rennie and I made lunch, and Rennie said I'm the best helper she ever had."

Gideon looked over at Rennie, who stood by the table, watching him with his children. The smile she gave him was hesitant. The smile he gave her was not. It spread over his entire face.

Her smile deepened before she turned away to clear the table. "Where is Nicki?"

"She must have gone straight to her room."

"How is she?"

"Fine, physically." Gideon lowered both children to the floor. "Trina, take Andrew and go find your sister. I think she's in her room. She really missed you." He squatted down to their level, rumpled Andrew's hair, rubbed his knuckles against Trina's cheek and kissed both of them once more.

"Wait a second." Rennie grabbed a clean dishcloth and dampened it under the tap. "Both of you come get wiped up." She carefully wiped faces and hands, then smiled at the children. "There, all clean." She playfully swatted their bottoms. "Go on, now. Do what your daddy says. Go see Nicki."

Gideon watched as they left the room, hand in hand, then turned back to Rennie. His eyes flickered over her, taking in the picture she made in her snug jeans and loose-fitting cotton shirt. Her hair was pulled back with combs in what he supposed was meant to be a no-nonsense style, but several strands had freed themselves to curl enchantingly around her face. The memory of her face, all flushed and sated after lovemaking, and framed by those same dark curls, flashed into his mind. He clamped down on that errant thought and finished answering Rennie's earlier question.

"Physically, Nicki's fine. The doctors at the hospital all say it was something of a miracle that she wasn't badly hurt, but she's really okay."

"I'm glad to hear that. I know you were worried."

He moved restlessly. "Yeah. But she's still confused and hurt. I tried talking to her this morning, but she doesn't want to hear anything I have to say, not even an apology."

"What are you going to do?"

"I don't know. I think deep down she knows what she did was wrong. She just won't admit it. There's a small part of me that says she should be punished, but most of me says she's been through enough. What do you think?''

Rennie was too surprised to answer at first. She hadn't thought he'd ask for her advice about disciplining his children, not this early in their relationship. She considered the problem carefully.

''I think you're right—she's been punished enough. Especially since Cheyenne was injured. Emily says Nicki loves that horse. I don't think there's anything you could do or say to her that will deliver the message better than the sight of her horse's knees.''

Gideon frowned. ''Was he cut up badly?''

''Bad enough that he's still at Emily's. We had the vet out to look at him. He should be okay, but there might be some scarring.''

''Could have been worse.''

''Yes, and I think Nicki will know it. Give her time.''

He grunted his agreement, then went to the refrigerator and started to open it. He caught sight of the drawing taped to the door. He smiled briefly and glanced at Rennie.

''Is this what Trina made for me?''

''Um-hmm. It's a horse.''

''Why does it only have three legs?''

''According to Trina, the other leg is broken.''

Gideon was surprised at his own chortle of laughter. ''Very literal-minded, isn't she?'' Rennie nodded. ''By the way,'' he said, ''what's she doing home from school so early?'' He checked his watch against the kitchen clock as if he thought it might be wrong.

''When she heard you were coming home today she begged me to let her stay home from school, 'just this once,' and I didn't have the heart to refuse. School's almost over for the year, anyway.''

''You're right. And besides, she's only in first grade. I

don't think she'll miss anything critical in one day." As he spoke he opened the refrigerator door, searching the interior for something edible. "You know, I forgot to warn you that I didn't have much fresh food in the house. I've been eating out in the bunkhouse with the men these last few months."

"Emily thought that might be the case, so she stopped in Carter's Junction yesterday and picked up a few things, enough for us to get by."

"Is there anything besides peanut butter and jelly?" He touched the smeared remains Andrew had left on his shirt and grinned. "I had an early breakfast and we didn't stop for anything on the road, so I'm starved."

"I can make you a ham and cheese sandwich. And there's some turkey left."

"Ham and cheese sounds good, but I can do it."

"I don't mind. Why don't you go see if Nicki's ready for lunch? What's her favorite?"

"Grilled cheese, but you don't have to go to all that trouble." He headed for the door.

"It's no big deal. How do you want your sandwich?"

"With everything. And make that two sandwiches while you're at it." The door swung shut behind him.

Rennie brought out a loaf of bread, then took everything she needed out of the refrigerator and busied herself with the sandwiches. It was unexpectedly satisfying doing things for Gideon, even something as prosaic as making his lunch.

She smiled to herself. It wasn't that she'd forgotten how Gideon looked or how she felt about him, but she hadn't been prepared for the impact he had on her senses. She'd forgotten how very *male* he was. When he'd walked through the kitchen door she'd wanted to do just what Trina and Andrew did: throw her arms around him and burrow against that masculine strength. She'd restrained herself, unsure of her welcome.

Rennie cut the sandwiches in half and arranged them on a plate, then added some potato chips. She set the plate at the head of the table, where Trina had previously informed her, "Daddy always sits there!" Next to it she put the bowl of fresh fruit that had been sitting on the counter. If Gideon wanted an apple or a banana he could help himself. Lastly, she filled a tall glass with milk and put it by his place, then turned her attention to preparing Nicki's lunch.

The grilled cheese sandwich was finished and already cooling before a tight-lipped Gideon returned without Nicki. "She's not hungry," he said tersely in response to Rennie's questioning look, before starting on his own food.

"Oh." She looked at Nicki's plate and sighed. She covered the plate with plastic wrap and put it in the refrigerator, then went back to cleaning the griddle.

She searched her mind for a safe topic of conversation. "I'll need to go grocery shopping sometime soon. As you said, there isn't much food in the house. I found some steaks in the freezer yesterday. I thawed them, so we'll have those for dinner tonight. And there's a package of lamb chops that we can have tomorrow night. But that's about it." She wiped her hands on a towel and pulled a piece of paper toward her. "I've never really shopped for a family, so I asked Emily to help me make up a list of what we need." She brought it over and put it beside Gideon's plate. "Would you look at it and see if I missed anything?"

He quickly scanned the contents of the list. "Looks good to me." He handed it back to her. "Let me know when you want to go and I'll take you in to Sheridan. We can go to the bank at the same time and have you added as a signer on my checking account. Oh, and that reminds me. I have something for you." He dug into his jeans pocket and pulled out a set of car keys. "These are yours."

"Mine?" Rennie took the keys and stared at them, puzzled.

"Yeah. I promised to buy you something more suitable to drive than your sports car, remember?"

"I remember."

He smiled. "So I bought you a new Blazer in Casper."

"What?"

He gestured with his head. "It's out front. I needed transportation back here, anyway, and there's a bigger selection in Casper than there is in Sheridan, so..." He picked up his second half sandwich and took a bite.

"I don't know what to say."

"Nothing to say. Just have a set of your car keys made for me and we're even." His eyes twinkled at her.

She shook her head at him as if to say, "What am I going to do with you?"

Whatever Gideon had intended to respond was forgotten when a wail arose from the front of the house.

"That's Andrew." He started to rise.

She pressed him back in his seat. "I'll go see what the problem is. You finish your lunch."

"You sure?" he said doubtfully as the wailing increased in intensity.

"At least let me try."

Gideon watched her shapely rear end, encased in jeans that lovingly hugged each curve, disappear through the swinging door. The sight triggered memories, like the firm, silky feel of that shapely rear end under his palms as he pulled her closer to deepen his thrusts. Like the feel of her legs wrapped around his thighs as he brought both of them to completion.

His body tightened involuntarily and he tried to clamp down on his wayward thoughts. *Get a grip on yourself,*

Lowell. It's the middle of the day, for God's sake, and you've got a week's worth of work to catch up on.

It didn't help much. He forced himself to concentrate on food, satisfying the lesser of his two hungers. When he'd polished everything off and Rennie still hadn't returned, he put his plate in the sink and went in search of her.

He found her in the family room, seated in the rocking chair with Andrew cuddled on her lap. She was humming, a soft, melodious tune he didn't recognize but which gently touched something deep inside him. It made Gideon think of dappled sunlight on a meadow, the lazy rustle of wind through tall grass, water tumbling over a streambed. From the way his son's eyes were sliding shut, he knew the tune was having the same calming effect on Andrew as it was on him.

Rennie continued to rock, even after Andrew's eyes closed completely. In a low tone she said, "It was time for his nap, anyway, so I thought I'd try to get him to go down. He's almost asleep."

The little boy's eyes fluttered open and he made a sound of protest. "Sshh," she told him softly. "It's okay. Close your eyes."

She began humming again, and Gideon recognized the lullaby as one from his own childhood. He stood rooted to the spot, his emotions in turmoil. There was something achingly poignant about watching Rennie with his son, the quintessential picture of eternal motherhood. Generations of Lowell women had sat in that rocker, babes in their arms, nursing, soothing hurts, lulling to sleep.

Johanna had sat there with Nicki, he remembered, and then Trina. The memories were as vivid and fresh as if it were yesterday and not years past. On those long winter evenings, while he sat at his desk and pretended to do his paperwork, he'd secretly watched Jo with their baby at her breast. Even though he'd been a shade envious of the bond between a nursing mother and child, it had been deeply satisfying, making all his hard, sometimes drudging work worthwhile.

Jo had never had a chance to hold their son in her arms, had never nursed him, had never sung lullabies to him. And Andrew had never known a mother's love, had never known the security of a mother's arms. Until now. Until Rennie.

Shaken, he realized he was standing on the threshold of a startling revelation. He abruptly pivoted and left the room, not wanting to face it, unable to deal with any more emotional upheaval in his life right now. At the front door he grabbed his Stetson and crammed it on his head. Then he went outside on the porch and leaned his arms against the railing, his muscles clenched tightly. He drew in several deep breaths and let them out, trying to calm himself.

He didn't need this. He didn't *want* this. He'd married Rennie to get a mother for his children, not to rip open the scars on his heart. It wasn't fair.

Fair? he jeered at himself. *You sound like Trina, complaining because she doesn't get to do all the things Nicki is allowed to do. What's fair? Is it fair that Jo died? Is it fair that Rennie be denied children of her own when it's obvious she's a wonderful mother? Is it fair to make comparisons between Rennie and Johanna, to compare what you feel for one against what you felt for the other?*

The last thought brought him up short. What he *felt* for the other? When had his love for Jo become the past tense? When had his jumbled feelings for Rennie coalesced into something more, something strangely akin to lo—

No! It's not true. I won't let it be true. I don't want to love Rennie. I loved Jo and she died. I love Nicki and look what almost happened. I can't go through this again. I just can't.

Work. That's what he needed. The mindless exertion of physical effort to wear himself out and keep him from dwelling on things he couldn't bear.

He jumped down from the porch and strode toward the barn.

The kitchen clock was chiming the hour when Gideon quietly let himself in the back door. Nine o'clock. The kids would be in bed already, but whether they'd be asleep was anybody's guess. Their normal routine was lights out at 8:00 p.m., but they never fell asleep right away. As soon as he cleaned himself up he'd check on them.

He pulled off his muddy boots and left them by the back door, dropped his hat on the kitchen table, then went into the bathroom off the kitchen and turned on the light. He caught a whiff of himself. He reeked of horse sweat and sheep. He peeled off his filthy clothes, stuffed them in the laundry hamper and stepped into the shower. He turned on the water and just stood there for a minute, letting the hot water sluice the dirt and sweat from his body, then lathered himself all over and quickly rinsed off.

He grabbed a towel off the rack and dried himself with it, then shrugged on the robe he kept hanging on the back of the bathroom door. He wondered idly if Rennie had had a chance to start on the laundry, which had piled up lately.

Rennie. He'd fought off thoughts of her for hours, but she kept creeping back. He'd sent word by one of his ranch hands that he wouldn't be back in time for dinner, so not to wait for him. Then he'd ridden off by himself, checking fences that didn't need checking.

As he finger-combed his hair, he told himself that Rennie was probably upset with him for leaving her to fend for herself with the children his first night back. He wouldn't blame her if she was, but he hadn't been able to face her in the state he'd been then.

Now it was a different story. He'd come to terms with some things on his solitary ride. He acknowledged that even though he couldn't, *wouldn't,* love Rennie, he wanted to recapture the closeness they'd found on their honeymoon, both in bed and out. He wanted to share his children with her, the joys, the worry, the fun. He wanted to sit with her in the evenings after the children were asleep and talk about everything and nothing. And he wanted to go to sleep with her in his arms and wake up the same way.

The only problem was, did Rennie want the same things from him? She'd married him for his children—he knew that. But in the short time they'd been married, it seemed as if she was willing to accept more. *She'd* come to *him* in his motel room. That had to mean something. Someone like her didn't jump into bed with a man unless she had feelings for him, even if that man was legally her husband. And the way she looked at him when she thought he wasn't watching, her face all soft and vulnerable, had to mean something, too.

Anticipation started a fire inside him as he padded through the house in his bare feet. He would apologize to Rennie, explain what he could, then take her to bed as he'd longed to do all evening.

But first he stopped at Andrew's bedroom door, then Trina's, then Nicki's. All three slept peacefully. In Nicki's room he stepped inside and pulled the covers back over her which she'd kicked off. She'd always been a restless sleeper. Even as a baby, he remembered, they'd had a hard time keeping her covered.

He leaned over and kissed her cheek, thanking God at the same time that she was home safe and sound. He never wanted to live through anything like these last few days again.

I won't let anything happen to you, Nicki, ever again. I promise.

He tucked the covers securely around her, kissed her once more, then left, closing the door behind him.

He opened his bedroom door, expecting to find Rennie waiting up for him, but she wasn't there. He flicked on the light and looked around, taking in everything in one glance. Not only was his wife not there, neither were any of her things. He jerked opened the closet. Only his clothes hung there.

Nice going, Lowell. If she ever intended to share a room with you, she obviously changed her mind.

Well, damn it, he wasn't going to give up that easily. If she wanted an apology for tonight, he'd give her one. God knew she deserved it. But he didn't intend to spend even one more night alone. Rennie was his now—she'd given herself to him. He was damned if he'd let his own stupidity keep them apart.

He headed back down the hall to what had been the housekeeper's bedroom, knowing that was the only place Rennie could be. He didn't bother to knock.

She was curled up on the bed in her nightshirt, reading, the bedside lamp casting a warm glow on her face. She looked up when the door opened, but didn't smile.

"Hi. You're back."

"Yeah."

She glanced at the clock on the nightstand. "Are you hungry? I saved some dinner for you. I could—"

"I scrounged something in the bunkhouse."

"Oh."

He took a step toward her. "Why are you here, Rennie?"

"What do you—"

He didn't let her finish that sentence, either. "Why are you here, in this bedroom, and not in mine? Ours," he corrected himself impatiently.

"I didn't know if I was welcome," she said with a quiet dignity that silenced him. She marked her place in the book and laid it carefully on the nightstand. As if she felt at a disadvantage, she slid off the bed and stood beside it. "When you walked into the kitchen this afternoon, you seemed happy to see me, and I thought...well, it doesn't matter what I thought, because tonight, when you didn't come home, I realized I was wrong."

Irrationally, her explanation angered him, his earlier intention to apologize forgotten. "Didn't you get my message?"

"Yes. I got your message," she said evenly, giving double meaning to the words. "I won't throw myself at you again."

"What the hell is that supposed to mean?"

"Keep your voice down. You'll wake the children."

That checked him. He repeated his question, quietly this time. She swallowed, and his eyes were drawn to the pulse beating in her throat.

"When I came to your motel room," she explained, color staining her cheeks. "Tonight, after I thought about it, I realized that I've put you in an awkward position. You could hardly tell me to my face that you don't...that is, I thought your not coming home was your way of politely telling me to keep my distance."

"Rennie, no." He took the two steps necessary to reach her and pulled her into his arms. She resisted at first, holding herself rigid, but when he said, "I'm sorry. Every time I turn around I hurt you, and God knows I don't mean to," she sighed and nestled against him.

"Then you weren't saying..."

"No! I was confused this afternoon. Seeing you with Andrew brought back...other memories." Johanna's name hung unspoken between them. "And too much has happened in the last few days. I needed time alone to sort things out in my mind. That's all. I never meant you to think I don't want you in my life." He tilted her chin up so he could see her face. "You're the best thing that has happened to me, to this whole family, in a long time."

He lowered his head and their mouths met in a kiss of reconciliation. It soon changed, however, as passion flared between them. Rennie moaned softly, straining to get closer. His lips ground against hers, taking them again and again, and she wound her arms around his neck, giving him back kiss for kiss. Without breaking the kiss, Gideon caught her behind the knees and lifted her in his arms, then carried her through the dark hall back to his bedroom.

Chapter 12

Rennie woke, the heavy weight of a man's arm across her waist anchoring her in place. For one minute she was disoriented, then she remembered. She was in Gideon's bed. She smiled drowsily to herself, luxuriating in the sensual pleasure of waking in the arms of her husband.

The shadowed room was early-morning cold, but she was warm under the covers, warm from the body heat exuded by the man curved against her back. Her gaze wandered around the part of Gideon's bedroom she could see without shifting position.

A man lived in this room. Of that there was no doubt. The furniture was austere, utilitarian, built to take the rough usage of a man with little time for anything but the bare necessities. Certainly no woman had had a hand in decorating this room, which was a startling departure from the rest of the sprawling ranch house. Everything looked fairly new, even the drab brown-and-tan drapes, and she surmised that he'd replaced all the furnishings in the room after Johanna's death.

Feeling a twinge in her hip from lying in one position for so long, Rennie stretched a little, careful not to wake Gideon. Small aches, wonderful aches, reminded her of last night.

They'd made love twice: the first time blazingly fast, a hungry wildfire raging out of control, consuming everything; the second time tormentingly slow, a phoenix rising from the still-warm ashes of their spent passion to rekindle the flames. Both times he'd made sure she was with him every step of the way, refusing to take his own pleasure until she was poised on the brink with him, sobbing for release. And both times their climaxes had been shattering.

"That's a Mona Lisa smile if I ever saw one."

Rennie felt as well as heard the rumble of Gideon's voice. She turned in his arms and snuggled up to him, her fingers tracing a random pattern on the strong muscles of his chest. "Good morning."

"Yeah." He smiled in satisfied agreement. "Yeah, it is." His hand journeyed possessively down her spine, over her hip, and back up to cup one rosy-tipped breast. He caressed it almost absently, rubbing his thumb over the nipple until it beaded, his eyes drifting shut. "What time is it?"

"Early." Rennie's heart began the all-too-familiar pounding associated with Gideon's touch, and she couldn't breathe. Would he always have this effect on her? God, she hoped so.

"How do you feel this morning?"

Correctly interpreting this husbandly question, she answered by hooking one leg over his and rubbing her inner thigh up and down his hip. She butterfly-kissed his raspy chin and purred, "I feel great."

"Oh, yeah? Me, too."

He slid his thigh between hers as their mouths met in a lazy, I've-got-all-morning kiss. His hands cupped her buttocks and pulled her closer, and she could feel his arousal, hard and throbbing, pressing against her stomach.

"What are you doing?" a childish voice asked.

They both froze, the mood abruptly destroyed by the innocently curious question. Rennie grabbed for the sheet, grateful when she discovered that it still covered them both. She twisted around as best she could, hampered by the sheet and by Gideon's arms and legs, which were tangled up with hers.

Trina was standing in the doorway in her nightgown, her hand on the doorknob. Rennie wondered how long she had been there, and felt her face turn a fiery red. Next to her Gideon began shaking with silent laughter.

"Stop that," she hissed at him. When he continued to laugh, she elbowed him in the stomach, hard.

He gave a very satisfying "ooph," then wrapped his arms tightly around Rennie to prevent her from inflicting further damage. He ducked his head and kissed her quickly, then looked over at his daughter.

"What are you doing up so early, sweetheart?"

"Nicki woke me up."

The grin left his face. His gaze sought Rennie's, and she stared back at him, then nodded confirmation of the thought that had sprung immediately to both their minds. Nicki had done this deliberately.

Gideon's lips twisted ruefully, then his gaze moved back to the doorway. "This is private, Trina. Close the door and go on back to your room. We'll talk about it later."

"Okay." The cheerful disinterest in her voice indicated to Rennie that Trina hadn't really seen or heard much of what had been going on between the two of them before her interruption. At least that was one fewer thing to worry about.

When the door closed, Rennie dragged the sheet off Gideon and wrapped it around herself sarong-style, stalked to the door and clicked the lock into place. Then she flicked on the overhead light and turned around to confront her husband.

He lay on his side, one arm propping up his head, completely at ease with his nakedness. For an instant she let herself be distracted. Just as she'd imagined the first night of their honeymoon, his tanned body was dusted all over with sun-kissed golden brown hair, especially his chest. She'd touched him everywhere, had felt the softness of that hair overlying the iron muscles beneath it, but she'd never seen him naked like this. He was truly magnificent, and obviously aroused.

He smiled an invitation and patted the bed. Rennie blinked, then stared at him in disbelief.

"You must be crazy if you think I can just pick up where we left off."

"Why not? The door's locked, Trina's gone back to her room, and the sun's not even up. We have time."

Rennie snorted and gave him a look that said, "Men!" She grabbed the oversize L.A. Lakers T-shirt she wore as a nightgown off the floor and pulled it over her head, oblivious to the fact that it was inside out. Muttering to herself all the while and irrationally getting worked up by the second, she shimmied out of the sheet, bunched it up and threw it at Gideon's head. He fended it off easily and laughed.

Frustrated, she picked up his robe and threw it at him, too. He dodged it, leapt off the bed and pounced on her. For a big man, he could move fast when he wanted to. He slung her over his shoulder and carried her back to bed, ignoring her struggles for freedom.

"What are you doing? Put me down!"

He complied, dropping her on the mattress. She bounced and tried to scramble away but he was too quick for her. He landed on top of her, catching most of his weight on his forearms. He didn't do anything else—he didn't have to. She was effectively pinned to the bed by the long, muscled length of him.

"What are you so worked up about?"

She pushed futilely against him. "Lots of things."

"Name one."

"Get off me and I'll tell you."

"Uh-uh. Tell me first."

Rennie gave up trying to dislodge him. It was impossible. And besides, even though she was annoyed and frustrated, it had more to do with the situation and the lost mood than with him.

"Why didn't you lock the door last night?"

"I didn't think of it—it's been a long time since I've had to." He grinned and waggled his eyebrows. "And I was distracted." He kissed her, a tantalizingly brief kiss. "I'll remember next time."

Her gaze traveled from his mouth to his eyes. "I…it was embarrassing."

"Yeah, but it's not the end of the world. I've been in more embarrassing situations than this. At least we were both decent." He chuckled softly. "I remember one morning, a few months after Trina was born, when Nicki walked in on Jo and me, and we were—" He broke off abruptly, his lighthearted expression draining away as if it suddenly occurred to him that it wasn't quite right to talk intimately about his first wife with his second.

"Sorry." He started to roll away from Rennie, but she wasn't going to let that be the end of it. Not this time. She rolled with him, ending up draped across his chest. She propped herself up.

"Don't do this, Gideon. Please. Not again."

"Don't do what?"

"Don't cut off your memories of Johanna, especially the good ones. I've told you before, you don't have to do that for me. She was a big part of your life and neither of us can pretend she wasn't. If I'm going to share your future, I need to share your past, too." She rubbed her cheek against his chest. "Don't shut me out."

He hesitated, then gently closed his arms around her. "I don't mean to. It's just…you make me forget…and then I remember, and I…oh, hell. I'm not saying this very well."

"You're doing all right. Don't stop." The male scent that was uniquely Gideon filled her nostrils, and she closed her eyes in frank enjoyment.

His big hand tangled in the curls behind her ear, alternately tugging and stroking. "I never thought things would turn out like this. It was only supposed to be a business arrangement."

"I know. You told me when we first met."

He continued as if she hadn't spoken. "I never expected anyone like you. How could I? There isn't anyone like you. And I never expected to be hap—" He stopped in midsentence. Rennie finished it for him.

"Happy." She raised her head, her face softly glowing as she dared to hope. "You never expected to be happy." Her eyes were shining. "Are you, Gideon? Do I make you happy?"

He stared at her, somber and reflective, his eyes puckered at the corners as he considered the question.

"Yeah. You do," he said finally, a strange, wondering expression on his face. "I never thought I'd say that to a woman again, but it's true."

Her heart overflowing, she had to tell him something of what she felt. "You make me happy, too."

"Do I?" Doubt crept in to replace the wonder. "With everything that's happened, how can you say that?"

"Because it's true." She touched a finger to his lips, tracing their shape. "When you smile at me, when you treat me as your wife, when you trust me with your children—those are the things that make me happy."

"Doesn't seem like much to me." He remained unconvinced.

"And...there's the way you touch me."

"You mean like this?" His hands slid down her body, making her shiver deliciously.

"You must know." She could feel the heat rising in her cheeks, but she faced him honestly. "I didn't know it could be like that. I didn't know *I* could be like that. I wanted to tell you that first night, but then you got the phone call about Nicki, and, well, there really hasn't been an opportunity since."

"So tell me now." His voice was like warm honey, deliberately seductive. His work-callused hand slid under the hem of her T-shirt and caressed the soft curves of her bare bottom. It should have felt rough against her delicate skin, but it didn't. It felt sinfully good. "Tell me," he repeated.

Rennie struggled to remember what the question was. "You're already too cocky as it is."

He grinned his best big-bad-wolf grin. "Cocky? You think so? Why don't you check for sure?"

She caught the double meaning immediately. "Oh, you..." She cuffed him playfully on the arm, her fist glancing off the eagle decorating it.

His eyes widened as a thought occurred to him. "Hey, you know what?"

"What?"

"I never got to see your tattoo." He rolled her over unexpectedly and wedged his powerful body between her legs. "Where is it?"

"Hah! I'll never tell."

"Then I'll just have to search for it," he teased, sliding both hands under her T-shirt. "More fun that way, anyway."

Blushing furiously, Rennie opened her mouth to tell him, when they both heard a child's sudden, frightened wail.

"That's Andrew." Gideon was off the bed in a flash, grabbing his robe and throwing it on. Rennie beat him to the door and unlocked it.

"I'll get him. This happened yesterday morning, too." She didn't wait for his assent. She ran down the hall, opened the door to Andrew's room and switched on the light.

The little boy lay hunched facedown in the middle of his bed, sobbing brokenheartedly. Rennie picked him up and cradled him in her arms, gently pressing his tousled head against her shoulder. He clung to her, tears soaking her T-shirt.

"Shh, it's okay. You're okay. I've got you." She stroked his head reassuringly and rocked him back and forth.

"Emmy, Emmy." He caught his breath on a sob. "I want Emmy."

"Aunt Emily's not here, sweetie, remember? But I'm here." She turned and saw Gideon standing in the doorway. "And Daddy's here. See?" She held the little boy so that he could see Gideon.

Andrew buried his face against her neck as fresh sobs broke from him. "I want Emmy."

"Let me take him."

Reluctantly she surrendered him to Gideon. "Shh," he said to Andrew, his voice calm and soothing. "It's okay." He began walking up and down the room with his son, his hand rubbing concentric circles on Andrew's back. Eventually the little boy quieted, and his arms crept around his father's neck.

In an undertone, Rennie said, "He woke up like this yesterday morning, and I was terrified. I couldn't find anything wrong and I didn't know what to do, except what you're doing now. I think maybe it's the strange room that frightens him. He's not used to it."

"But it's always been his room."

"How long has it been since he lived in this house?" she reminded him. "Even a few months is a long time for a child his age."

Pain flashed across Gideon's face, and Rennie's heart ached for him. It wasn't by Gideon's choice that Andrew had been denied the chance to live in his own home, to recognize his own bedroom.

Movement in the doorway to Andrew's room made Rennie turn her head. Trina and Nicki both stood there.

"My goodness," Rennie said with forced cheerfulness. "Everybody's awake now. Who's ready for breakfast?"

"Me. I am," said Trina. "I'm starved."

Andrew's head lifted from Gideon's shoulder and Rennie turned to look at him. "Hey, pardner. Are you ready for breakfast, too?" He nodded slowly. "What would you like?"

He sniffed and rubbed his eyes with a little fist, then said, "Waffos."

"Yeah, waffles!" Trina chimed in.

Rennie looked at Nicki. "Waffles?"

Nicki glanced at her father and nodded reluctantly.

"Then waffles it is."

That day set the pattern for the ones to come. Rennie made breakfast in the large, airy kitchen, with Trina's dubious help, while Gideon, already dressed in jeans and a plaid shirt, drank his morning coffee at the table and read out loud articles from the local weekly newspaper. In one corner Andrew played noisily with two pot lids and a ladle. And Nicki fed the cats in another corner, beside the stove.

Rennie smiled to herself at the domestic scene they all made, and sent up a small prayer that things could stay this way, at least for a while. They'd all been through enough emotional turmoil to last them a long time.

She'd found a waffle recipe in one of several cookbooks stacked beside the stove and hoped it would turn out okay. As she folded beaten egg whites into her waffle batter according to the recipe, she noted that whoever had planned this kitchen had done a good job of taking advantage of natural light. The window over the sink faced east, the windows by the large kitchen table, south. Even though the sun wasn't up yet, fingers of early-morning light found their way in. It reminded her of her grandmother's kitchen in the homestead on the Circle F when she was growing up. And she remembered her tiny grandmother standing in that kitchen, teaching her the basics of cooking in much the same way she was now teaching Trina.

Her smile deepened. She poured batter into the big four-square waffle iron, closed the lid, checked the recipe again and set the timer. As she got down plates from the cabinet she began to hum to herself.

Gideon glanced up from the newspaper. "What song is that? It sounds familiar."

"It's an old hymn my grandmother used to sing to me, 'Be Thou My Vision.' I've always loved it."

She resumed her humming, and from the corner Nicki looked up, an arrested expression on her face. Neither Rennie nor Gideon noticed.

The waffles turned out perfectly, to Rennie's relief, and

after breakfast, Nicki and Trina cleared the table, stacking the dishes on the counter while Rennie washed syrup from Andrew's hands, face and hair. She smiled to herself. She didn't know how he'd managed it, but there was syrup on his eyelashes, too.

"All clean," she said finally, dropping a quick kiss on his baby mouth. She set him back on the floor in the corner, where he resumed his drum solo. She turned around to see Gideon retrieving his Stetson from a nail by the door, where he'd hung it this morning when he came in from doing his chores.

"I've got a horse I have to check on in the barn," he said, "and then I need to see a man in Carter's Junction. I can take the girls with me this morning and drop them at school to save you a trip." Both girls brightened at that. "But we'll have to leave by seven."

Rennie glanced at the clock on the stove. "That gives Nicki and Trina a half hour to get ready for school. Shouldn't be a problem. I can finish up here, and I'll make sure they're outside and waiting for you by the time you're ready to go."

"Okay." He started for the door, then he remembered something and he turned around. "I almost forgot. When did you want to go to Sheridan to do your shopping?"

"I don't know. I don't want to wait for the weekend, but the timing's kind of tricky. According to Emily, Andrew takes a two-hour nap every day right after lunch, and someone has to pick the girls up when school lets out at three, so no afternoon during the week is good. How long will your meeting take this morning?"

"Not more than a couple of hours. I should be back by ten."

Rennie considered things, then nodded. "That sounds good. Andrew and I will be waiting for you."

"All right." He stood there a moment, obviously undecided about something, then he made up his mind. Ignoring the interested gazes of his daughters, he crossed the kitchen, leaned down and kissed her, taking his time about it.

When he finally ended the kiss, Rennie stared at him in a dazed fashion. "What was that for?"

He settled his hat on his head, then tugged at the brim in the way that was becoming familiar to her. "Ask me tonight and I'll tell you." His wicked grin was back. "See you in a bit."

Ten o'clock came and went, with no sign of Gideon. Fifteen minutes later Rennie checked her watch for the third time, glanced down at Andrew who was starting to fidget, then went inside the house for a toy to occupy him.

No sooner had she stepped back onto the front porch than Gideon's pickup truck drove up, pulling a horse trailer. Gideon got out.

"Sorry I'm late," he called as he went around the back. "Took me a little longer than I thought." He unlatched the trailer gate and let down the ramp, then disappeared inside.

Rennie put down the box of blocks she'd just brought out, picked Andrew up and walked over. "I wondered where you were. I thought you were just meeting someone in Carter's Junction. I didn't know you were going to Emily's also, to fetch Nicki's horse."

"I didn't." Gideon carefully backed a horse out of the trailer, a compact chestnut mare that looked familiar to Rennie.

"Sweetwater!" A soft whinny answered her. Rennie looked from the horse to her husband. "Gideon, you didn't!"

He smiled, took Andrew from her and handed her the

lead rope. "She's yours, Rennie. I called her owner from Casper and arranged to buy her."

"But...why?" She stroked the mare's nose with her free hand. "I mean, you have plenty of horses. You didn't need to buy another one just for me."

"I wanted to. I saw how you felt about her and how she responded to you. That kind of rapport with a horse is something special."

Andrew was wriggling in his father's arms, trying to pat Sweetwater, and Gideon shifted him so he could. "Be gentle," he told his son firmly. "Be very gentle." Then he looked down at Rennie. "And I wanted a way to thank you for rescuing Nicki."

The tiny leaves of a new emotion unfurled inside her, but she didn't recognize it for what it was. Confused and uncertain, she said, "You still didn't have to do this. Having Nicki back safe is thanks enough."

"Yeah, but I know how dangerous it was and how much courage it took to do what you did. I should have told you at the time, but I didn't. I just wanted you to know how much it meant to me." He hesitated, then added, "I told you last night that you were the best thing that's happened to my family, and to me, in a long time. I wasn't just saying that—it's the truth." He cupped her cheek gently, then bent and brushed his lips over hers. "And I thank God for sending you to us."

The memory of that day remained with Rennie for weeks afterward, sustaining her through the inevitable difficulties and problems that arose.

She wrote an optimistic, rambling letter to Jess and received a terse one in response. It came in a plain white envelope with no return address, and was simply signed

"Jess," just as she'd requested. She hated the subterfuge, but she wasn't taking any chances. She replied the next day.

"I'm home now," she wrote. "And I'm happy."

Everything she longed for seemed to be within her grasp. Andrew and Trina quickly became attached to her, and she to them. Trina was a joy to mother, always trying to help, always asking questions, and most important, always wanting to be kissed or cuddled. All the love and attention Rennie lavished on her was reaping its own reward. And the bundle of inexhaustible energy that was Andrew kept her running from morning to night, but she loved it. A hundred times a day she responded to his call of "Wemmy!" He brought her things: a pebble he found in the yard, a button that fell off his shirt, and once, a still-wiggling worm which she thanked him for before discreetly disposing of it.

And her relationship with Gideon was thriving. She went to sleep in his arms every night, her body damp and sated from his lovemaking. Every morning she woke to find herself still held within his embrace. And they talked. In the evenings after the children were asleep they discussed the minutiae of their respective days. To an outsider it might not seem much, but Rennie knew those shared, peaceful moments out of their hectic days were drawing them closer than she had dared hope.

Only Nicki remained a problem. When Gideon was around, Nicki was polite and helpful, although still a bit sullen. It was a different story altogether when he wasn't there. Rennie had never known anyone who could silently convey resentment and dislike as well as Nicki could, without ever actually resorting to outright rudeness.

Then things began disappearing. Little things to begin with: a shopping list, a pair of earrings, a book she was reading. At first Rennie scarcely noticed, thinking she'd just misplaced them. But when school finally let out and the girls were around all day a pattern began to develop, and Rennie's suspicions inevitably settled on Nicki. She refused to tell Gideon. This was between Nicki and her, and Rennie was determined to work it out on her own.

Rennie and Gideon had been married a month when Emily Holden stopped by for a visit. The friendship that had begun the night Nicki ran away had grown in the ensuing weeks. Emily was a few years older than Rennie, but they had a lot in common, not the least of which was their love of children, Gideon's children especially.

Emily knocked at the kitchen door, and when no one answered, stuck her head inside the screen door.

"Anybody home?"

"Emily!" Rennie swiped at her tear-stained cheeks and pasted a welcoming smile on her face. "What brings you out here?"

Emily's bright eyes didn't miss a thing. "I had some free time this morning, and I thought I'd stop and see how you're doing."

"I'm fine," Rennie said with false brightness. "Can you stay awhile? Where are the boys?"

"They went fishing in the mountains with Jim. The doctor told him he needed to slow down, take a day off every now and then. Which he refuses to do, of course. So I had a little chat with Seth and Matt, and they talked their grandfather into this fishing trip."

The two women shared a conspiratorial smile about the male of the species, then Rennie pulled out a chair at the table for Emily and said, "Can I get you something? Coffee? Ice tea?"

"Black coffee sounds good, if it's fresh."

"If there's one thing I know about running a ranch house," Rennie said as she got down a coffee cup from the cabinet, "it's to always keep a fresh pot of coffee on the stove." She filled the cup and set it in front of Emily. "How about a piece of apple cobbler? I tried that recipe you gave me last week."

"Well—" Rennie could see Emily struggling against temptation "—a small piece might tempt me."

"One small piece coming up." Rennie fetched plates and forks, then cut a piece of cobbler for Emily and one for herself. "Here you go."

Emily took a bite, savoring it. "Mmm, it's good." She watched Rennie push her piece of cobbler around the plate, then said, "I know it's not my business, but what's so wrong that you have to cry in the middle of the day?"

Rennie stopped and looked up. She tried for a smile and failed miserably. "Oh, it's nothing. Really."

"Um-hm. I always cry over nothing, too."

"You'll think it's silly."

"I doubt it."

Rennie hesitated, then said, "I…misplaced my wedding ring. I took it off when I was scrubbing the kitchen floor. I…thought I left it on my dresser, but when I went back to get it, it…wasn't there." This time she succeeded in forcing a smile, but it was a wan effort. "See, I told you it was silly."

"It's not silly. I know exactly how you feel. Maybe you put it somewhere else and just forgot."

Rennie shook her head. "I've searched everywhere. Twice."

"Maybe one of the children found it. Have you asked them?"

Rennie's eyes shifted away. "No, I…Andrew's asleep, and the girls are playing outside."

If Emily suspected Rennie was hiding something, she

kept her thoughts to herself this time. She patted Rennie's hand consolingly. "It'll turn up. Wait and see."

Emily took another bite of her apple cobbler and changed the subject. "How are things with Gideon?"

If Rennie thought it strange to be confiding in Johanna's sister about Johanna's former husband, she ignored it. Emily was a friend. And she needed a friend right now.

"Things are…good," she said. Then she looked up shyly. "Better than good, actually."

"I'm glad. For him and for you." Emily hesitated, then said, "You know, Jo would have wanted him to marry again. She loved Gideon very much, and she'd want him to be happy."

"He is happy." Rennie spoke from the heart. "At least, as happy as he can be with Nicki the way she is."

"Is she still making trouble for you?"

"I don't mean that. I mean her not speaking." Rennie stopped, suddenly taken aback. "How did you know Nicki was causing problems?"

"I didn't. But knowing her, I guessed."

So intent were they on their conversation that neither woman saw the silent shadow that crept up to the kitchen screen door and peered inside.

Emily shook her head. "It doesn't seem fair, does it. After everything you went through the night she ran away—figuring out where she'd gone, finding the spot where she went over the cliff, climbing down to rescue her—after all that, it just doesn't seem fair she should treat you badly."

A gasp from the doorway drew their attention. Nicki was standing there.

Chapter 13

Rennie's chair scraped across the kitchen floor as she stood up. Nicki's shocked immobility told her the girl had overheard something that had profoundly affected her. She took a step toward her, but before Rennie could say anything, Nicki suddenly bolted.

Rennie went after her. She tossed a few words over her shoulder to Emily about watching in case Andrew awakened from his nap, but didn't wait for a response. The screen door slammed open when she hit it running, rattling its hinges. She caught a flash of movement as Nicki rounded the corner of the house, and she followed.

"Nicki, wait!" But Nicki just darted around a parked pickup truck and headed for the horse barn. The door was open and she ran inside, disappearing into its shadowed interior.

Although her hip protested with an angry twinge, Rennie didn't slow until she entered the barn. When her eyes adjusted to the dim light, she began searching for the girl. She went first to Cheyenne's stall, thinking to find Nicki there, but without any luck. Then she systematically went from one stall to another, most of them empty, peering inside each one.

A slight rustling sound made her pause. Rennie cocked her head, listening intently. There it was again. Overhead. She found the ladder leading into the hayloft. She climbed it quickly.

Nicki was huddled in the far corner, curled up into a tight ball of misery. She couldn't fail to hear Rennie's approach but she ignored it as if by doing so she could make Rennie go away. Nicki wasn't crying. Rennie almost wished she were, because it would have made things easier.

So instead of putting her arms around Nicki as she wanted to, Rennie sat down beside her and waited. She wrapped her arms around her knees and watched the dust motes swirling in a shaft of sunlight from a window above them. And waited. And waited.

Eventually her patience was rewarded. Nicki uncurled slowly, raising a dry-eyed face so full of pain and remorse that tears sprang to Rennie's eyes. Her heart ached for Nicki, and she knew from her own experience the emotions the girl was feeling.

"You took my wedding ring this morning, didn't you?"

The question obviously hadn't been expected, and Nicki's eyes widened in surprise. Guilt replaced the surprise and she nodded slowly.

"And all those other things, too?"

A quick bob of her blond head confirmed it. Although filled with guilt, her eyes bravely met Rennie's. Something in their depths reached out to her, an appeal for understanding and forgiveness she probably wasn't even aware of. Rennie carefully trod the path through emotional quicksand, knowing that the wrong approach now could ruin everything.

"I knew it was you. I'll bet you're wondering why I didn't tell your father." The girl hesitated, then nodded, and Rennie said gently, "I kept quiet because I knew it would hurt him deeply, and I don't ever want to do that."

She was close, very close. Nicki's lips were trembling and she swallowed visibly. Rennie pressed on. "Do you love your father, Nicki?"

Her stepdaughter gulped and sniffed. Her hands were tightly clenched, fingers wrapped around fingers. Rennie longed to touch her, but held back.

"I think you do. I think you love him more than anything in the world. Sometimes, when we love someone that much we get scared that the person we love will stop loving us. Or leave us." She paused, then added softly, deliberately, "Or die."

Nicki moved convulsively, then was still.

"In our fear we do things that make it look like we don't love them at all. My father died when I was fifteen. I loved him more than anything, and I felt my world had come to an end. I was angry with God for taking him away from me, and I was angry with my father for leaving me when I loved him so much. But he wasn't there, so I took that anger out on the whole world, including my mother. I carried that anger for a long time.

"When my mother remarried I was doubly angry with her. I told myself, 'She never loved Daddy, never. How could she marry someone else if she did?' I said some hateful things to her, things I didn't really mean in my heart. But I never got the chance to take them back. I never got the chance to tell her how much I loved her. She died, Nicki. She died before I could."

A sob burst from Nicki, then another, and another. She

covered her face with her hands, her whole body shaking as she fought not to cry. Without thinking Rennie reached over and pulled the little girl into her arms. Nicki resisted for only a moment, then her slender frame collapsed against Rennie, seeking comfort and absolution.

Rennie cuddled her close, resting her cheek against Nicki's bright head, stroking her hair, and making calming, comforting sounds, easing her stepdaughter's pain.

"Shh. It's okay." The simple words, echoes of the same words Gideon had used to comfort Andrew when he cried, seemed to be exactly what Nicki needed. She buried her face against Rennie's shoulder and wept.

Rennie just held her and let her cry, knowing the healing power of tears. After a long time the tears ceased, but Nicki made no attempt to free herself from Rennie's embrace.

Into the silence floated the mundane sounds of the horses below, snorts, the stamp of a shod hoof, soft nickers. Outside the barn, she heard a truck drive up. A door slammed and male voices rumbled. Yet Nicki still clung to her and Rennie refused to abandon this opportunity to gain the girl's trust.

"You've been angry for a long time, Nicki. Angry and scared. Those emotions don't leave much room for love. Don't you think it's time you let them go?"

The body in her arms stiffened as if in protest, then relaxed once more. Her nod was almost imperceptible, but Rennie felt the slight movement. She smiled softly over Nicki's head.

"Your father's a good man, and he tries very hard to be a good father. He makes mistakes sometimes, but he loves you all very much and he does his best for you. That's why he married me. He wanted you and Trina and Andrew to have someone to love you and help him take care of you. Someone who wouldn't leave. He never meant to hurt you.

He'd rather die than do anything to hurt his children. You know that in your heart, don't you?''

Again that slight nod. Rennie tightened her hold, knowing that her next statement would be the riskiest of all.

"When you care about someone, their pain becomes yours. That's why I had to find you when you ran away. I *had* to, Nicki, because I care about your father. I'm not really very heroic or brave, but you ·were missing, and it was tearing him apart. We *had* to find you. Can you understand?''

Nicki pulled away and stared at Rennie for several heartbeats, her young face mirroring her internal struggle to comprehend and accept these very grown-up concepts.

Rennie reached over, tucked a strand of pale, fine hair behind Nicki's ear, and smiled crookedly. "I already love Andrew and Trina. I want to love you, too. Won't you let me?''

Two tears trickled down Nicki's cheeks. She wiped them away but others replaced them. Her lips parted as if to speak, but no words came. She squeezed her eyes shut in frustration, and when they opened again they were filled with such yearning intensity that Rennie's heart broke for her.

Nicki's hand darted out and brushed at the straw in front of her. Rennie started to reach for that small hand, but drew back at the last second when she realized what the girl was doing. Having cleared a small patch away from the wooden planking, Nicki was writing something in the fine layer of straw dust that remained. Reading upside down, Rennie made out the words *I'm sorry*. Nicki looked up and their eyes met, contrition in one pair of eyes, understanding in the other.

"I know you are," Rennie said softly.

Nicki cleared away another patch of straw and began

writing again. The words *Forgive me?* took shape. Once more they gazed at each other in the barn's dim light.

"Of course I do." Rennie cupped the girl's cheek with one hand, her thumb stroking away the last of the tears. "It's okay, Nicki. We all do things we're sorry for later. But we can't change the past, no matter how much we might want to. We just have to live with it and do our best to learn from it, to become better people *because* of the past rather than in spite of it."

A ghost of a smile flickered over Rennie's face. "It might not seem like it to you right now, but you're lucky you're learning all this so young. I learned the lesson rather late." The smile faded. "Something really bad happened to me once. I was in an accident and I was hurt for a long time afterward. I had a lot of time to think. And I learned some things that changed me—" Rennie pressed her free hand to her heart "—in here."

She saw the question in Nicki's eyes and tried to answer it. "I guess the most important thing I learned is that love is never wasted. Never. Loving someone isn't safe. People die, Nicki. You and I both know it. But that doesn't mean we shouldn't love them. If you love someone, they can't ever really die, because they live on in your heart for always." Rennie's eyes filled with tears. "My parents will always be a part of me because I love them, just as your mother will always be a part of you. And that's the way it should be."

Nicki's face crumpled and she began to weep again, then somehow they were both clinging to each other and crying together.

"We're going to be all right, Nicki," Rennie whispered between the sobs that shook them both. "Everything's going to be all right."

* * *

Coming out of the barn into the sunlight was a shock. Rennie and Nicki stood in the doorway for a minute, blinking against the startling brightness. Feeling just a bit disoriented, Rennie shaded her eyes and looked around. A distance away, four men stood in earnest conversation by the sheep pens, one much taller than the other three, and she easily recognized Gideon.

He must have seen the two of them emerge from the barn because he raised his arm briefly in acknowledgment. He stood there for a minute watching them. Rennie glanced down at her stepdaughter and saw the tension in her body and the longing on her face.

"Go to him, Nicki." The girl looked up at Rennie, doubt in her eyes. "He loves you, sweetheart. Go on."

Nicki needed no other urging. She took three steps forward, then broke into a run. Rennie watched as she raced across the barnyard, skirted the corral and headed for the sheep pens with wings on her heels. Nicki threw her arms around her father, only to be picked up and crushed in Gideon's embrace. The other men stepped back and turned their heads, as if to give the boss a little privacy.

A wave of emotion swept through Rennie, for both father and daughter. "You did it," she whispered to herself. "You did it." Tears prickled, but she refused to let them fall. She'd already shed enough of them today. Besides, what was there to cry about? They'd made a start today, she and Nicki. They still had a long way to go, but things were going to be all right, and that was cause for celebration, not for tears.

Suddenly she remembered something. "Oh, my Lord. Emily!"

That night Gideon walked into their bedroom just as Rennie emerged from the bathroom, drying her hair with a towel. He stood just inside the door, enjoying the tantalizing view of slender thighs revealed beneath her Lakers T-shirt every time she raised her arms.

"Paperwork done?" she asked.

"Yeah. Finally."

"Did you check on the children?"

"Yeah. Sound asleep."

She rubbed the ends of her hair a few more times, then laid the towel over the back of a chair and picked up a comb. She sat in the middle of the bed, tucked her legs under her, and began combing her hair to help it dry faster.

Gideon watched for a moment, mesmerized by the repetitive movements of the comb through Rennie's damp curls. Then he shook his head, moved into the room and began unbuttoning his shirt with one hand. He pulled it off and tossed it in the direction of the clothes hamper.

He unsnapped his jeans and said, "What was that all about this afternoon?"

In the middle of fluffing her bangs, she didn't bother looking up. "With Nicki, you mean?"

"Yeah."

Rennie put down the comb and faced him. Her slow smile came from the heart. "I think Nicki and I reached an understanding."

"What about?"

"Life."

His brows drew together in puzzlement. "Say again?"

"We had a long conversation about a lot of things. It was a little one-sided verbally, I admit, but I think we were able to communicate pretty well just the same."

He sat on the edge of the bed, causing it to tilt downward, and she had to catch herself from tumbling over. "I still don't get it," he said, pulling off his boots.

"Well, some of it's kind of private, between Nicki and me."

That clearly didn't set well with him. "I don't think anything to do with my daughter should be kept from me," he said, with a slight emphasis on the word *my*. He dropped the second boot beside the first and stood up, hands on hips.

"It's not like that, Gideon, believe me."

"Does it have anything to do with her behavior lately? With the things she's been doing to you behind my back?"

Rennie's jaw dropped. "How did you know about that?"

"I didn't. I had my suspicions, but no proof. You just confirmed them for me."

"You didn't say anything."

"I was waiting for you to tell me."

She picked up the comb again and ran it through her hair for something to do. "I didn't want you to know," she said finally.

"Why?"

"I wanted to handle it on my own." Her eyes beseeched him. "Try to understand. This was something Nicki and I needed to work out by ourselves."

"Have you settled things with her, then?"

"I think so. We've made a start, anyway."

"Good. It was worrying me." He stretched, rolling his shoulders to relieve the dull ache between his shoulder blades. "Lord, I'm beat. If there's one thing I hate it's sitting at a desk going over numbers. Even with that new computer software I bought last year, it's a hassle."

"I'd offer to help you, but I'm hopeless at bookkeeping. And computers just don't seem to like me."

He unzipped his jeans and stripped them off, taking his briefs with them, and Rennie averted her gaze. Even after a month of sharing a room with Gideon, of sleeping every night in his arms, she was still shy around him when it came to nudity. He seemed to have no self-consciousness about his body, but then, why should he? He was a man in the prime of his life—tall, whipcord lean, and with the musculature of a man who worked, rather than worked out.

The memory of last night, when he'd unexpectedly joined her in the shower, rose fresh in her mind. She'd tried to hide her body from him, but he'd refused to let her. He'd traced the scars crisscrossing her flat stomach with a touch so gentle she'd felt like weeping. But he hadn't let her do that, either. His soapy hands had caressed every inch of her, arousing her unbearably, then he'd persuaded her to do the same for him. When they could take no more, he'd rinsed them both off, carried her back into the bedroom and made love to her. She hadn't even noticed until afterward that he'd deliberately left all the lights on.

Gideon dumped his dirty clothes in the hamper and said, "I'm going to take a shower. Want to come scrub my back for me?"

She knew he was teasing her, but she couldn't help it. She blushed.

He chuckled. "You are so damned cute when you do that." He strolled over to the bed, leaned down and kissed her thoroughly. "Wait up for me," he whispered, his fingers sliding under her T-shirt to brush tantalizingly against the butterfly tattoo at the top of her right thigh. "I won't be long."

Two weeks later Rennie lay in the dark, listening to the slow, measured sound of Gideon's breathing. He was asleep. She knew she should try to sleep, too. Morning came awfully early in this household. His internal clock woke Gideon at four-thirty, and his movements in bed always woke her, no matter how tired she'd been the night before. Maybe it was some kind of sensual radar—they often made love first thing in the morning. Even though she was definitely not a morning person, waking up to Gideon made waking up worthwhile.

Sometimes he'd pull her on top of him, coaxing her to take the lead while his hands lazily explored her soft curves. Other times he'd be in too much of a hurry, drawing her beneath him, parting her legs and taking her on a fast trip to sweet oblivion.

It seemed he always desired her, night or morning, just as she desired him. But lately it seemed as if something was different. Not with Gideon exactly, because he satisfied her physically, just as he always had. He seemed to have a sixth sense about her, somehow divining just where she needed to be touched at exactly the right moment. And though they didn't always reach the peak together, he never left her unsatisfied. He made her feel special, cherished.

But sometimes when they made love she found herself almost holding her breath, as if waiting for something else to happen, something that never did.

She sighed and turned over, her cheek seeking a cool place on her pillow. What was wrong? Why couldn't she sleep? She'd had insomnia for the past two weeks, ever since she and Nicki... But that couldn't be it. Working things out with her stepdaughter should have relieved her mind, not burdened it.

Gideon stirred beside her, almost waking, but not quite. His arm tightened around her, and he murmured something she didn't catch. She lay very still, forcing her breathing to slow as she feigned sleep. She didn't want him to wake up. He worked too hard and he needed his rest. Besides, if he woke he might ask her what was wrong, and what could she tell him?

What *could* she tell him? Her life was everything he'd promised, and more. The children were thriving. Andrew no longer woke in tears, and when he called for someone it was Rennie's name he called. Trina was blossoming, growing more secure with each passing day.

And Nicki? Rennie wasn't foolish enough to believe that everything was resolved where Nicki was concerned. But they'd made a start that Friday two weeks ago, and she was slowly gaining Nicki's trust and affection.

Last Sunday, for the first time, Nicki had kissed her goodnight. Gideon had seen both girls to their respective rooms and had tucked them in, while Rennie put Andrew to bed. But on the way back from his room Rennie had double-checked on Trina and Nicki. Trina had already been asleep so Rennie hadn't lingered, but Nicki had been awake and restless. And after she'd straightened Nicki's tangled sheet, Rennie couldn't resist lightly brushing her lips against Nicki's forehead.

"Go to sleep," she'd whispered as she bent over her. "It's late."

Rennie had started to rise, when Nicki abruptly slid her arms around Rennie's neck, hugged her and kissed her cheek.

Rennie's hand stole to her cheek, feeling the kiss even now. Of all the kisses she'd ever received from a child, that had been the hardest won, and consequently meant the most.

"What's the matter? Can't sleep?" The deep rasp came out all as one word. Without opening his eyes Gideon shifted position and pillowed Rennie's head against his shoulder.

"It's nothing. Go back to sleep."

He didn't say anything, but his hand began kneading her bad hip as if he thought she was hurting but didn't want him to know. After a few minutes he said, "Better now?"

Although her hip had been fine before, she said, "Yes. Thanks."

He continued the massage for a few minutes more, but eventually his hand slowed, then stilled, and she felt him slide back into a deep sleep.

Rennie could have cried. What was the matter with her? Why couldn't she accept what she had and be happy? Why did she feel so empty?

The next afternoon, while the girls were playing outside and Andrew took his nap, Rennie sorted through a seemingly never-ending pile of laundry. Her shoulder blades ached from bending over, and she straightened for a moment, then sighed and blew her bangs off her forehead in exasperation.

There were a lot of chores in this household, and although Gideon and his daughters helped, most of them were her responsibility. She hadn't realized before she came here just how much work children could be, nor how many clothes they could go through in a week. And doing the laundry was the one thing she disliked the most. But there was no help for it.

Suddenly Nicki and Trina burst into the room. "Rennie, come quick! There's something wrong with Shadow!" Trina was almost in tears. They dragged her into the utility room, where the cat was mewling piteously in a corner, her swollen body wracked with contractions.

Rennie recognized the signs and let out a sigh of relief. She explained what was happening, and together she and the girls found a shallow box, lined it with soft, clean towels and put it in the utility room for Shadow to use. Then in breathless wonder they watched three tiny kittens make their way into the world.

At the dinner table that night, Nicki's normally animated face wore a thoughtful expression, while Trina chatted endlessly about what they'd seen. Gideon responded with just enough interest to keep her going, and Andrew, indignant that he'd been left out of the afternoon's adventure, had to be physically restrained from getting up from the table to see the new kittens.

"You can see them later," Rennie told him firmly, but it wasn't until Gideon said the same thing that the little boy finally subsided in his chair.

After dinner, Rennie excused the girls from helping with the dishes. "Go on," she said indulgently. "I know you're dying to see the kittens again."

"Thanks, Rennie." Trina scrambled from the table. She latched on to Gideon's hand. "Come on, Daddy," she said, self-importantly, "I'll show you where they are. But you have to be really quiet. Rennie says Shadow will get upset if we aren't *really* quiet."

"Hold on for a second." Gideon picked Andrew up. "Aren't you coming, Nicki?" She shook her head and began stacking the dirty dishes on the table. Gideon gave her a considering look, then left the room with Trina and Andrew.

Nicki waited until the others were gone, then sought out pencil and paper for the question that had obviously been on her mind all afternoon. She wrote something, then handed the paper to Rennie.

Are you going to have a baby? Rennie read.

Sharp pain stabbed through Rennie at the unexpected question, and for a wild moment she mourned what might have been, if only the accident had never occurred. A child, Gideon's child growing within her, created from love.

Then sanity returned. If not for the accident, she wouldn't even be here, would never have met Gideon, would never have married him.

Rennie looked at Johanna's daughter, all her earlier guilt returning in full force. If not for the accident, Nicki would never have suffered through the loss of her mother—Johanna would still be alive. And Nicki would be a normal, happy, *talkative* nine-year-old.

Badly shaken, Rennie still managed to find her voice. "No, Nicki. I won't ever have a baby."

Nicki picked up the pad of paper and scribbled several sentences, then handed it back to Rennie, who read it out loud. "Mama was married and had babies. Aunt Emily was married and had babies. Connie Peters, our first housekeeper, got married and had a baby. I thought all married women had babies."

Rennie swallowed against the lump in her throat, then pulled out a chair and sat down. She met her stepdaughter's curious eyes. "Not all married women do, Nicki. I won't."

The girl tilted her head and raised her shoulders as if to ask, "Why not?"

"Remember when I told you I was in a bad accident?" Nicki nodded. "I was hurt inside in a way that means I can't have children of my own."

Nicki leaned over and wrote, *Never?*

Emotion welled in Rennie, rising dangerously close to the surface. She shook her head. "No. Never."

Once more the girl scribbled something, then turned the pad so Rennie could see. *Did you want to?*

It was the last straw. Rennie covered her face with her hands and sobbed once as the old, haunting pain came back in full force, joined by a new pain she only now recognized. She pressed her fingers against her eyes, straining to keep back tears that refused to be held back. She sobbed once more.

"Wemmy's cwying." The voice belonged to Andrew. He tugged at her arm. "Why you cwying, Wemmy?"

Rennie dropped her hands and gathered him into her arms, drawing him onto her lap. She squeezed his dear little body close and pressed her damp cheek against his hair as a third sob escaped.

"Rennie?" There was a frightened waver in Trina's voice. "What's wrong?"

Suddenly Gideon was there, gently taking Andrew from her and setting him on the floor. Then he crouched beside her chair, checking her hands and face for injuries. "What's the matter? Are you hurt?"

She shook her head, sobbed and covered her face again, huddling in the chair. She couldn't stop crying. Nicki's innocent questions had chipped away at the dam of her emotions, and now the flood waters overwhelmed her. *Did you want to?* kept echoing in her head, and the reminder of how much she *had* wanted babies of her own kept the tears flowing full force.

But when Rennie heard Gideon sternly ask Nicki if she'd done something to make her cry, she knew she had to respond.

"She didn't do...anything," Rennie forced out between the sobs that shook her whole body.

Gideon plucked her from the chair and sat down with her on his lap. "Rennie, stop this. You're making yourself sick."

She tried, she really did. "I...can't."

"Rennie, please. You're scaring the children."

The children. She was scaring the children. The words became a litany in her mind, until she finally calmed down a little. She gulped, sniffed and rubbed the back of her hand against her nose. "I need...a tissue."

Trina darted off and returned with a whole box. "Here, Rennie."

Rennie took a deep, shaky breath. "Thank you."

She grabbed a couple of tissues from the box, mopped her eyes and blew her nose. Her vision cleared, and she glanced from Trina's scared expression, to the bewilderment on Andrew's face, to Nicki's troubled look.

"I'm sorry." Her apology was to Nicki. "It wasn't your fault. You…didn't know."

Gideon started to say something, then thought better of it. He stood up with Rennie in his arms. "Nicki, you and Trina finish the dishes for Rennie, okay? And keep an eye on Andrew. I'm going to put Rennie to bed."

He carried her out of the kitchen and down the long hallway to their bedroom. He didn't say a word the whole way, nor did he speak until he'd stripped off her clothes, slipped her nightshirt over her head and settled her under the covers.

He brought a damp cloth from the bathroom and wiped her face gently, then set it aside. He tilted her face up to meet his gaze. His eyes were very green in his tanned face as he took in her pallor and felt the slight tremors that still shook her.

"Are you okay now?" he asked finally.

She nodded.

"Can you tell me what that was all about?"

In a voice scarcely above a whisper, she said, "Nicki asked me if I was going to have a baby, and I told her I…couldn't."

"Oh, Rennie. I'm sorry."

"I thought I'd dealt with it, Gideon, but I guess I was wrong."

"It's obviously been coming for a long time." He was silent for a moment. "Didn't you go through any counseling for it?"

"Yes, but I don't think I ever really grieved. I went through the denial and depression stages, but I never let myself mourn. I guess I never really accepted it, even though I told myself and everyone else I had."

"But what brought it on *now?*" Perplexity showed on his

angular features. "I can't believe that one question from Nicki could trigger this kind of emotional explosion if you hadn't been primed for it."

The last piece of the puzzle fell into place in Rennie's mind. "You brought it on," she said before she realized it. She caught her breath sharply and covered her mouth, but it was too late.

"What?" He grasped her arms and pulled her closer. "What did you say?"

There was no going back. She could only go forward. "It was you," she whispered.

He shook his head in denial. "What have I done to make you unhappy?"

"Not unhappy," she explained, looking at him but not really seeing him. "Happy. But it wasn't enough," she said to herself. "That's why I haven't been able to sleep these past two weeks. I've been grieving."

"What do you mean?"

She focused on the face that had become so dear to her, noting each subtle nuance of expression. "I didn't understand until just now." Her eyes were very dark in her pale face, but the words flowed out of her in a cleansing stream. "It was *our* babies I was grieving for, Gideon. Yours and mine. Because I love you."

Chapter 14

Rennie's words went through Gideon like a whirlwind, shaking him to the core.

She loved him.

He hadn't wanted to face it, hadn't wanted to deal with the consequences, but somehow he'd known. Rennie would always follow her heart. He'd convinced himself that all they shared was chemistry, friendship, sexual attraction, and any of a dozen other words, when all the while he'd known deep down in the secret recesses of his soul that what she felt for him was love.

What had she said? Love. Babies. Their babies.

For one brief moment he remembered Johanna carrying their children, remembered the joy, the wonder. But close on the heels of those memories came a picture that could never be—Rennie carrying their baby, her body rounded with the promise of new life, her face soft and glowing with love. The ache in his heart for that child that they would never have shook him more than he thought possible.

"Rennie." He pulled her into his arms and held her tightly, both giving and receiving comfort for the grief that he finally understood.

"I guess I didn't want to admit it, even to myself." The words were muffled against his shirt. "We had an agreement, and you kept your side of the bargain."

"The hell with that," he said roughly.

"No. It's important, Gideon. You've kept your promises to me. It's not your fault I fell in love with you."

"Rennie, I—"

Whatever he was going to say was lost when the door handle to their bedroom rattled impatiently. It was followed by the sound of a small hand slapping at the door. "Wemmy!" came a voice from the other side. "Wemmy!"

"Damn!"

Gideon's softly spoken curse exactly echoed Rennie's sentiments. Much as she loved Andrew, she could have wished him anywhere but here at this precise moment.

"Wemmy!" Andrew's voice rose in volume and the door handle rattled again.

"You'd better open it, or he'll start crying," Rennie said.

Gideon briefly tightened his hold, then reluctantly released her and went to open the door. Andrew marched inside, his bottom lip trembling ominously.

"Wemmy." It was a piteous sound, and Rennie couldn't resist it. She patted the bed beside her.

"Come on up."

The little boy tried, but the bed was too high. Gideon lifted him and settled him next to Rennie, but he scrambled onto her lap and laid his head on her breast. She curved her arms around him and hugged him close, and he burrowed against her.

"It's okay," she told him. "I'm not going anywhere."

"Daddy?" Gideon turned and saw his daughters standing in the open doorway. "Can we come in?" Trina pleaded.

He glanced at Rennie, who nodded. He faced the girls again and said, "All right. For just a minute."

Trina crept inside, but stayed close to the door. Nicki did the same, but where Trina's eyes were wide and afraid, hers held guilt and trepidation.

"Don't be scared," Rennie told them. She reached deep inside herself and found a reassuring smile. "I'm okay." She looked at Trina and held out her hand. "But I could really use a hug and a kiss right now."

Trina didn't hesitate. She ran to the bed and climbed right up, throwing her arms around Rennie's neck and kissing her. Rennie held her tightly, returning the kiss many times over.

"I love you, Rennie," Trina said, her voice wobbling.

"I love you, too, sweetie. You'll never know how much."

Andrew raised his head, not wanting to be left out. "*I* wuv you, Wemmy."

She kissed the tip of his nose. "And I love you, too." Then she looked over at Gideon's oldest child, her heart in her eyes. "Nicki?"

Nicki walked slowly toward the bed, but stopped just short of it and hung her head, as if she still feared Rennie blamed her for what happened. Rennie shifted Trina to one side and reached out to touch Nicki's hand.

"It wasn't your fault," she said softly. "It was mine. You didn't do anything, and I'm sorry I made you feel that you did." Nicki lifted her chin and their eyes met. "Won't you forgive me?"

With a choked cry, Nicki threw herself at Rennie, and they clung to each other. "I love you, Nicki," she said, "I love you so much. Don't ever doubt that."

Then somehow all three children were embracing her,

clamoring for hugs and kisses that, between laughter and tears, she divided equally among them. As if from a distance, Gideon watched the touching tableau they made, his children clustered around Rennie, basking in the charmed circle of love she created so effortlessly. Love that extended to him.

Then Rennie looked up and smiled at him, a smile so radiant it took his breath away, and suddenly it was all so simple that he marveled how he could ever have been so blind.

He loved her.

Adrenaline surged through his body. God, it had been staring him in the face all this time. Why had it taken him so long to realize he loved her? That he needed her the way he needed air, water, food? It had taken Jo's death to make him understand how precious and rare had been the love they shared. Why hadn't he seen that he had something equally precious in Rennie?

Love and Rennie. The words met and mated, fitting together the way he and Rennie did. Perfectly.

More than anything he wanted to take her in his arms and hold her, just hold her, reassuring himself that she was his now, in a way he'd never dreamed she could be.

And if they hadn't had an audience, he'd have done just that, and more. But now wasn't the time. First, he had to put his kids—no, *their* kids—to bed.

Then, Rennie, he promised her silently, *then I'll tell you the words I long to say and you long to hear.*

But it was not to be. His kids were too emotionally wound up to go quietly to bed. Between baths, nightclothes, brushing teeth, two bedtime stories for Andrew and a drink of water for Trina, it took him forever to settle them for the night. Then he stole five minutes for a quick shower in the bathroom off the kitchen. By the time Gideon finally returned to the master bedroom, Rennie was fast asleep, one hand tucked beneath her cheek.

Disappointment sliced through him. He'd eagerly anticipated this moment for the past hour and more, his newfound love for her burning white-hot. He ached, not just in body, but in soul. He wanted to tell her what was in his heart, then watch her eyes as he took her with the words of love trembling between them.

He touched her shoulder, but she didn't even stir. The faint shadows under her eyes bore mute testimony to her exhaustion, both mental and physical, and he told himself he'd be a selfish bastard if he woke her now. He pushed his disappointment aside. Morning would come soon enough. For now he'd have to be content with holding her.

Gideon stripped off his robe and slid naked into bed beside her. He punched up his pillow and shoved it under his head, then reached over and gently drew Rennie back against him. She sighed but didn't waken. His body responded to her proximity with predictable results, but he ignored it as best he could. He slipped one knee between hers, curved his arm under the soft swell of her breasts, then closed his eyes and tried to sleep.

Sleep refused to come. He was too keyed up, his mind playing back scenes from this evening, from the moment he'd found Rennie in tears, to her startling declaration of love, to his even more startling discovery that he loved her, too.

It shouldn't have been such a surprise. I should have seen it long ago. Why didn't I? Rennie brought laughter and love into my life again, and she gave me back my children. She loved them, and me, and she turned this house into a home once more. How could I help but love her? And why did it take me so long to realize it?

What a barren wasteland his life had been without her, a desert where he had wandered aimlessly for so long he'd forgotten the cool, clean, life-giving taste of water. Rennie's love was like water for his thirsty soul, and he needed it, and her, forever.

His arm tightened around her. *You gave me gifts beyond price, sweetheart, and in exchange I gave you nothing. Nothing but promises that were easy to keep. Promises...*

That was it. There was the answer that had eluded him, the reason why he had denied for so long the love growing between them. It all came down to a promise. Not one he'd made to Rennie, but to Johanna.

He'd promised Jo that he would take her and their children to visit her parents, who had retired to southern California a few years before. But when the time came to make good on his promise, an outbreak of pneumonia had threatened his prize-winning merino flock and he'd begged off the trip. Jo, Nicki and Trina had flown to California without him.

And as a result, Jo died.

It was his guilty conscience, not just his love for Jo, that had kept him from reaching out for love again. All this time he'd thought he had no love left in him to give, had thought that part of him had died with Jo. But the truth was harder to accept. He'd been afraid of love, afraid he'd fail another woman as he had failed Jo.

He'd been a coward long enough. It was time he faced the truth and forgave himself. Only then could he be free of the past, free to love again.

It wasn't quite dawn when Gideon's pickup truck pulled up to the cemetery entrance. He parked and turned off the engine.

He hadn't wanted to leave Rennie to come here. After

lying awake for so long he'd finally slept, then had wakened at his usual time, with his wife still in his arms. Her baby-soft skin, warm and rosy; the scent of her, a unique combination of delicate perfume and Rennie; the dusky curls tickling his chin—all these things had pulled at him to stay. But he knew what he had to do.

Gideon grabbed the bouquet from the seat next to him and pushed open the truck door. With a firm tread he made his way in the predawn light through the older section of the cemetery. He stopped in front of his parents' graves for a moment's quiet reflection, then moved on. It was only a short distance from there to Johanna's resting place.

He removed his hat and set it on the gravestone, then crouched to place his floral tribute in the container embedded at the base. Dew still clung to the petals, and Gideon wiped his damp hands on his jeans as he stood up. He'd haphazardly plucked the flowers in the dark and the odd mixture reflected it, but he'd wanted flowers for Johanna, today of all days.

He reached over and traced the words carved on the tombstone, then abruptly thrust his hands in his back pockets. "Hey, Jo, it's me," he said softly.

Having said that, he glanced down at the scuffed tips of his boots, suddenly at a loss for words. How to say what was in his heart? Then it came to him.

"You probably already know it, Jo, but ever since you died I've blamed myself. I didn't know I did. Guess I didn't want to know. It wasn't until I fell in love with Rennie that I realized it." He exhaled strongly, relieved to have finally spoken the words.

"Yeah. I love her. I haven't told her yet, but I will. I just had to talk to you first, though, had to clear my conscience before telling her." He paused a moment, then said, "I made you a promise. I broke it. I wish I hadn't, and I'm sorry. But it's something that can't be changed, something I have to live with. And it's time I forgave myself. I hope you forgive me, too.''

He watched the first fingers of morning steal over the earth like a lover's hand. The sky turned a rosy blue. Tiny creatures of the night scurried past his motionless figure, seeking sanctuary. And still he waited. Finally, with the rising sun came a gentle breeze that ruffled Gideon's hair in passing.

His eyes glistened, but he smiled. "I still love you, honey. Part of me always will. But there's room in my heart for both of you now.

"Rennie's a lot like you, inside, where it counts. But she's different, too, just as the love I feel for her is different. I'm not the same man I was before. And I know now that you're my past. Rennie is my future.''

Gideon leaned over to touch the gravestone one last time, in a final farewell. "Goodbye, Jo.''

He settled his Stetson on his head, pulling it low over his eyes. Then, with a free heart, Gideon headed for home. He never looked back.

Rennie was sitting on the front porch steps, sipping from a cup of black coffee, when Gideon drove up in a swirl of dust, parked and jumped out.

"Good morning," he called out. "You're up early.''

"So are you. I didn't even hear you leave.'' Even though her insides were shaking, she took pride in the fact that she managed that much with at least a semblance of calm.

He strode around the front of the truck, his boots kicking up more dust, and came to sit beside her. His large frame crowded her, and she inched away to give him more room. His eyes creased into a smile. "Got enough of that to share?''

"Um-hm. But it's not very hot. Let me get you a fresh cup." She started to rise, but he stopped her with a strong hand on her arm.

"No, don't bother. I'd rather share yours if you don't mind."

Rennie sank back down onto the steps. "I don't mind."

He took the cup from her and deliberately turned it so that his lips touched the same spot on the rim where hers had been. He took a long swallow, then handed it back to her.

He looked out over the ranch, which was already alive with activity, and asked, almost too casually, "Where are the kids?"

"Still sleeping." She sipped her coffee, telling herself she only imagined it tasted sweeter now. "After everything that happened last night, I decided to let them sleep in for once."

He nodded slowly and said, "That was probably a good idea. I thought you might sleep in, too. That's why I tried not to wake you."

He turned his head suddenly and caught her watching him. His eyes were very green, and she wondered whether he was remembering the night before. He didn't say anything, though, and Rennie wasn't about to ask him.

Instead, she said, "Where did you go so early this morning?"

He gazed down at her for a moment before answering. "I went to the cemetery."

"Oh."

If he hadn't been watching her so carefully he would have missed the slight trembling of her lips before she controlled it. He reached over and brushed her bottom lip with his thumb. She turned her head to avoid his touch, but he caught her chin and brought her back to face him.

"I went for a reason, Rennie. Don't you want to know why?"

"No. I don't think I want to hear this."

"I think you do." He ran one finger under her chin, sending shivers of awareness through her, and tilted her face upward. He studied each feature, taking his time about it, even though each one was already imprinted on his heart. "You are so beautiful," he finally whispered, only a fraction of a second before his mouth sought hers with a tender kiss. When he drew back she stared up at him, her eyes wide and vulnerable.

"Ask me," he said huskily. "Please ask me."

She forced the words out. "Why did you go?"

"To talk to Jo." Rennie closed her eyes against the stab of pain and guilt, but they flew open at his next words. "To tell her I've fallen in love with you, and to say goodbye."

She blinked, then caught her breath as the meaning sank in. "What did you say?"

"I said I love you, Rennie."

She couldn't quite take it in, and she shook her head. "Don't say that if you don't mean it."

"I mean it."

Because she so desperately yearned for it to be true, she wouldn't let herself believe him. Not yet. She searched his face, her eyes begging for the truth. "You're not just saying this because of what I told you last night, are you? I couldn't bear it if you're only saying it out of pity."

"Rennie…" His arms enfolded her, pulling her onto his lap, and his mouth descended for a reverent kiss that left no doubt in her mind. But he wasn't finished. "Does this feel like pity?" he whispered as he claimed her mouth again. Lips clung and withdrew, tongues touching, then dancing aside. He raised his head a fraction of an inch and groaned, "Rennie, I love you."

She melted into his embrace, a believer at last. For the briefest of seconds a tiny voice whispered in her mind that she didn't deserve to be this happy, but she refused to listen. She loved and was loved, and nothing else mattered.

Her head found its home in the hollow between his neck and shoulder, and she let herself revel in the rapid thud of Gideon's heart, the snugness of his arms encircling her, as if he couldn't bear to let her go.

"When did you know you loved me?" she asked eventually, a lover's natural curiosity coming to the fore.

"Last night. Or rather," he amended, "I finally let myself admit it last night. I think I must have loved you ever since I saw you on that ledge with Nicki, so scared and so determined not to let it show. Or maybe it was even earlier. I don't know." He was silent for a moment. "And you?"

"I think it was the night we were stranded on the mountain," she confessed. "But I couldn't admit it, either."

"Why do you think it took us so long?"

"Maybe we weren't ready to hear it."

"Yeah, maybe you're right." He rested his cheek against the top of her head. "But I'm ready to hear it now."

She smiled softly. "I love you, Gideon."

How long they sat there after that, Rennie neither knew nor cared. The sun advanced in the sky, chasing away the last of the early morning shadows. From a dreamy distance she heard a telephone ringing, but she ignored it. Finally it ceased.

But a minute later the front screen door opened with a hesitant squeak, and footsteps skittered across the porch. "Rennie, it's the phone for you."

Gideon released her reluctantly, stealing one last kiss to tide him over, then one more after that before they both turned to face Trina.

"Who is it?" Rennie asked.

"Aunt Emily."

"I wonder what she wants," she murmured to herself as she stood up.

"She's probably calling about tonight." At Rennie's questioning look, he added, "I stopped in town and called her. I wanted some time alone with you, so I asked her if she'd take the children just for tonight."

"Oh." Rennie's slow smile was breathtaking. *Gideon had planned for them to be alone together!* "What did she say?"

"She said yes."

That afternoon Rennie put Andrew down for his nap, then just stood and watched him sleep for a few minutes. Love welled up in her at the sight of him, so like Gideon. He slept the same way, too, with a sort of reckless abandon. She saw the years spreading out in front of her, years of watching Andrew grow into the man his father was. And she saw herself as his mother, holding him, loving him, guiding him, and someday letting him go as all mothers must. He was Johanna's child, but he was hers, too.

In that moment she let go of the grief she'd denied for so long. She would always regret the loss of the children she'd never bear. That sorrow would reside in its own private corner of her heart all her life. But the sharpness of the pain would fade over time. She knew that now. She had the life she'd dreamed of all those years ago, maybe not quite as she'd envisioned, but then again she herself was different from the girl who'd dreamed those dreams.

We all change, Rennie thought. *We all adapt. And we all compromise. Life is never exactly as we plan. We just do the best we can with what we have and try to build a life for ourselves rich in love and loving. That's what Gram tried to teach me, only I was too young to understand.*

I have so much—Gideon's love, Gideon's children. It's enough for one lifetime.

A movement out of the corner of her eye made her turn. Nicki stood in the bedroom doorway, watching her watch Andrew. Rennie motioned for silence, then glided quietly from the room, closing the door behind her.

"Did you need something, Nicki?"

The girl shook her head slightly, but there was something in her expression—wistfulness? sadness?—that made Rennie put her arm around Nicki for a quick hug.

"Then would you like to help me make some brownies? Your dad really liked those mint ones I made last time, so I thought I'd make them again. Trina is coloring, so it'll just be you and me."

Nicki nodded and smiled up at her, and Rennie said, "Come on, then." Arm in arm they moved to the kitchen.

It wasn't until after the brownies were baking that Nicki broached the subject that was on her mind. The pen and paper that were her only means of communication were brought out again, and once more Rennie vowed to herself to find some way to break down the silence barrier.

Nicki wrote quickly, then pushed the pad toward Rennie. *You really love Andrew, don't you?*

"Um-hm. Very much."

And Trina?

"Yes."

Nicki scribbled something, then hesitated before showing it to her. *And me? Do you really love me?*

Rennie nodded. "Yes, Nicki. I really do," she said softly. "I hope someday you'll believe that."

Nicki's brow furrowed and she bit the end of the pen, then wrote, *Would you still love me if I did something really bad?*

Rennie raised her eyes from the paper. Nicki was watching her anxiously. "Of course, Nicki," she said, reaching over to clasp the girl's hand. "I would love you no matter what you did. And so would your dad. It might make us sad, but we would never stop loving you."

Despite the sincerity in Rennie's voice, Nicki didn't look convinced. *What about my Mama? Would she still love me?*

"Oh, sweetie, of course she would. There's nothing you could do that was so bad your mother couldn't forgive you." Rennie felt herself on the verge of discovery. There was something here that she couldn't quite put her finger on, something terrible, in Nicki's mind at least, behind all these questions. She held her breath, hoping against hope that Nicki's next question would reveal something more.

Nicki sat lost in thought for a while. Finally she pulled the pad of paper back and wrote, then turned it for Rennie to see. *I'm sorry I made you cry last night.*

"You didn't, sweetie. It was me. Just something I had to deal with. I didn't know it would hurt so much to be reminded about never having children of my own." She smiled reassuringly. "But I'm okay now. Really I am. Please don't worry about me."

Nicki's hand was still for a moment, then she wrote, *Is that why you love us? Because you can't have children of your own?*

"That's part of it," she admitted, refusing the temptation to hedge the truth. "And part of it is because I love your father so much and you're his children. But Nicki—" she squeezed the girl's hand "—every day I love you more and more because of who you are, inside."

The timer on the oven buzzed. Rennie leaned over and kissed Nicki's cheek before rising. She took out the brownies and set them on the counter to cool. She sniffed appreciatively.

"Don't those smell good?" She flashed Nicki a smile,

and the girl nodded eagerly. "Your father's going to love them."

The chocolaty aroma brought Trina running. "Mmmm! Brownies! Can I have one?"

Rennie shook her head. "Not this time. These are for tonight." She pulled down the cookie jar. "But you can have some of the peanut butter cookies we made yesterday."

Trina pouted, but only for a minute, and Rennie almost laughed at how eagerly she reached for the cookie jar. Soon both girls were sitting at the table, munching happily and sipping at the milk Rennie had given them. Rennie began the topping for the brownies.

"Guess what." she said absently, frowning over the recipe, then measuring in the peppermint extract. "Aunt Emily has invited you to sleep over tonight at her house. She's going to rent that new video you were asking about last week and let you stay up late to watch it. Doesn't that sound like fun?"

The silence that greeted her words made her swing around. The apprehensive look on both faces wiped the smile from Rennie's. She dropped the mixing spoon. "Sweeties, what's wrong?"

Tears trembled in Trina's eyes. "Will you be here when we get back?"

Then Rennie understood. To both girls, and probably Andrew as well, staying with Emily was equated with loss—their mother, all the housekeepers, even their father. Why hadn't she and Gideon thought of that?

She moved to the table and crouched by Trina's chair. "Do you want me to be here?" Trina nodded. Rennie turned and asked the same question of Nicki, who hesitated only a second before nodding also. "I'm never going to leave you," she said huskily. "Never. And when you get back, I'll be right here, waiting for you. You'll see."

"Promise?" Trina threw her arms around Rennie's neck and Nicki followed suit. She hugged them close.

"I promise."

That evening Rennie and Gideon stood arm in arm by the front porch, waving and watching the taillights of Emily's station wagon recede from view. When they finally disappeared, he turned to her, pulling her fully into the circle of his arms.

"Alone at last," he said with a playful growl.

She laughed a little. "I miss them already."

"Then we'll just have to see what we can do to take your mind off them." He waggled his eyebrows at her.

"Oh?" She drew that question out and arched a brow at him. "What did you have in mind, cowboy?"

This time he laughed. "It's been so long since I've had a night free like this, I'm not sure. We could go into Sheridan, take in a movie, or check out the bars for a live band and do a little foot-stomping. It's up to you."

Rennie glided one finger down the side of his face and smiled at the shiver that ran through his body. "I'd rather just stay home."

So would he, but she deserved to be romanced. "Is that what you really want?" he asked softly.

"More than anything."

"Me, too."

Their lips met briefly, then he swung her into his arms and carried her inside.

Chapter 15

The house was unnaturally silent without the children. Rennie was almost tempted to whisper, it was so quiet.

"You can put me down now," she told Gideon.

"Not a chance, Mrs. Lowell. I'm carrying you over the threshold."

"You already did."

"Uh-uh. The front door doesn't count." He flicked off the light in the living room with his elbow. "It's the bedroom door that matters."

"Is that so?"

"Um-hm."

"How come I never heard that one before?"

His teeth flashed white in the semidarkness as he carried her down the hall. "You've been living in California too long."

"What's that supposed to mean?"

"You had to come all the way to Wyoming to find a man, didn't you?"

She gasped, then laughed. "I think you just slandered an entire state."

He shouldered open the door to their bedroom. "Yeah, well, let 'em sue me." He put her down carefully, then cupped her cheek and turned her face upward for his kiss. Long seconds later, he whispered seriously, "I'm just glad you came here, whatever the reason."

"There are millions of men in California," she whispered back. "Good men. Real men. But none of them were you."

Irresistibly drawn, their lips met again in a kiss that left both of them breathless and hungry for each other. Gideon broke away first.

"Damn." He adjusted the fit of his jeans. "I wasn't going to start anything just yet." His gaze was tender, rueful. "But when I'm around you I don't think. I feel. And you feel too damn good in my arms."

"That's the nicest compliment you've ever given me." Rennie moved to embrace him, but he backed off.

"I need a shower," he said.

"You always say that," she teased gently, sliding her arms around his waist despite his halfhearted attempt to elude her.

"Because it's true."

She buried her face against his shoulder and breathed deeply. "You smell the way a man should at the end of the day," she said dreamily. "I like it."

He chuckled. "I smell like horses and sheep."

"With a touch of leather and soap thrown in."

"I'd prefer a touch more soap and a lot less of all the rest. Come on. I'll let you scrub my back."

She tossed her head. "Oh, now I get it. You just want me along to do all the work."

"I have to save my strength." He nipped at her lower lip. "For later." His hand closed around hers and he would have led her into the bathroom, but she pulled back as she remembered something.

"Wait. I have an idea." At his quizzical look she gave him a slow, seductive smile that started smoldering fires burning inside him. "Trust me. You'll love it." She touched the base of his throat exposed by his open cotton work shirt, then slid her fingers slowly down to his belt buckle. "Stay here."

She left him standing in the middle of the room, and he watched as she went to the dresser, pulling something out of one of the drawers, shielding it from view with her body. She closed the bathroom door, and he heard the water running in the tub for what seemed like a long time. The water finally stopped and the door opened.

Rennie stood in the doorway. Her dark curls were artlessly tousled, making him think of mornings after, and she was wearing the peignoir from their honeymoon and nothing else.

The smoldering fires she'd ignited earlier burst into flames. The peignoir hid nothing. It enhanced. It clung to her slender form at breast, hip and thigh the way his hands wanted to do. She looked soft and sexy and so damned beautiful his body reacted with a surge of desire that had him shaking.

She walked toward him. Walked? No, what she was doing couldn't be called anything as mundane as walking. She sauntered, the filmy fabric of her robe floating around her. When she finally reached him, she tilted her head and gave him a saucy, sexy smile.

"You look like you could use a bath, cowboy." She slowly unbuttoned his shirt all the way down and pulled it out of his jeans.

"Yeah." Was that his voice, that strangled sound?

She slipped the shirt off and let it fall to the floor. Her

fingers played over his bare chest, teasing, tormenting, working their way downward. "We've got two kinds of baths in this hotel," she drawled, unbuckling his belt and drawing it out of the belt loops, taking her sweet time about it. "A regular bath is seventy-five cents." The belt dropped from her hands. "A French bath is two dollars."

The connection clicked, and a hint of a smile played over his lips. His right hand slid into his jeans pocket and came out empty. So did his left one. "Sorry, ma'am," he said with a woeful expression. "I'd purely love one of those French baths you're offerin', but I'm flat broke."

She stepped back and eyed him up and down. "Are you good for it?"

"Oh, I'm good for it, ma'am," he said, the glint in his eyes leaving no doubt as to the double meaning intended.

Her response was a throaty laugh that sent fire surging through his veins. Then slender fingers grazed his fly and his already uncomfortable jeans grew impossibly tight.

"Rennie…"

When she popped open the top button of his jeans he thought the rest of the buttons would pop open as well. And when she rubbed her knuckles back and forth against the hardness beneath the soft denim, he learned a whole new definition for the word *ache*.

Just when he thought he couldn't take any more, she swirled away in a froth of fabric and lace and sauntered toward the bathroom, tossing him a come-hither look over her shoulder that sizzled his toes.

"Why don't you come on back, cowboy."

She never made it to the door. Gideon caught her before she took another step, lifting her high in his arms. She squealed in surprise.

"What are you doing? This isn't the way it goes."

"You have your fantasies," he told her with a wolfish smile. "I have mine."

He caught her mouth with his, capturing and conquering her tongue, drawing the willing prisoner into the moist cavern of his mouth. She twined her arms around his neck and gave herself up to his kiss.

He carried her into the bathroom, maneuvering through the door with difficulty because he refused to release her passionate mouth. Then he lowered her slowly, letting her body slide down his. They stood there for an endless moment, wrapped in each other's arms, caught up in the fantasy, surrounded by their love.

When he finally let her go she swayed, unable to stand on her own. She leaned toward him, steadying herself against the hard planes of his body. Her scantily covered bosom rose and fell, the soft swells of her breasts tormenting him as they brushed his chest with each breath.

Eventually she regained enough control to continue. Her hands glided down to the front of his jeans, and fumbled just a bit as she unbuttoned the remaining buttons on his fly. Gideon thought he'd die of frustration by the time she got them all undone, but he wasn't about to interfere.

She slid urgent hands inside the waistbands of both jeans and briefs and began skimming them off together. That's when he stopped her.

"I'd better take my boots off first, don't you think?"

She laughed softly. "I guess I'm not that good at this." With obvious regret she removed her hands, but not until they'd stolen one last caress.

He braced himself against the doorframe and pulled off his boots in record time, tossing them into the bedroom. "You're better than you think," he said as he stripped off his clothes, then straightened to his full height. Her admiring gaze affected him like a physical touch, and his body responded wildly. "But now it's my turn."

He tugged at one end of the single bow tying Rennie's diaphanous wrapper and drew it from her body, draping it over the towel bar. He grasped her slender waist and pulled her close, noting the delicate pink flags coloring her cheeks when their naked bodies brushed.

"Every time I think I know you, you surprise me," he whispered, loving everything about her—from shy blushes to sexy fantasies. A sudden tightness in his chest made breathing difficult. "Just who are you, Rennie, really?"

Her eyes never leaving his, she took his hand and placed it over her rapidly beating heart, a heart that he knew beat for him alone. "I'm the woman who loves you."

He closed his eyes and swallowed. "And I love you so damned much it scares me. If I lost you..."

"You're never going to lose me, Gideon. Never." She strained against him, offering her love and herself as one.

His fingers slid through her hair, anchoring her head in place for a kiss, but she wasn't going anywhere he didn't go. She pressed her body all along his, trembling slightly, but Gideon knew it was from desire, not fear.

"Wrap your legs around me," he urged, lifting her with powerful arms.

She did as he commanded, the soft flesh of her thighs gripping his hips with surprising strength. He groaned, caught her lips for one more kiss, then stepped into the oversize tub and sat down. Water sloshed against the sides of the tub in a tidal wave, some splashing onto the floor. Neither cared. The water lapped at their heated bodies, an elemental, sensual caress, and they both shivered.

Fantasy gave way to reality, the reality of lips and hands and overflowing hearts. They bathed each other slowly, building the anticipation to fever pitch, testing the limits of their endurance.

Gideon was the first to break. "No more," he said, catching her wrists and dragging her hands away, bringing them up to his face. "Not this way. Not this time." He pressed a kiss into each open palm, then let her go.

He rose, water streaming from his magnificently aroused body, and stepped out of the tub. "Stay there," he told her, quickly drying himself off. Then he helped her from the tub and dried her carefully. The slight roughness of the towel made her vibrantly aware of every inch of skin it touched, and even places where it didn't. Her hair was damp where she had lain against him at one point, and he rubbed it dry as well. Afterward, she would have wrapped the towel around herself, but he took it away from her.

"The scars don't matter, Rennie. Don't hide from me. Please."

She met his gaze and knew there was no reason to. Not anymore. "I won't. Never again."

He carried her into the bedroom. He drew back the covers and laid her on the bed, then just knelt beside her for a moment, gazing down at her with such undisguised love and desire that Rennie's heart nearly burst. She held out her arms to him mutely, and he came down into her embrace.

Despite the height of their mutual arousal, or perhaps even because of it, they weren't in any hurry. This wasn't sex, it was love, and they both wanted to savor the difference. This was the true beginning of their marriage, and everything that had gone before faded into insignificance.

In planning this night Rennie had put clean sheets on their bed, and the fresh-scented, fine linen was soft and cool beneath them. Gideon stretched out beside her, propped up on one arm, two fingers tracing a pattern from her shoulders to her sensitive breasts.

"You are so beautiful, Rennie. Just like you were that first night you came to me. I've never forgotten."

Her heart skipped a beat, then sped up. "I wanted to be beautiful—for you."

"You were. Like something out of a dream, my dream. When I'm ninety I'll still be able to close my eyes and see you standing in that doorway, so beautiful you took my breath away."

His hand sought and found one rosy-tipped peak. His fingers circled it, drawing shudders of pleasure from Rennie and sending hot pulses through his manhood.

She shifted onto her side so her hand could reach him and inflict the same exquisite torture he was inflicting on her. Her fingers discovered the flat disk of his nipple, tracing the nubby outer ring, then moving toward the tiny center.

"I wanted you so much that night," she said, her voice as soft as velvet. "I was so nervous I was shaking, but I wanted you. Just like I want you now."

"God, I love you, Rennie. Now and always."

"Oh, Gideon." She kissed him, and it was like throwing gasoline on burning coals. Their mouths clung, as did their hands, and they moved restlessly closer, legs tangling.

The waiting, the anticipating, was over. He parted her legs and drew them up on either side of his hips, settling within the cradle they created. He entered her with a sure thrust, making her gasp and quiver with intense pleasure.

He filled her, just as she'd filled him. He'd been so empty, so alone, and now she stood within that empty place inside him, filling him with so much love he didn't know how to tell her. So he showed her.

He found her mouth with his, tasting the sweetness that was like no other. Then he ducked his head in search of more unique flavors, rasping his tongue across the hardened tips of her breasts, loving the way she shuddered and tightened around him.

His hips began a primeval rhythm, stroking in and out of her clinging warmth, alternating between shallow and deep. He told himself to be gentle, to go slow, but she wouldn't let him. She took him, all of him, inside her, locking her ankles around his thighs and urging him on with soft moans and clutching hands.

He had no control left. Again and again he thrust his surging body into her eager depths, thinking each stroke *must* be the last, but unable to govern his body's continued plunges toward completion. And then he couldn't think at all, just feel. He was so hard, achingly hard, and her softness measured him, swallowed him, engulfed him.

The end came swiftly. Rennie stiffened beneath him, arching upward and crying his name, her body's involuntary pulsations drawing him in deeper. His muscles clenched for one last lunge. Embedding himself in her throbbing, welcoming heat, he surrendered the essence of life.

Trembling, drained of almost all strength, he used the last of it to lower his body on hers, careful not to crush her. He shifted slightly, removing some of his weight, but still staking a primitive claim. Peace invaded him, the aftermath of the storm that had raged only a moment before. He brushed his lips against the tantalizing softness of her throat, then pillowed his head in the hollow between her arm and her breast.

He sighed, a deep, contented sound, curled his arm around her waist and gently nuzzled the velvet peak so near to him. As he drifted into sleep, he whispered the thought uppermost in his mind.

"I love you, Rennie."

Rennie lay awake, exulting in the weight of Gideon's

body on hers. The warmth of his breath against her breast sent shivers of aftershocks throughout her system.

That he'd fallen asleep so quickly didn't bother her. He'd already given her more than she'd ever imagined. His control had deserted him for the first time in all their times together, proving beyond words his need for her, as great as her need for him.

She caressed him gently, savoring the precious knowledge that he loved her, and envisioning the future they would build, together.

Then her conscience tugged at her heart, reminding her that any life she built with Gideon was based on a lie. A silent lie, but a lie, nevertheless. *I can only hurt him by confessing the truth,* she pleaded with that still, small inner voice. *He loves me now, and he's happy. Isn't that what matters?*

But it took a long time to convince herself.

Gideon woke from a light, dreamless sleep, in the arms of the woman he loved.

"You're awake." The voice was Rennie's, but the tone was one he'd never heard from her before. It hinted at all sorts of wonderful, highly pleasurable things, and held a touch of possessiveness that was akin to the way he felt about her. *Mine,* it seemed to say, an emotion he'd become very familiar with recently.

He stretched indolently. "How long have I been asleep?"

"About an hour."

"Damn." But the word was uttered without heat. "I had big plans for tonight, and none of them included sleeping."

Rennie peered at the clock on the nightstand. "It's still early, only nine-thirty."

"Good." He yawned and stretched again, then rolled onto his back, pulling her to sprawl on top of him. "So tell me,'' he said with a soft, teasing drawl, ''any more fantasies you'd like to try out?''

She chuckled deep in her throat, cuddling against him. ''This is the best one I can think of,'' she told him, smiling but serious. She pressed a quick kiss against his shoulder. ''Just being here with you, knowing you love me.''

His throat ached suddenly, and his voice turned husky. ''I do, you know. I haven't had a lot of practice saying it lately, but give me time. I'll get better.''

She rubbed her cheek against the downy hair covering his chest and snuggled closer. ''You've done all right so far.'' She reached around behind her and grabbed a corner of the top sheet, drawing it over them.

''Cold?''

''Just a little.''

''I'll warm you up.''

His hands trailed down her back, leaving tingling warmth in their wake. He stopped when he reached her buttocks, cupping them in his big hands and pulling her flush with his body. He was already semiaroused, and she angled one leg to allow him to fit better at the juncture of her thighs.

''Mmm. I like that,'' he rumbled.

''Me, too.''

''Yeah?''

''Yeah.''

''What else do you like?''

She raised her head and gazed at him, her heart in her eyes. ''Everything you do to me.''

That earned her a kiss. He lifted her so he could reach her mouth, then lingered over it. When he finally let her go, his hands slipped down to tease the sides of her breasts. She made a breathy little sound, and he felt her nipples tighten. His sex responded predictably, swelling and surging upward.

"Open for me," he whispered, and when she did he slid inside. Her body closed around him, and he groaned in satisfaction.

She braced herself and pushed downward, forcing him deeper, and deeper still, until he was buried to the hilt. She moaned, rocking a little, and moaned again.

"Hold still," he told her, wedging a hand between their bodies. His fingers found her, stroking through the folds of her body and caressing the tiny nub of flesh there. She tensed and arched away from the unbearably arousing touch, but he caught her with his other hand and held her firmly in place.

"Don't fight it," he whispered against her ear. "Let it go."

She caught her breath on his name and did just that, her head thrown back, her body exploding with mindless pleasure. She sank down on his chest, gulping air into her depleted lungs. She lay there for several minutes, unable to move. When she finally recovered, she propped herself up to look at him. She was a little shocked at the swiftness of it all—from arousal to satisfaction had taken only moments. She searched his face and asked, "Why did you do that?"

He gave her a very satisfied, very male smile. "It was one of *my* fantasies."

"But you didn't..." She licked her dry lips.

"Yeah. I know." He thrust his hips upward, pressing his swollen flesh deep inside her, then rolled them both over. "Now it's my turn."

Afterward they both dozed, their bodies one lump beneath the covers. Finally Rennie stirred inside the cocoon of warmth they'd created. Awake already, Gideon shifted to accommodate her.

"What time is it?" she mumbled.

"After midnight." He carefully brushed her hair away from her face and drew her into the curve of his arm. She nestled there for a few moments, her eyes closed, then smiled and sighed. It was an exhausted but contented sound.

Her eyes still closed, she asked, "How long have you been awake?"

"A few minutes."

She yawned, then swallowed dryly. "I'm thirsty." She yawned again and snuggled closer to Gideon, almost dozing off once again.

"Hey. Wake up." He shook her gently. "Rennie, come on. Wake up."

"I'm awake." She yawned a third time.

He laughed and sat up, bringing her with him. His lips grazed hers. "Come on, sweetheart. You're thirsty and I'm starving. Let's go raid the kitchen."

"Okay." She slipped out of his arms and plopped back onto the pillows.

He laughed again, and the mattress sagged as he moved to the side of the bed. That was the last Rennie knew before the mattress dipped beneath his weight once more.

Gideon punched up his pillow and settled back against the headboard, then lifted her boneless body and propped her against his shoulder. He reached for something and held it to her lips. "Drink."

She obeyed, and cold milk slid down her throat. She shivered and her eyes flew open, awake at last. She shivered again and pushed the glass away. She frowned at him.

He set the glass on the nightstand, then grabbed a fistful of covers and pulled them up, tucking them under her arms. Satisfied, he picked up the pan of mint brownies she and Nicki had made that afternoon and held it out to her. "Brownie?" She shook her head. "I hope you don't mind if I help myself, then," he said, suiting his actions to his words.

Still dazed from sleep, she silently watched him eat three brownies in quick succession, washing them down with gulps of milk. "Sure you don't want one?" he asked after the third brownie had disappeared.

She shook her head again, watching as he licked chocolate mint frosting from his fingers, then finished the last of the milk. She still hadn't said anything when he moved the brownie pan and the glass to the nightstand.

He tilted her chin up with one slightly sticky finger for a chocolate-and-peppermint-flavored kiss. "I forgot how hard it is to wake you up in the middle of the night," he said when he was done.

Nothing made much sense to her after such a short amount of sleep, and she gave him a quizzical look.

"Remember when we were stranded in the mountains by the rain," he reminded her, "and I was supposed to wake you for the second-shift fire watch?" She nodded, the memory slowly coming back to her. "You did the same thing you did tonight, told me you were awake, then went back to sleep."

"I remember," she said, smiling a little now.

He slid down beneath the covers, taking her with him. Their arms went around each other. "It's one of the little things I love about you," he said, cuddling her close.

"Really?"

"Yeah."

"Tell me more."

He laughed. "Let me see. I love the way you blush when I tease you about sex." He whispered something scandalously earthy, and she blushed on cue and hid her face. "God, I do love that."

"What else?" she said from the depths of his shoulder.

"Well, it's kind of selfish, I know, but I love the way you always try to please me in small ways."

"You mean, like baking mint brownies because they're your favorite?"

"That's exactly what I mean." He twined his fingers with hers.

"I just want you to be happy."

"I am. You make me happy, Rennie, just by being here."

"I'm glad."

He was silent for a moment, then said softly, "But I guess the thing I love the most is the way you've taught me to believe in love again." In the privacy of their bedroom, in the middle of the night, he could say these things to her. "After I lost Jo I built a wall around my heart. I didn't want to love you," he confessed. "I wanted to stay safe behind that wall. But you tore it down, and showed me that the only thing worse than loving and losing is not loving at all. I couldn't help loving you, Rennie. I just wanted you to know."

"Oh, Gideon." She gave him a misty smile. "I couldn't help loving you, either." She laid her hand over his thudding heart and kissed him.

Rennie woke early the next morning, feeling well and truly loved. Filled with unusual energy, she still lay beside Gideon for a while, watching him sleep the same way she'd watched Andrew sleep the day before.

Finally she touched her fingers to her lips and transferred the kiss to his cheek. She slipped from the bed, careful not to waken him, and padded barefoot to the bathroom. She winced a little and thought about taking a bath to ease her various aches, but decided she'd shower in the bath off the kitchen, instead. And she'd wait until Gideon was awake before cleaning up the mess they'd left in this bathroom the night before.

She grabbed her nightshirt from behind the bathroom door and pulled it over her head. She might have come a long way in overcoming her physical shyness around her husband last night, but she wasn't the type to go traipsing naked through the house, even if they were alone.

She grabbed her toothbrush, crept into the bedroom for her comb and a pair of clean undies from the dresser, then crept out and made her way toward the kitchen.

Fifteen minutes later, showered, teeth brushed, and with her freshly washed hair curling damply around her face, she reentered the kitchen with a sense of purpose. Gideon would be famished when he woke, and she wanted to have breakfast ready for him. Humming softly, she ground coffee beans and started a pot of coffee, then gathered the ingredients for buttermilk pancakes, one of his favorites. She mixed the batter in a squat pitcher, and put it to one side. Then she set the table for two, using the good china for a change.

She smiled to herself as she made a fresh pitcher of apple juice, another of Gideon's favorites, and set it in the refrigerator to chill. At the same time she took out the maple syrup and set it on the table, remembering his words of the night before. *"...I love the way you always try to please me in small ways...."*

It was true, and she enjoyed doing it. Even such a simple thing as making his favorite breakfast gave her pleasure, and if it meant she was hopelessly old-fashioned in that respect, well, that was all right with her.

But was it really old-fashioned? Or was it that love, true love, took more pleasure in the giving than the receiving?

"Well, there'll be plenty of giving *and* receiving now,"

she said out loud, hugging the words to her heart. "Gideon loves me. *He really loves me.*"

With nothing left to do, she poured herself a cup of coffee and leaned against the kitchen counter to drink it. And that's when the tiny, niggling doubt crept back into her mind.

But would he love you if he knew the truth? Would he love you if he knew who you really are? He loves Rennie. Would he, could he, love Francesca Renee?

A loud rapping at the front door echoed through the house, startling her out of her uneasy reverie. Who could be dropping by this early on a Sunday morning? She set down her coffee cup, spilling it in her haste, and hurried into the living room, hoping to quiet whoever it was before they woke Gideon. She swung the door open, ready to give the untimely visitor a piece of her mind. But instead, her mouth fell open in astonishment.

How could it be? There stood *Gideon*, his hand raised to knock once more.

Chapter 16

But Gideon's asleep! How could he...

Then she noticed the subtle differences. Only someone who was intimately familiar with Gideon would see that his hair was just a shade more golden than this man's, and his body just a fraction deeper through the chest and shoulders. And the tiny network of lines etched around Gideon's eyes from squinting into the sun were missing.

There was only one person this could be, however, and she named him. "You must be Caleb. I'm Rennie. Gideon's wife." She pushed the screen door open, offering him her hand and a tentative smile. "Won't you come in?"

While she'd been observing him, he'd been doing the same to her. "I figured you must be the new bride." His tone was noncommittal, as if he were reserving judgment. He shook her hand briefly. "Where's Gideon?"

"He's still asleep," she blurted out, then felt herself flushing as if Caleb knew what she and Gideon had been doing the night before.

Caleb eyed her again, and she could almost see him revising his opinion of her, but whether that was good or bad, heaven only knew. Before he could say anything, a strong, bare arm came around her waist.

"I'm awake now," Gideon told her unnecessarily, dropping a kiss on her upturned face. Then he looked at Caleb and grinned. "You son of a gun. Why didn't you warn us you were coming?" He grasped Caleb's out-thrust hand, shook it, then clapped his brother on the back. "Damn, it's good to see you. Come on in."

Caleb's grin matched Gideon's as the two men moved into the living room. "It's good to see you, too. Hope I didn't come at a bad time, but I didn't know until yesterday I was even going to be in the area. I had a last-minute charter flight to Casper, and I figured what the hell, I might as well come on up the rest of the way, see you and meet your new wife."

Gideon's eyes softened with love and pride when Caleb mentioned the word *wife*. He turned and drew her into the curve of his arm. "I'm glad you did. This is Rennie," he said. "Rennie, meet my brother, Caleb."

"We've already sort of met."

"Yeah." Caleb grinned wickedly. "I couldn't believe it when your blushing bride said you were still in bed." His dancing eyes took in Rennie's bare legs beneath her T-shirt, and the jeans Gideon had pulled on so hastily he hadn't finished buttoning them. Caleb made a chiding sound with his tongue. "And on a Sunday morning, too."

"Hey, none of that." Gideon faked a punch at his brother. "You're embarrassing Rennie."

"Sorry." But he didn't look the least bit repentant. He continued to grin, looking so much like Gideon at his lighthearted, teasing best that Rennie couldn't be annoyed, despite her embarrassment.

"It's okay." She glanced up at Gideon. "There's a fresh pot of coffee in the kitchen. Why don't the two of you go ahead and help yourselves while I get dressed."

Gideon held her close for a second. "Don't be long," he murmured for her ears alone before he released her.

Both men watched her slender figure retreat down the hall toward the master bedroom. When the door closed behind her, Caleb darted a sharp look at his brother, a tiny frown forming. "She looks sort of familiar. Do I know her?"

Gideon shook his head. "I don't see how. She's not from around here. Maybe she reminds you of someone."

"Maybe." Caleb shrugged it off and followed Gideon into the kitchen.

Gideon hesitated for only a moment when he saw the romantic breakfast setting Rennie had arranged for the two of them. He pushed the regret aside, knowing there would be other mornings for them. How often did he get the chance to see his brother?

He poured coffee into two large mugs and handed one to Caleb. "So when did you get in?"

"Last night." Caleb leaned against the counter and took a sip of coffee, testing it, then made a sound of pleasure and drank deeply. "I was planning to call you for a lift, but I ran into Rory Daniels. Remember him?" Gideon nodded. "He's married now, has a little place outside Sheridan. He offered to put me up for the night, and he lent me his old pickup truck this morning. I have to bring it back this evening, but I've got to be in Casper tomorrow afternoon, anyway, to pick up my charter, so it works out all right."

"So soon? You just got here."

"Yeah, well, you know how it is. Charter flights aren't so plentiful these days that I can afford to pass up whatever business does come my way."

"You're not in trouble, are you? I have some money in the bank. It's not much, but you're welcome to it."

"No. Thanks, anyway. I'm doing all right. It's just that the bank doesn't own me yet, and I'd like to keep it that way. But thanks for the offer."

"Any time. I mean that."

"I know. And that goes for me, too."

The two men shared a look of brotherly affection and understanding that transcended time and distance. They drank their coffee in silence, savoring the strong bond between them as they savored the strong brew.

"I got your letter a while back," Caleb said finally. "Sorry I didn't make it to the wedding, but I was running a charter down to Mexico and I didn't get your message or your letter until it was too late."

"It's okay. I understand."

"I would have been here if I could, you know that."

"Yeah. I know."

Caleb was silent for a moment, then said diffidently, "I know it's none of my business, but I sort of got the impression from your letter that this was an 'arranged' marriage."

"Yeah."

"And Rory Daniels told me Rennie answered your ad for a wife. Is that true, too?"

How long ago that seemed. "Yeah. But things have changed since then."

"Seems to me you're in love with her." The statement was almost a challenge.

"Yeah. I am." A tinge of wonder colored his next words. "And she loves me."

"I'm glad. You deserve it after everything that's happened."

Rennie bustled into the kitchen wearing jeans and a

lavender T-shirt sporting the words It's Better in the Big-horns. The two men turned at the interruption.

"I made up the bed in the spare bedroom," she said, smiling at Caleb. "How long can you stay with us?"

"I have to leave this evening, I'm afraid."

"Oh, no." She glanced at Gideon to see how he would take this news, but he only smiled ruefully and shook his head.

"He already told me."

"I knew this visit would have to be short, but I did want to meet you, Rennie," Caleb said. "And I wanted to see my nieces and nephew. Not to mention this guy here," he added, indicating Gideon. "It's been too long." His brows drew together. "Speaking of your kids, I would've thought they'd be up by now."

"They're not here," Rennie said. Delicate color surged into her cheeks as she remembered why. "They spent the night with their aunt, but she'll be bringing them home after church."

"Emily? Jo's sister, Emily?" He slanted a look at his brother, and when Gideon nodded Caleb said, "Last time I saw her was at the funeral." He stopped awkwardly, suddenly remembering Rennie's presence and realizing how sensitive this subject was for both his listeners. "Sorry. I wasn't thinking."

"It's all right, Cal," Gideon assured him, putting down his coffee cup and stepping to Rennie's side, smiling down at her. "Rennie and I have talked about Jo before." He glanced back at Caleb. "It's not a problem for us."

Caleb's gaze moved from Gideon to Rennie, then back to Gideon, as if seeking the truth behind his brother's statement. Then he relaxed a little and said seriously, "I'm glad to hear it." He stared into his coffee cup for a moment, then turned and tossed the dregs into the sink.

The awkward moment passed, and Gideon set his coffee cup on the counter. "Well, I've got chores to see to. You can help me, Cal." He laughed at the expression of mock horror on Caleb's face. "Come on, Cal. It's not that bad. Give me a minute to get some clothes on, and then I'll give you the nickel tour. You can think up excuses not to help me while I'm gone."

The kitchen seemed empty once Gideon left it. For want of anything else to do, Rennie busied herself with setting a third place at the table. That done, she glanced hesitantly at Caleb. For the first time, he smiled at her without reservation.

"You've been good for him," he said softly. "Anybody can see that."

"I'm glad you think so."

"My brother is a very lucky man."

Rennie shook her head and opened the refrigerator, taking out the juice pitcher. "I'm the lucky one."

"I don't think so. I know what he went through when Johanna died. I never thought he'd fall in love again, never thought he'd open himself up to that kind of vulnerability again, but he has. You must be a very special woman to have gotten through to him."

She put down the pitcher. "I loved him," she said simply. "That's all."

"You loved him." Caleb's voice held a strange bitterness. "You say that like it's nothing, Rennie. Don't you know that it's everything?"

They stared at each other for a moment, then Caleb muttered an oath and strode from the room. Rennie watched him go, wondering what had caused his sudden outburst.

The murmur of deep voices from the living room was followed by the opening and closing of the front door, and she knew the two brothers had gone out. They'd be back soon, though, and they'd be ready for breakfast. If Caleb's appetite was anything like Gideon's, she'd need a double batch of everything just to keep pace. She pulled out the flour, then stopped abruptly, realizing her hands were shaking.

Delayed reaction. That's all it was, she told herself sternly. Delayed reaction to the mention of Johanna's death so soon after she'd been thinking about her own involvement in it, and how Gideon would feel if he knew. And Caleb's reminder about what Gideon had suffered after Jo died certainly hadn't helped any.

As she had so many times before, Rennie silenced her guilty conscience, then started on the pancakes. Fifteen minutes later the men walked through the kitchen door, laughing.

"I can't believe you fell for that," Caleb said, his good humor obviously restored.

"Fell for what?" Rennie slid warm stacks of buttermilk pancakes onto plates and set them on the table. Gideon caught her as she turned and dropped a kiss on her cheek. He must have taken the time to shave when he'd gone to dress, she thought distractedly, because the golden stubble of beard was gone. "Fell for what?" she repeated as he went to wash his hands at the kitchen sink.

"Gideon was telling me about your imaginary pig, Squeaker," Caleb said as he joined his brother at the sink. He elbowed Gideon. "Talk about gullible. I would have seen through that story in a minute."

"Hey," Gideon protested, wiping his wet hands on a towel, "I'm not gullible. If you'd heard Rennie tell that story you'd have believed it, too. Nobody can tell a more believable tale than Rennie. Nobody."

"Guess it's a good thing she doesn't have any dark secrets, then," Caleb teased. "Otherwise you'd be in a world of hurt."

Rennie froze, but neither man saw it. Gideon came over to where she was standing and put his arms around her, drawing her flush against his body. "There aren't any secrets between us," he said, softly, warmly. "Not anymore." He kissed her gently, his eyes full of love and contentment. And trust.

It was the trust in his eyes that shredded her heart. She almost told him then, guilt fresh on her conscience. Only Caleb's presence stopped her. She couldn't do that to Gideon, couldn't hurt him in front of witnesses. He had such faith in her. When she told him, *if* she told him, it would have to be in private, where the only witness to her betrayal of his trust would be her.

So instead of blurting out the truth or bursting into tears, choices denied her, she pasted a smile on her face. "Breakfast is getting cold," she said, sliding out of her husband's embrace. "Better sit down and get started."

She moved to the stove and turned up the fire under the griddle, then poured out more circles of pancake batter on it. Her hands trembled, but she completed the task, knowing she had to have *something* to keep her busy or else she'd break down and confess all, despite her resolve. It took everything she had to maintain a semblance of calm.

It was amazing what the human body could do when pushed to the limit. When survival was at stake, people had been known to lift objects many times their weight, perform feats of tremendous courage, face certain death without flinching.

Only the thought of survival kept Rennie going through that breakfast. She sat at the table with the two men, responding appropriately when spoken to, and pretending to eat, when all the while she was secretly considering and discarding a dozen approaches to telling Gideon the truth.

Caught up in their discussion of old times and filling each other in on what was happening in their lives now, neither Gideon nor Caleb realized how far removed Rennie was from them, lost in her own thoughts.

Breakfast was long finished when Caleb laughed at something Gideon said, and added, "Knowing you, you'll probably offer too much."

"I don't think so." Amused, Gideon leaned lazily back in his chair. "And in any case, you probably don't remember the first thing about what makes good grazing land."

"That sounds like a challenge to me." Caleb's eyes were sparkling. "I say we ride over there and look at it. Then we'll see who's right."

"You're on. Want to come with us, Rennie?"

The sound of her name jolted her, and she raised questioning eyes. "I'm sorry, I wasn't paying attention. What did you say?"

"Caleb and I are going to take a look at the piece of land I'm thinking about buying. Do you want to come with us?"

"What land?"

"Haven't you heard anything we've said in the past five minutes?" She shook her head. "Remember I told you last week Walter Houseman was retiring and selling out?"

She thought a moment. "Yes."

"I'm thinking about making him an offer for that piece of land adjacent to ours. Caleb and I are riding over to look at it. Want to come?"

"I'd better not." If things had been different, she would have loved to go with them, but she had two very good reasons for staying behind. She only voiced one of them. "Emily will be bringing the children home soon, and I promised them I'd be here when they got back." She looked at Gideon, her heart in her eyes. "It's important that I be here, just as I promised, especially for Nicki and Trina."

"I understand. Want me to stay with you?"

"We don't have to go, Rennie," Caleb interjected. "It was just an idea."

"No, you go on," she said, looking from one to the other. "Caleb's only going to be here today, so you won't get another chance before he leaves. Besides, it'll be more fun with just the two of you."

They both started to deny it, but she wouldn't let them finish. "I have plenty to keep me busy this morning, anyway," she added as a clincher, "and you'll just be in my way." She rose and began clearing the table.

Gideon came up behind her so quickly she didn't even know he was there until his arms closed around her waist. He kissed her cheek and nuzzled her ear, then whispered a few sweet, loving words about what a wonderful, understanding wife she was. It was evidence of Rennie's distraught state of mind that his words both soothed and exacerbated her pain. When his lips found hers for one last kiss, she turned in his arms and held him tight. Then she let him go.

"Go on," she urged, her voice husky with held-back emotion.

Gideon watched her with a puzzled expression for a moment, but she wouldn't look at him. Finally he glanced away and said, "Come on, Cal. Let's see if you still know how to saddle a horse." Caleb answered with an insult of his own, and the two men laughed.

Rennie stood where she was as two sets of boots clomped across the kitchen floor. The screen door creaked open, then slammed shut behind them. Masculine voices and laughter floated back toward her, then faded away.

You have to tell him, Rennie. You'll have no peace of

mind until you do. The little voice was back, louder now
than ever before.

"I can't." Spoken aloud, she winced at the cowardly
sound of those two words.

You have to. You can't go on like this.

"I have so far," she whispered.

If he loves you, he'll understand. And forgive.

"And if he doesn't understand? If he can't forgive me?"
The anguished words were torn from her. "What if I lose
him?"

Then you never had him to begin with. Rennie's conscience was implacable. *This lie has to stop. Don't you see?
It's the only way. And you're the only one who can put an
end to it.*

There was never any other choice. She saw that now. She
would tell him tonight, after Caleb left, after the children
were asleep. And all she could do now was pray, pray that
Gideon loved her enough to forgive the deception.

She didn't cry. Some things went deeper than tears.

Caleb and Gideon rode south. Skirting a stand of scrub
pine and a dry wash, they cut through a ravine as familiar
to both of them as their own backyard, following it as it
angled westward, then southward again. The walls of the
ravine were high at first, towering over their heads, but
slowly dwindled down to where they could see over the top,
and eventually petered out to nothing. Gideon headed west
from there, treading on the long shadows cast by the early
morning sun.

When Caleb drew up alongside him, Gideon pointed toward the mountain range looming before them and broke
the silence. "Remember when we used to go climbing in
those mountains?"

"Yeah." Caleb's grin flashed. "I suppose you're going

to remind me of the time I broke my leg up there and you had to pack me out on the back of a horse.''

Gideon chuckled. "As a matter of fact, I'd forgotten about that."

"Sure."

"No, really. I was thinking about something that happened just a few weeks ago. Nicki ran away right after Rennie and I were married, and ended up lost on the mountain nearest Carter's Junction."

"How'd you find her?"

"I didn't. Rennie did."

"Rennie? I thought you said she wasn't from around here."

"She's not. Don't ask me how she knew, but she and Emily somehow figured out where Nicki was heading, and went after her." He glanced at Caleb. "Nicki had fallen down the side of a cliff, and Rennie climbed down after her. Scared stiff she'd fall herself, she did it, anyway."

"Sounds like she's got a lot of grit."

"Yeah. She has that, all right."

"Is Nicki okay? She must be, or you would have said something before now."

"Yeah. She still doesn't talk, but otherwise she's fine. She and Rennie are really close now. In fact, all the kids love Rennie. She's been a good mother to them." Gideon's tone was deep, reflective, and rich with satisfaction.

"You really love Rennie, don't you."

Gideon pulled up for a moment, leather creaking, and Caleb did the same. The two brothers faced each other. "I told you I did."

"Yeah, but I don't think I've ever seen you quite like this, not even with Johanna."

Silence followed. Gideon looked out toward the mountains, morning haze still clinging to them. Finally he said,

"I'm older, Cal. I know what it is to lose the most important person in my life. Maybe that's why what I feel for Rennie is more...intense than what I felt for Jo. I don't know." He stopped, tightening his hands on the reins, and looked at his brother. "Don't get me wrong. If Jo hadn't died I would have loved her all my life, and been content with that. But she did. And now I have Rennie."

He searched for the words that would explain what she meant to him. "It's like riding through mile after mile of scrub with no direction, heat and dust choking you, thirst building up until you're so parched you start chewing on the reins. And just when you think you'll die if you have to go one more step without water, you stumble on a mountain stream. Water—pure, sweet, life-giving water. You didn't know it was there, but somehow you found it, and you thank God for it." He paused for a moment. "That's Rennie."

Rennie had just finished clearing the table when she heard a car door slam. She put the last of the dishes on the counter, wiped her hands on her jeans and headed for the living room. The front door burst open and the children swarmed in, surrounding her.

"Rennie, we missed you!" Trina's tight hug was followed by Nicki's quick embrace, then Andrew threw his arms around Rennie's legs.

"Wemmy! I mithed you!"

"I missed you, too, sweetie. All of you." She picked him up and squeezed him close, pressing her lips against baby-soft skin. But all too soon he wiggled out of her arms and she reluctantly let him go.

"Can we show Aunt Emily the new kittens?" Trina pleaded, and Andrew chimed in eagerly, "Kittens!" But Rennie shook her head.

"I don't think that's a good idea right now. Shadow doesn't like it when we all crowd around, remember? Maybe another time, when they're older."

Trina obviously wanted to argue the point, but Andrew was quickly distracted when he spotted their other cat, a tabby named Marmalade, who spotted him at the same time and took off running. Andrew was right behind her.

Rennie chuckled and looked at Nicki and Trina. "So, did you have a good time? Were you good for Aunt Emily?"

Nicki nodded and Trina said, "Um-hm. And guess what? We watched a video, and we made popcorn, and we got to stay up until *ten* o'clock. And we were almost late for church today because Andrew didn't want to get up."

Rennie glanced at Emily, standing in the doorway. "Sounds like you had your hands full."

Emily smiled. "It wasn't too bad."

"We really appreciate it. Thank you."

"Any time. I hope you and Gideon enjoyed yourselves." Her eyes held just the faintest hint of a twinkle.

"Oh, yes. Yes, we did."

"What did you do, Rennie?" Trina tugged at her arm. "Did you and Daddy watch a video like us?"

Rennie turned pink under the interested gazes of her two stepdaughters. "No, we…um…we just took a bath and went to bed early."

Trina made a face. "Oh, yuck. That's no fun."

"Depends on your point of view, doesn't it?" teased Emily in a quiet aside that only Rennie heard. Their eyes met, and despite the foreboding fear hanging over her, she had to smile.

"Yes, it does," she answered.

"Listen, I've got to run." Emily began to edge out the door. "The boys are in the car and I have things to do at home. I'll call you later and you can tell me all about it. See you."

Rennie followed her out onto the porch and called after her, "Thanks again, Emily, for everything." Emily waved, hopped into her station wagon and drove off.

She watched until the car had disappeared from sight, all the while wondering if she'd ever see Emily again. And if she did see her, would Emily forgive her once she knew the truth? So many people were tangled up in her deception. Not just Gideon and the children, but Emily and everyone else she'd come to know and care about here.

She went inside and looked at Gideon's daughters. Oh, God. What would they think of her when they heard who she was? Would they hate her? Would they blame her? How could she have done this to them?

None of her inner thoughts showed on her face when she smiled gently and said, "Guess what? Daddy and I had a visitor this morning, and guess who it was?" Of course, no one could guess, so she quickly added, "Uncle Caleb."

Trina caught her breath and said, "Uncle Caleb! I remember him! He looks just like Daddy, remember, Nicki?" When Nicki nodded and grinned, Trina jumped up and down and said, "Where is he? Where is he?"

"Calm down, sweetie. He's not here right now. Daddy and Uncle Caleb went riding, but they'll be back soon. Why don't you and Nicki take your things to your rooms and put them away. Then you'll be all ready to see him when they come home."

"Come on, Nicki." The two girls scooped up their knapsacks and raced down the hall.

Rennie sagged against the wall. *Forgive me, Nicki. Forgive me, Trina. I just wanted the chance to love you. I never meant to hurt you in any way. I only wanted to make it up to you. Please understand. Please.*

* * *

"Come on, Cal. Admit you were wrong."

"Okay, 1 was wrong." Caleb mounted and pulled his horse around. "You're the best sheep rancher that ever lived."

Gideon laughed and tucked the binoculars back in his saddlebag. "No, I'm not, but I do know good grazing land when I see it. And I'm no sucker. Just because *you* could always goad me into doing what I knew I shouldn't doesn't mean anyone else can." He swung into the saddle. Although he'd enjoyed this time with his brother, he was eager now to get home. "Let's head back down."

"What's your hurry?" Caleb threw him a mischievous grin. "Missing someone already?"

"Yeah." It wasn't quite a growl.

"Afraid she won't be there when you get back?"

"No, not really." His voice dropped and turned serious. "But sometimes I think how easily I could have missed finding her, and it scares me. If I'd never run that ad for a wife, if she hadn't somehow seen it out in Los Angeles and decided to come here, if I'd turned her down because she didn't 'look' like a rancher's wife—as I said, sometimes it scares me."

Curiosity and a niggling feeling that he was missing something made Caleb ask, "Did you say Rennie's from Los Angeles?"

"Yeah. Crazy, isn't it? I run an ad for a wife in Wyoming, and a woman in California happens to see it."

"That's it!" Caleb snapped his fingers triumphantly. "Francesca Whitney!"

"What?" Gideon's horse danced sideways, from an involuntary jab of Gideon's boots and an unusually slack rein. He pulled the gelding up sharply and slewed in the saddle to face his brother. "What did you say?"

"It's been bugging the hell out of me who Rennie reminds me of. It just now came to me. Francesca Whitney."

"You must be mistaken." Gideon paled under his tan.

Caleb shook his head. "Nope. That's who she looks like, all right. Of course, Francesca Whitney was just a kid when I saw her, seventeen or eighteen at the most. That's what threw me off. But Rennie could be her sister."

"No. It's not possible...." Gideon grabbed Caleb's arm. "Cal, do you know who Francesca Whitney is?"

"Sure. She's J. T. Whitney's stepsister. You know who I mean. The corporate raider. I remember them because when their parents' private jet went down in the mountains outside Tahoe, Whitney chartered every available plane to help in the search, mine included. I only saw her once, but you don't forget something like that."

"Oh, God, it can't be." Gideon jerked on the reins, spinning the horse on its hocks.

"Hold on now." Caleb's expression betrayed his bewilderment. "I didn't say Rennie *was* this woman. I just said she looks like her. Hey, wait!"

But Gideon was already spurring back the way they came, heedless of the danger. Caleb shouted after him.

"What's Francesca Whitney ever done to you?"

His answer came on the wind.

"She killed my wife!"

Chapter 17

Not Rennie, Lord. Don't let it be true.

The words pounded through Gideon's brain in terrible counterpoint to the pounding hoofbeats as he rode at breakneck speed. He didn't want to believe it. Rennie, his love, his life, *couldn't* be Francesca Whitney, couldn't be the woman responsible for Johanna's death.

But too many questions he'd ignored before came back to haunt him.

It had always puzzled him that she'd come all the way to Wyoming to answer his ad rather than writing. What had she said? *"I wanted to meet you in person, so I just took a chance."* Even more puzzling was how she happened to come across his ad in the first place. Puzzling, that is, unless she'd deliberately sought out information about him.

No, that didn't make sense. If Rennie *was* Francesca Whitney, why had she waited two years?

Then it hit him. The accident. She'd been in a coma, then in physical therapy. She'd told him, only he'd been too blind to see. She had still been recovering; she couldn't have come any sooner.

Click. Like a bullet inserted into the chamber of a .45, the first piece of evidence slid into place with deadly ease.

And why had she been so willing to marry a stranger, especially after the things he'd said to her when they met? Her reasons had seemed a little weak, but he'd been so pleased to finally find someone who met his qualifications that he'd glossed over them in his mind. But now it made sense if you added guilt to the equation, guilt over her involvement in Jo's death.

Click. The second bullet slid in beside the first.

Then there was that odd, almost defiant look in her eyes when she'd told him her name that first day, as if she expected it to mean something to him. It hadn't, of course, but she'd stood there for a moment afterward, waiting. Waiting for him to recognize her?

Click. And a third bullet dropped into its chamber.

And what about that stepbrother of hers. What was his name? Jess. That was it. *J* for Jess as in J. T. Whitney? A man whose name carried weight even here in Wyoming. What had Rennie said about him that night on the mountain? Very little actually, and only now did it occur to Gideon that she'd never mentioned his last name. But he remembered something else she'd said that night. Her mother and stepfather had died in a plane crash.

Click. Bullet number four joined the others.

Then doubt assailed him. It couldn't be true. It just couldn't. It had to be a series of coincidences, however unlikely. It wasn't possible that Rennie had deceived him for so long. No one could live such a lie unless they were an unbelievably good actress, unless...

Despite the sun's warmth Gideon felt a cold chill run through him. What had Caleb said just that morning? *"Talk about gullible. I would have seen through that story in a minute."*

And his own response. *"Nobody can tell a more believable tale than Rennie. Nobody."*

Click went the fifth bullet. The evidence was mounting. The .45 was almost loaded.

Gideon rode into the barnyard like a man possessed, pulled up hard and swung down from the saddle before the gelding even stopped. He threw the reins at his startled foreman and headed for the house. For the first time in his memory he left his horse for someone else to cool down and groom. He had something more important to tend to.

The house was cool, dim and welcoming, but Gideon was in no mood to appreciate it. He heard sounds from the kitchen—no doubt Rennie was in there. But he wasn't ready to confront her. Not yet. Despite his suspicions, he still hoped, *prayed,* that there was another explanation. He loved her. If he was wrong, if he accused her unjustly, his lack of trust might destroy the very thing he needed most—Rennie's love.

So he made for the bedroom, not sure what he was seeking, but certain it would be there if it was anywhere.

He hesitated in the middle of the room for a moment as memories of last night played back swiftly through his mind. Loving Rennie, being loved in return. They'd been so close, almost one in spirit as well as in flesh. Did he really want to know that it was all a lie?

But what if she's innocent? If I don't prove it, I'll never know for sure. I'll always have that suspicion in the back of my mind, and Rennie will sense the difference. It's not fair to her, or to myself. I have to know the truth, either way.

In the end, the damning evidence was pathetically easy to find.

It was in the bottom drawer on her side of the dresser, a small pile of papers tucked under a stack of folded blue jeans. He shuffled impatiently through them. Most meant nothing to him. A letter with no return address caught his eye, and after a momentary hesitation he opened it. It was from her stepbrother, but it revealed no clues and was signed simply "Jess." Gideon tossed it aside, picked up the next item and felt his world crashing down around him.

A Montana birth certificate. For Francesca Renee Fortier.

His fingers trembled as he smoothed out the folded paper and read it once more. There was no mistake. *Francesca.* The name leapt off the page, too unusual to be a coincidence. Not on top of everything else.

Click. The sixth bullet entered the revolver's last chamber with the discovery of the only physical piece of evidence. The cylinder spun, then locked into place, and the hammer was cocked. Then the gun took aim directly at his heart.

He squeezed his eyes shut. "Rennie." He wasn't even aware that he'd spoken. All he knew was the ice-cold feeling of betrayal, a betrayal that went so deep he couldn't begin to see bottom.

Like an old man, he stood up and walked toward the kitchen, her birth certificate clenched in his hand. He pushed open the kitchen door.

"Francesca." He forced the damning name through frozen lips.

Rennie dropped the pitcher she was holding and it shattered on the floor, spilling its contents and sending shards of glass flying. She swung around, her eyes wide with fear and guilt.

Gideon's last hope vanished, a hope he hadn't even

known was still in him until it was gone. Without realizing it, he let the swinging door go and it closed behind him.

"It's true, then," he said, slowly walking toward her, glass crunching beneath his boots. "You're Francesca Whitney."

No more lies, Rennie told herself, even as tremors shook her. *No more lies.* "How did you know?" she whispered.

"Caleb recognized you. I didn't want to believe it." He opened his fist, displaying the crumpled birth certificate. "But then I found this."

"I was going to tell you."

"Were you?" The ice encasing him began to crack under the weight of his anger. "When? When you got tired of the charade?"

"No!" She faced him bravely. "I decided this morning I couldn't lie to you anymore."

"How convenient. Too bad I don't believe you." Though softly spoken, his tone was filled with contempt.

"Gideon, please—"

"Why did you do it? Why did you come here?" His face contracted in pain and he pulled her close, his hands digging into her soft flesh. "Damn it, why did you marry me?"

"I…" Rennie tried to remember, but Gideon was holding her too tightly. She couldn't think.

"Was it a game? Just to see if you could do it, is that it? Just to see if you could fool us all?"

"No!"

"Then tell me why, damn you. Why?"

In her room Nicki heard her father's voice raised in anger, and froze. Her insides began to shake as she remembered another angry voice from long ago. Anger directed at her. She tried to block it out, but the voices from the kitchen blended in with the memory, making it impossible.

Nicki covered her ears and whimpered. Why was Daddy yelling at Rennie? Daddy never got angry. Why now?

The kitchen reverberated with fury barely held in check, the fury of a man betrayed. Gideon scarcely knew what he was saying anymore, the words pouring from him in a molten stream.

"I blamed myself for Jo's death. Did you know that? All this time I blamed myself because I promised I'd take her on that visit to California, and I didn't go. For two years I've lived with guilt that should have been yours."

"Don't, Gideon." Raw pain laced her words. "Please don't."

He steeled himself against the inexplicable softening inside him. "You're going to hear. At the time, the police said that they couldn't tell who was responsible. I believed it then. I don't now. Did your stepbrother buy them off?"

"No! That wasn't what happened!"

The kitchen door opened a crack. Neither Rennie nor Gideon noticed.

"Then why did you come here, unless guilt brought you?"

"I *did* feel guilty, but I—"

He pounced on her confession. "Wasn't it enough that you took Johanna's life? Did you have to take everything that was hers—her children, her home, her husband?"

"It wasn't like that!"

"No? Then tell me. What was it like? Tell me, *Francesca*." Violence hovered on the edge of his control.

"Don't call me that!"

"Why shouldn't I? It's your name. Francesca. Whitney." Gideon spat the words at her, and they fueled his anger. He shook her. Hard. "Damn you! Was it all lies? Was it?"

"No!"

He couldn't bear it. He thrust her away from him and swung around, his chest heaving, his hands fisted in impotent rage. Fresh pain welled up inside him, pushing him beyond reason. Rennie. Johanna. The women he loved. One was dead and the other never existed except in his mind. Francesca Whitney had robbed him of both.

Gideon turned to confront Rennie again, and he came closer to hitting a woman in that moment than he'd ever thought possible. Words became his fists. "How could you lie to me and then sleep in my arms? How could you?" Rennie flinched as if he'd struck her. Gideon didn't give her a chance to answer before hammering the next blow home. "And how could you steal my children's love after killing their mother?"

"No, Daddy! No! It wasn't Rennie, it was me!" Gideon and Rennie both whirled as Nicki stumbled into the kitchen, tears streaming down her face. "I did it," she said, her voice cracking from disuse. "I killed Mama."

Gideon stood rooted to the floor, shocked into immobility. Nicki was talking! God, he'd prayed for it so long he'd almost given up hope. But what was she saying? Her words didn't make sense.

But Rennie understood instantly. She flew to Nicki and enfolded her in her arms. "No, honey, no. You didn't kill her. It was an accident."

Nicki clung to Rennie, sobbing. "It was my fault." Nicki's knees buckled and she sagged against Rennie. The dead weight was too much for Rennie, but she refused to let Nicki go, and the two of them sank to the floor.

The girl burrowed into Rennie's embrace, and Rennie pressed the blond head against her breast, rocking, soothing, cradling the shaking body. "Shh, Nicki. It's okay. Everything's going to be okay."

Nicki's torrent of grief continued unabated, and tears

trickled down Rennie's face. Her eyes flashed to Gideon in mute appeal. The look freed him and he moved swiftly. Kneeling beside them, he lifted Nicki into his arms and she turned to him with a wild cry.

"Daddy!"

She buried her face against his shoulder, her tears soaking his shirt. Gideon held his daughter so desperately tight he was afraid he might hurt her. But there was no way he would let her go.

"I'm sorry, Daddy." The anguished words were muffled.

"It's okay, Nicki, whatever it is."

"Don't…hate me."

Gideon's heart cracked wide open. "Oh, baby, I could never hate you. Not for anything."

"I did it." She sniffed and wiped her face against Gideon's shirt. More tears oozed from her swollen eyes. "I didn't mean to, but I did."

Gideon's face was wet, too.

"What, baby? What did you do?"

Nicki hiccuped. "Trina and I were fighting in the back seat. Mama told me to stop, but I didn't." She sniffed again. "I said something mean to Trina and she started crying. Mama turned around to yell at me and the car swerved." She caught her breath on a sob. "And then…"

"It's okay, Nicki." He kissed her forehead and his arms tightened around her. "It wasn't your fault. It was an accident." Gideon's gaze met Rennie's over his daughter's head, tears in his eyes, as he rasped, "I still love you."

Was he saying it to Nicki or to Rennie? Not even Gideon knew.

A noise from the doorway made them all turn their heads. Caleb stood there with Andrew in one arm and Trina beside him. Andrew's mouth was puckered as if he were about to cry, and Trina wasn't much better.

"I found them in the hall," Caleb said softly, looking down at Gideon. "I think you scared them."

"Wemmy." Andrew squirmed and pushed against his uncle's chest until Caleb lowered him to the floor. He ran to Rennie and threw his arms around her.

She held him tight, wondering if this was the last time she'd ever hold him, this child who'd stolen her heart with just a smile. Would she ever see him smile again?

Her eyes squeezed shut, then opened to find Gideon's gaze locked on her. She averted her face and cleared her throat. "I think we could all use something cold to drink, don't you think so, Andrew?" He nodded solemnly. "Trina? Nicki?" A chorus of hesitant yeses answered her. She rocked back on her heels and stood up, Andrew still in her arms. She glanced at Caleb. "There's glass all over the floor in here that I have to clean up. Will you take the children to the front porch for me? I'll make some lemonade and bring it out."

"Sure. No problem." Caleb lifted Andrew and perched him against his shoulder, then took Trina's hand. "Are you coming, Nicki?"

Nicki looked at her father with hope and fear. "Daddy?" Her voice broke in the middle.

He hugged her once more, kissed her tenderly, then set her on her feet and stood up himself. "Go with Uncle Caleb, baby. I'm not angry with you. I promise."

"Are you coming out soon?"

"Yeah." He gave her an encouraging smile. "I have to talk to Rennie, but I'll be there in a minute."

Still shaking, Nicki stood her ground. "You aren't going to yell at Rennie again, are you?" Fresh tears threatened. "I don't want you to yell at Rennie."

"No, baby." He could barely swallow past the lump in his throat as his little girl defended the woman she'd come to love against all odds. "I'm not going to yell at Rennie anymore. Now, go with Uncle Caleb."

Silence filled the kitchen after they left. Rennie avoided looking at Gideon, knowing she just couldn't take any more right now. At some point she'd have to face him, but not at this moment.

She skirted the worst of the mess on the floor and took down a plastic pitcher, then held it under the water tap.

"Rennie."

"Not now, Gideon. Please."

"We have to talk."

She struggled for composure. "I know. Just…not now, okay?"

He didn't say anything, and Rennie quickly measured sugar and lemon juice into the pitcher of water, stirred it, then added ice cubes from the freezer. She brought out a serving tray and set four glasses on it, then added a fifth glass for Gideon and stared at it. Last times. So many last times to remember. Was this another?

All at once she knew she couldn't go out there and pretend everything was all right. Everything *wasn't* all right and never would be again.

"Could you…" Her voice was clogged with unshed tears. "Could you take this tray out for me? I have to pick up the glass and mop the floor."

"You go. I'll take care of the glass."

"No." She turned and faced him, even though it broke her heart to do so. "Nicki needs *you* now. She needs to believe that you forgive her."

He took a step toward her, his hand outstretched, but she whirled around, so close to breaking that she had to grab on to the edge of the sink to keep from falling. "Please, Gideon. Please. Just go."

His hand dropped to his side. He didn't understand why

her rejection ripped through him, or why the sight of her distress aroused his protective instincts. He didn't understand why it still mattered.

With a muttered oath he did as she asked, grabbing the tray so roughly the glasses rattled dangerously, then stalking from the kitchen. The kitchen door swung back and forth several times before settling into place.

Rennie stood there for a moment, pale and motionless, all her dreams shattered like the pitcher she'd dropped.

The sun had long since set and the children were already in bed with lights out when Gideon came inside to check on them. He went from Andrew's room to Trina's, and found them both fast asleep, then entered Nicki's room. She was quiet, and he thought she was sleeping, too, but when he tucked the covers more securely around her, she turned over.

"Daddy?"

"Shh. It's late," he whispered, stroking her hair soothingly. "You should be asleep."

He'd spent most of the afternoon with Nicki. Although she hadn't said it in so many words, he'd figured out that all this time his daughter had been afraid to speak, afraid she'd cause someone else's death that way. Nicki had talked until her voice was hoarse and strained, but he let her keep going, knowing she needed to unburden her soul. And though he knew it would be a long time before she stopped blaming herself for her mother's death, he thought she'd taken the first steps on the road to recovery.

"What's going to happen now, Daddy?"

He sat down on the edge of her bed. "What do you mean?"

"Is Rennie going away?" Gideon didn't answer because

he couldn't. Then Nicki said, "I used to wish she'd go away, you know."

"I know, baby," he said huskily.

"But now I don't. I don't want her to leave. Are you still mad at her?"

He swallowed hard. "I don't know, Nicki," he said honestly. "I just don't know." He leaned over and brushed his lips against her forehead. "Get some sleep now. We'll talk about it in the morning."

Gideon stood up and walked out, closing the door softly behind him. He stood in the hall for a moment, listening to the silence all around him, then sighed and headed for the front door.

When he stepped out onto the porch he was wound up tighter than a watch spring, and he leaned one hip against the railing, longing for a cigarette. But instead of going down to the bunkhouse and bumming one from his foreman, he crossed his arms and stared into the cloudless night sky.

Caleb was long gone. He'd left as planned, after dinner, a somber dinner that Rennie had prepared but that the two brothers had shared with only the children. But before he'd left, Caleb had taken him aside for a moment, and now Gideon finally had the time to mull over his twin's parting words.

"It's none of my business," Caleb had said brusquely. "I know that. But I'm going to butt in, anyway."

When Gideon didn't respond, Caleb said, "I don't know why she came here. But I know why she stayed. That woman loves you. No matter what she might have done in the past, she loves you."

"Did she tell you that?"

Caleb's voice roughened. "She didn't have to. A blind man could see it."

As the scene replayed itself in his mind, Gideon considered the possibility that Caleb was right. But where did that leave them? Now that the sharp pain of Rennie's betrayal had dulled somewhat, he didn't know where to go from here. He didn't know what he wanted anymore. He knew he should feel angry, hurt and betrayed, but somehow that wasn't what he was feeling at all.

But she lied to you, he reminded himself.

Yes, but she loved me, too. That part wasn't a lie. And she loved the children. That wasn't a lie either.

But she killed Johanna.

No, I can't blame her for that. Not after what Nicki said. Rennie was really the innocent party. And she's paid dearly for someone else's mistake.

Gideon shifted position and looked out at the vast expanse of stars above him. It reminded him that Rennie had once described Wyoming's night sky to him, and he searched his memory for her exact words. Diamonds on blue velvet. That's what she'd said. And she'd said something else, too, something about the stars making her realize how insignificant their problems were in the grand scheme of things.

The grand scheme of things.

If Rennie hadn't come here, if Nicki hadn't grown to love her, if none of this had ever happened, would Nicki have regained the use of her voice? Or would she have lived on in silence forever? God only knows.

And only God knows how I'll survive without Rennie.

The thought came to him out of nowhere, and all at once he knew. He didn't *want* a life without her. It didn't matter anymore how or why she had come to them. The only thing that mattered was that she was inextricably woven into the fabric of all their lives. He couldn't tear her out of his heart or his life without destroying everyone's happiness, including his own.

With that conclusion the tension drained slowly out of him, and he relaxed. He had his answer now.

In the shadows beyond the reaches of the yard light, Rennie watched Gideon walk out onto the front porch and lean against the railing. Even from this distance she could see the rigid way he held himself, could feel the tension radiating from him. She longed to comfort him, to ease his pain, but knew she had forfeited the right.

So instead of going to him, she turned away and slipped into the barn to say goodbye to Sweetwater, not knowing if she would have the chance later. She fed the mare a carrot and told her how beautiful she was, then she buried her face in the horse's mane and wept.

Afterward she mopped her eyes with her shirttail, then tucked her shirt back in and ran her hand over Sweetwater's nose one last time.

"I'll miss you, girl," she said. "You'll never know how much. But I can't take you with me. Even if I could, you wouldn't want to go. You'd be miserable in Los Angeles. You'll be much happier here, just as I was." She choked on the last words. "Just as I was," she whispered once more. Tears threatened again, but she suppressed them. "Goodbye, girl."

As silently as she had entered the barn, she left it.

Suddenly Gideon knew he was no longer alone. A movement in the shadows alerted him, but he'd sensed her even before that.

"Rennie." His voice was deep and low.

She crossed the barnyard and came to stand at the foot of the porch steps. In the eerie combination of light cast by the moon overhead and the yard light, he saw that she'd been crying. Her eyes were swollen, but her softly rounded face was set in determined lines.

"We have to talk," she said.

"Yeah." He stood up straight and looked down at her. "We do."

She seemed composed, almost too composed, as if she'd somehow blocked out all emotion, and not at all like herself. "I'd like for you to listen to me first, without saying anything," she said quietly. "Then, when I'm done, I'll listen to anything you have to say. Can we do that?"

"I think so."

"Good." She rubbed her hands over her bare arms, nervous, but intent. She drew a deep breath and let it out slowly, as if unsure where to start.

Finally she said, "When I came here in answer to your ad, I'd only recently learned about Johanna's...death. You see, I had no memory of the accident, and I was in a coma for almost a year afterward. When I came out of the coma I was facing a long, difficult period of physical therapy if I ever wanted to walk again. And of course, I'd sustained those internal injuries you already know about. Because of the latter, I was in such a state of depression that Jess decided to keep me in the dark about Johanna. He's very rich and...powerful, and used to having his own way. And he's always been very protective of me. I think you can understand that."

"Yeah."

"Well, as I said, I'd just found out about Johanna, and the news devastated me. I couldn't leave things as they were. I felt responsible. So I hired a private investigator to find out about her family."

"And that's how you saw my ad?"

"Yes. I don't know if I really intended to go through with it, but I came out here with the idea of applying for the job as a way of making restitution. Afterward, after I'd done it, Jess told me I was crazy to think it could work." She smiled sadly.

"Anyway, when I drove onto the Rocking L I felt like I'd come home. I began to believe I really could do this. And then I met you."

"Rennie—"

"No, please let me finish first." He nodded reluctantly and she continued.

"I think I knew when I met you that you were different from anyone I'd ever known. It wasn't love at first sight, but I was attracted to you, and it scared me, especially under the circumstances. But you offered me something more than just the chance to make it up to Johanna Lowell's family. You offered me things I desperately needed then—a place to call home, and children who needed me. I never lied to you about that, Gideon. I hope you can believe me."

"I do."

Her brief smile never reached her eyes. "I'm glad," she said simply. Then the smile faded. "I tried not to think about Johanna, tried not to think about what would happen if you found out who I was. I just tried to make you happy. And then I fell in love with you.

"It wasn't until you told me you loved me, too, that I realized what I'd done was wrong. You trusted me, and I'd lied to you. A lie of omission, but a lie just the same.

"I really was going to tell you the truth. I thought, if he loves me enough to forgive the deception, then what we have is the real thing. And if he can't forgive me, then we never really had anything to begin with.

"But you found out before I told you." Her dark eyes were sad and bleak. Then she glanced away and added with quiet finality, "And I guess I have my answer."

The silence stretched between them. In the distance they

heard a lone coyote crying to the moon, while nervous sheep baaed in response. And in the barn restless horses nickered softly to one another.

Gideon took a step forward. "Is it my turn now?" She nodded, but refused to look at him, and her moonlit profile was the most vulnerable thing he'd ever seen. "Then I'll tell you what the answer is. But I have to know something first."

"What is it?"

"Do you still love me?"

She turned her head and stared up at him, her heart in her eyes, then whispered, "Yes."

He took her hand in his. Her hand trembled, then stilled, as he curled his fingers around hers. "And I love you, Rennie."

She just stood there for a moment, unbelieving. Then with a choked cry she threw herself into his arms.

"Oh, God, Gideon. I'm sorry," she said, fighting back tears. "So sorry. I never meant to hurt you."

"The only way you could really hurt me is if you stopped loving me."

"Never. I'll never stop loving you."

Her reward was a fierce kiss that took her breath away. Then he wrapped his arms around her, needing the melting softness of her body against his just as he needed the love she'd given him so freely. With a heartfelt sigh she fitted herself against him and closed her eyes.

"I'm sorry, Rennie." He ran his hands slowly over her arms where he'd grasped her so roughly that morning, as if searching for the bruises he knew he'd left on her delicate skin. "I never meant to hurt you, either." His conscience smote him. "That's not true. I wanted to hurt you the way I'd been hurt. But not this way. Never this way."

Her eyes flickered open and she raised her face to his. "I

know." She caught his right hand and carried it to her lips, then cradled it against her cheek. "But if you can forgive me, I can forgive you."

Gideon's throat tightened with an upsurge of emotion, and his eyes stung. "Cal was right," he said when he finally trusted his voice enough to speak.

"About what?"

He told her what Caleb had said just before he left. "But I already knew, deep down. Even when I was accusing you, I think I knew. I was just afraid to believe it."

"Why afraid?"

"Because I need you so much."

She brushed his lips with her fingertips. "Is that bad?"

"Only if you don't need me, too."

"I do, Gideon. I always will." She nestled closer, locking her arms around his waist. "I need the things you've given me," she said softly. "A family. A home. And your love. More than anything, I need your love."

His hold tightened. "Then you don't ever have to look anywhere else for what you need. I love you, Rennie. Now and forever."

She laid her head against his heart and smiled mistily in the darkness. "Promise?"

"I promise."

*   *   *   *   *

Where love comes alive™

SILHOUETTE *Romance™*

From first love to forever, these love stories are for today's woman with traditional values.

Silhouette® *Desire*

A highly passionate, emotionally powerful and always provocative read.

Silhouette®
SPECIAL EDITION™

Emotional, compelling stories that capture the intensity of living, loving and creating a family in today's world.

Silhouette®
INTIMATE MOMENTS™

A roller-coaster read that delivers romantic thrills in a world of suspense, adventure and more.